NORTH
OF THE
BRAZOS

Also by Keith Remer

In the Midst of Wolves

Run River Run

The Aristocracy of Caddo County

Killing Bardoe, Book One of the Calamitous Breed Trilogy

Blood City, Book Two of the Calamitous Breed Trilogy

The Hiding Place of Thunder

NORTH OF THE BRAZOS

By

KEITH REMER

Honey Lee Press
Oklahoma City

First Honey Lee Press trade paperback edition March 2020
Manufactured in the United States of America
10 9 8 7 6 5 4 3 2 1

Print ISBN 978-1-7341015-3-9
eBook ISBN 978-1-7341015-4-6
Library of Congress Control Number: 2020904774

For just a really good man and wonderful friend,

Randy Stelter

Without him, I'd not had this story

ONE

The 105 inch curved screen of the LG television amplified tears streaming down a dark face. The resolution magnified horror in the woman's eyes and emphasized inner-city terror etched in every crease and wrinkle. The beads of sweat, fuzz on her upper lip, and the crookedness of her stained teeth in a gaping mouth might have been missed on a smaller screen. The woman wailed as the Chicago television reporters allowed her to express profound torment between gasps for air.

"Another . . . dead baby . . . my last one . . . but nobody cares . . . not even God."

From his plush chair centered on the giant screen, Charles Atkinson thumbed the power button and watched as agony faded to black. He sat safely inside a New York mansion far removed from the suffering mother. Yet, "Sir" Atkinson mumbled under his breath, "I care, dear lady." He forced himself out of the comfort of rich leather before speaking again.

"Enough! This must be dealt with," his voice boomed. "Donning?"

"Yes, sir?" his personnel assistant responded from the far end of the cavernous study.

"It was the poor woman's third child to die violently."

"Yes, sir," Kenneth Donning said as approached his long-time employer.

"And she is just one of what? Hundreds? Thousands, more likely, who have lost beloved children to this hideous cancer devouring our beloved nation."

"More than likely thousands, I would assume, sir. I can have it researched if you'd like."

"Not necessary. We can better spend our time and resources," Atkinson mumbled, as his mind momentarily took him back nearly a year to a trip he'd taken to Dallas, Texas. It was there while on business that he'd became familiar with a most bizarre criminal trial playing out in south Texas.

Atkinson looked his dear confidant square in the eyes. "I want you to reach out to those two men down on the Brazos River in Texas."

Kenneth Donning reacted in the exact manner Atkinson expected. His surprise and concern registered on his broad face and in his words. "But they pleaded innocent and were acquitted by a jury."

"Of course, they were," Atkinson smiled wearily. "However, that clip you found for me on the internet clearly explained why. You surely remember the clip of the District Attorney down there speaking to reporters after the trial."

"I do, sir," Donning sighed.

"That DA was outraged. He called it a blatant case of jury nullification. We both know that means the jury knew they were guilty as charged, but decided to acquit them anyway. So, yes, they were acquitted by a jury of *Texans,* whom I believe, possessed a high and appreciative tolerance for justified vigilantism. Not a quality, I fear, we New Yorkers can so easily embrace."

"I can't even imagine, sir, how to approach those gentlemen."

"May I suggest, Ken, that you simply inform them one of the wealthiest men in America has an assignment that suits their impressive training, service, and willingness to right wrongs with extreme violence."

"Sir, in all the national coverage, both consistently denied . . ."

"Kenneth?"

Donning exhaled a sigh. "Okay, sir. What will you expect of them?"

"Simply to rid Chicago of the consuming cancer. I will provide specific details before you depart for Texas."

"And what do I offer, sir?"

"Anything they want, and everything they need."

"Will you then excuse me to start making all arrangements?"

"Of course, but one more thing."

"Yes, sir?"

"We will need someone inside the Chicago Police Department to provide information and cover."

"I will get my staff on that as well," Donning said as he nodded and turned to leave.

Atkinson let him walk halfway across the lavish room before calling his name.

"Ken?"

Donning stopped and turned back, "Yes, sir?"

"Three to five years is not much time at all. But it's all I have to make the profound differences we've discussed. Our society, our way of life, *these United States of America*, depends on us taking drastic actions. The police have their hands tied with the bonds of political correctness, and the courts refuse to even as much as acknowledge the constitution. It is high-time good men act in ways that might seem, initially, horrific and senselessly brutal. However, in the end, the means will produce a most necessary outcome."

Donning did not stand so far away that Atkinson could not see the sadness that assaulted his expression. "I will not fail you, Sir Atkinson."

"You never have, Colonel Donning."

* * * *

Four months later on the south side of Chicago

"Fuck dat man, Latrisha, she just look at yo' tiny dick, and laugh 'til it turns soft as yo' brains," Slash taunted as he administered a good-natured shove to Tink's bony chest.

"Shee-it!" Tink responded, "That girl see my dick, she won't never want to see another!"

P-Wac stood beneath the glow of the streetlight, taking in the banter of his three subordinates along with the heat of the late night air, while constantly moving his head to scan for signs of danger. The oldest of the four, but still a baby gangster, P-Wac took his responsibilities seriously. Soon he would no longer be a juvenile, and possessed a burning desire for bigger and more profitable duties. P-Wac knew senior members, and more importantly, senior members knew P-Wac.

"Fuck, Slash, you and Tink, all you talk about is dicks. Makes me wonder 'bout you bitches," Nine Mil contributed to the conversation.

P-Wac chuckled, but could not join in as the three others upped their insults and escalated their antics to initiating animated combative gestures. He knew they wouldn't really fight. They never did. It made no sense to fight among themselves when so many enemies threatened from all sides. He let them go. Let them have their fun until . . .

"Jee-zus! Check this shit out, man," P-Wac interrupted, and sharply nodded his head toward the street in front of them.

The three others stopped their horseplay as if ordered to do so, and immediately went on alert. They focused their attention on the object of P-Wac's signal, a beast of an automobile moving slowly towards them.

"Mutha fuck," Slash exclaimed, "Who be drivin' a monster like that?"

"Don't know," P-Wac mumbled.

"It's a Hummer, and a bad-assed one, too. All black. Clean as fuck. Be ominous as shit, man," Nine Mil said.

"Ain't never seen it before," Tink added.

That's what bothered P-Wac. It certainly did look ominous, and it did not belong here. Did not fit. P-Wac knew the dudes that could drive such a car on this turf, and none of them did.

"Could be Hot Wire, P-Wac," Slash said. "Ain't no wheels he can't jack, man."

"Could be," P-Wac nodded. He hoped so.

"Best be Hot Wire. Or the evil lookin' bitch might end up bein' mine," Nine Mil said.

"Be cool, Nine Mil," P-Wac warned. He'd started developing his gut warnings at the age of ten. At the moment they sounded like a siren.

The four grew silent as the super-sized SUV came to a stop in the street a mere fifteen feet to their front. Deep and throaty pipes testified to the tremendous power of the engine beneath the hood.

Windows darkened as black as death concealed who and how many sat inside.

"Shit. Looks like the devil him own self's wheels," Tink all but whispered.

"No shit, Tink," P-Wac did whisper.

For tormenting seconds, the Hummer simply sat and grumbled like a pissed demon. Suddenly, the front doors started to open, but in a most unusual way. They were not being pushed open from the inside, but slowly opened in unison accompanied by a distinct sound of hydraulics. P-Wac wondered what kind of car needed hydraulic doors. No light shown from inside the Hummer. Until the last second, the lack of light concealed the existence of two tall and stout figures that emerged from the driver and passenger seats, slowly, but at the exact same time and in the exact same manner. Like a pair of robots.

"*What the fuck?*" Slash snickered.

"*Bitches playing dress-up?*" Tink chuckled.

"*Ain't believin' my fuckin' eyes,*" Nine Mil chimed in.

P-Wac knew what the fuck, and wanted to agree with Nine Mil, except, seeing was believing. Seeing made his guts clinch.

* * * *

2 a.m. in a Long Island mansion

Charles Atkinson sat upright in bed at the sound of soft rapping on his bedroom door. As he'd done for the past five years before going to sleep and upon awakening, he stared at the empty spot and unused pillow next to him. Patricia could never bless him with children. They'd grown old together, and then she died. He missed her still.

His everything left him with nothing but a tremendous fortune. Of which, he'd spend every last dime to have her back. That being impossible, and having no blood kin to pass it down to, he could now use every last dime to right awful wrongs in memory of his beloved Patricia.

"I'm awake" Atkinson called toward the door.

The door swung open and Ken Donning stepped in clad in his business attire.

"It is done, sir. I just received word over secure lines that the operation was a success. The first four targets and two body guards are dead."

Atkinson simply nodded his head. He did not relish the outcome, but believed with all his heart that no other alternatives existed. He'd solemnly taken on the responsibility of doing what the police could not, and what legislatures and courts would not.

"All went as planned with the warehouses, safe-houses, escape routes, and intelligence?"

"Many millions spent insured they did, sir."

"More millions spent than what my holdings produce in a week's time?"

"Yes, sir."

"Than two weeks' time?"

"Not quite, sir."

Atkinson nodded again. "Well, then, it was well spent."

This time, Donning took his turn to nod.

"You did well, Colonel. We started a movement that will soon spread to every city across this great land."

"That will depend on news coverage, sir."

"There will be plenty of that."

"Sir, all they will have is six dead, counting the two body guards, and no suspects."

"Yes, but *who* died . . . and *how* they died . . . will be news. And with the deaths to come, it will spread like wildfire."

"A wildfire we will never be able to contain," Donning said with fatigue sounding in his voice.

"Nor should we. Now, get some rest, Ken. You'll need to be at your best to oversee the events to follow."

* * * *

P-Wac knew of such shit. He'd spent long summers at his grandfather's house in New Mexico. The old man grew up on a ranch, rode horses, still wore a hat and boots, and loved anything western. P-Wac had no interest, thought it all bullshit, but still, the old man introduced him to the likes of John Wayne, Clint Eastwood, and a host of other white bad-asses, and even a few black one's as well. The message always proved the same. They were the kind of men you didn't cross, and if you did, you wouldn't do it again. When they came riding in, you'd best ride out. Because when they came riding in, they'd mess somebody up in some bad-ass way. What P-Wac now wondered . . . did it mean the same when they drove up in a Hummer?

Strange? No, *unfucking believable.* Something out of a movie, but this was no movie. This was the streets. Some of the meanest in Chicago.

"These mutha fuckas ain't be for real," Slash shrugged.

P-Wac considered it real as shit. He doubted the other three knew the long black coats the two men wore that reached down below their calves were called dusters. And these two were damned sure dusty, as if they rolled in dust. Even the black hats on their heads were caked in it. Made P-Wac think they'd just come from the country doing whatever kind of things that made *cowboys* dusty. Slash, Tink, and Nine Mil had seen plenty of dudes wearing bandanas, but P-Wac knew they'd never seen them tied around necks and pulled up to cover faces. *Unfucking believable.* Dark pant legs disappeared into the tops of tall boots, and even more *unfucking believable*, the boots bore spurs. *Fucking spurs?*

"You mutha fuckas must be lost," Tink shouted the first words exchanged.

P-Wac shot Tink a quick and ugly look, and Tink acknowledged the admonishment by taking a slight step backwards. Sure, the light on the tall pole didn't shine all that brightly, but couldn't Tink interpret the looks in these white dudes' eyes? No, he'd most likely never seen Clint Eastwood squint and look all crazy-eyed. But, P-Wac had.

"What do you want?" P-Wac called out to the men in a voice he hoped sounded neutral instead of challenging.

The man on the passenger side took a step up on the curb, and the driver calmly strode to the front of the Hummer. Their movement opened the dusters, and P-Wac had clear view of two sets of old-style pistols worn backwards with butts forward. Out the corner of his eyes, P-Wac saw Nine Mil reaching beneath his t-shirt.

"Fuck that, Nine Mill! Just chill, nigga," P-Wac growled.

"Good advice," the man on the curb chuckled. "And what do we want? We don't want nothing."

"Then why are you here?" P-Wac questioned.

The man doing the talking looked P-Wac hard in the eye with his squint-eyed craziness.

"Devon Davies," the cowboy started. "Also known as, DD, also known as, D-Killa."

Slash moved in front of P-Wac. "Fuck yo' crazy ass, man. We ain't givin' you no word on D-Killa."

P-Wac pulled Slash back. The talking cowboy slowly shook his head.

"No. We're here to give you the word on D-Killa."

"And what would that be?" P-Wac asked hesitantly.

The man chuckled a second time. "Word is . . . He's dead. Died in an ugly manner. His top three in line, well, they died with him. Whoever moves up to take their places will get the same, *or worse.*"

Nine Mil gave into rage, this time sticking both hands up his shirt. Before P-Wac could respond, both cowboys' arms crossed in front of their stomachs and four pistols came out in a flash.

"Pull 'em, young'un," the spokesman said too calmly. "You might be fourteen. You might be fifteen. But, point a gun, and you are old enough to die."

"No, Nine Mil!" P-Wac shouted. "Chill the fuck out, bro!"

"Fuck, P-Wac, them old revolvers, they gots only six rounds a piece. I have two pieces with fifteen in each. Fuck them!"

P-Wac started to speak, but the cowboy beat him to it. "We only need eight. One for each of your two eyeballs. We'd use the remaining four to blow off your dead and shriveled dicks. Want your mama to see you that way, boy?"

"*Boy?*" Nine Mil screamed, but did not go for his guns.

P-Wac stepped in front of Nine Mil. "Why don't you two go on now and play cowboys and Indians some other fuckin' place?"

Both men kept their guns pointed. The speaker did not chuckle this time.

P-Wac turned to the silent one in front of the Hummer. "Shit, man, can't you talk?"

This one cocked his head as if to study P-Wac. What little face showing above the bandana looked much darker than the talking cowboy's skin. Long black hair extended from beneath his hat to touch his shoulders.

"I am a cowboy," the longhair grumbled. "And I'm a Comanche. I don't play at being either."

Then, as if out of some crazy fantasy western set in the dead middle of the hood, the cowboy Indian dropped both guns to his side. With an index finger in each trigger guard, he started slowly twirling the guns forward around his fingers. As he gradually raised his hands, the guns spun faster. At shoulder height, he crossed his arms over his chest, and effortlessly reversed the spin to a backwards motion. He twirled them around his fingers so fast that they seemed to lose their form. Suddenly, he let go of both revolvers, and for a split second, they spun in thin air before being grabbed by the opposite hands that set them free. In the wink of an eye, both guns were rotated butt forward and dropped smoothly into their holsters. Without another word, he started back toward the driver's door and slid into the car.

The cowboy on the curb kept his guns pointed while backing to the Hummer and disappearing into the passenger seat. The hydraulic noise sounded again as the doors swung shut. But the car did not move an inch.

"FUCK . . . THIS . . . SHIT!" Nine Mil screamed, pulling two autos from beneath his shirt. Slash pulled a gun as well. P-Wac watched as both emptied what bullets they had toward the car. Those that hit the car zipped and zinged, causing little metallic sparks, but amazingly, left no noticeable damage.

After Nine Mil, Slash, and their guns were left spent, the sinister SUV pull away from the curb and crept slowly out of site.

* * * *

P-Wac stopped to catch his breath a few doors down from D-Killa's safe house. He'd sprinted the entire fifteen blocks with his mind racing far ahead. It just could not be true, and he didn't care to approach the two men posted at the door like some panting and frightened little bitch. He took long seconds to fill his lungs and clear his thinking. *D-Killa dead?* Bullshit. It just could not be. D-Killa, Poptop, Gee-Gee, and Doc Blood all dead? No possible way. Besides, to kill those three, someone would first have to get by the guards posted at the doors. No ten dudes could do that. Two cowboys, no matter how wicked they appeared, damn sure couldn't execute such a feat.

P-Wac managed to walk the remaining distance to the safe house at a slow and cocky pace. No lights shown from inside, but no cause for alarm because they never did. Covered windows kept the inside in and outside out. P-Wac called out to the dark front stoop, identifying himself, and waited for an invite before climbing the few steps. The dudes up there always occupied the shadows instead of standing out as clear targets. Maybe they didn't hear him? P-Wac called again, but just a tad louder this time. Still, no answer came in turn.

Not good. Not fucking good at all.

P-Wac drew in a deep breath and started slowly up the steps, talking as he went.

"Aye, niggas! It's me P-Wac. Don't shoot my ass. It's just me, P-Wac. What the fuck? Where the fuck you at?"

The post stood deserted. From the lights out on the curb, P-Wac observed two pools of thick and dark liquid on the concrete landing.

He bent for a closer look and only then spotted the dislodged teeth. Releasing a barrage of foul language, P-Wac jumped aside, stumbled, and fell against the wall next to the door. The door that stood ajar.

Run Mutha Fucka run! Get the fuck gone!

P-Wac fought back the instinct. Maybe someone in the house needed his help. Not that he truly gave a fuck at this point, but saving anyone privileged enough to be at this house, could only push him way up the ladder. He reached into the waistband of his jeans to retrieve the Glock he'd borrowed from Nine Mil before racing off to get his ass in this jam.

P-Wac held it way out in front of him and used it to push the door open.

"Yo, D-Killa? Hey, Doc Blood? Anyone in the fuckin' house?" He shouted with a tremor in his voice he could not control. No response came from inside, and he forced his feet to move. Move the feet, the body has to follow.

He'd never been in the house. Way too small-time for that shit to happen. He felt relieved the lights were already on. At first anyway. Just past the entryway, P-Wac discovered the carnage.

"*. . . Died in an ugly manner . . .*"

No fucking shit. P-Wac knew death. Had already seen his fair share, but not like this. He dropped the gun, and started to shake. He moved in circles. He threw gang signs, and didn't know why. He babbled. He sputtered. Lots of *shits* and *fucks*, and *Jesus, Jesus, Jesus, Jesus . . .* Until he heard the footsteps at his back. P-Wac leapt for the gun.

"POLICE! Show your hands, motherfucker! Get away from that goddamned gun!"

* * * *

13

Detectives Sean Scully and Mark Penn pulled up chairs and plopped worn-out asses in front of the legendary Lieutenant Ely Elmore.

"Tell me about it," Elmore barked.

Scully cut his eyes toward Penn, the senior of the two. He'd gladly let the older detective try to explain the hideously screwed-up scene they'd been working for the past six hours. Scully trusted Penn to know where to start in telling what they knew, what they didn't, and what they could only assume. He depended on his partner to do a decent job of explaining the inexplicable. Too, Scully's mind already felt fucked enough without it being fucked with further by the gruff and burly Lieutenant of Detectives.

"Never seen nothing like it, Boss," Penn started.

"You've been on the job over twenty years, Penn," Elmore said, "How can these six dead gang-bangers be any different than any other six dead gang-bangers?"

Scully fought off a sudden and foolish urge to laugh out loud. He wouldn't want Elmore to think he was laughing at him.

"Let me just start at the beginning," Penn tried again.

"Always a good fucking place to start," Elmore grimaced.

Mark Penn took a deep breath and flexed his shoulders, no doubt trying to release tension. "Dispatch took the call from a pay phone in Detroit, Michigan."

Elmore sat upright and moved his chair closer to the desk. "Detroit? Why the fuck would it come from Detroit?"

"Have no idea, but, it gets better, or worse," Penn nodded. "We listened to the tape. The voice, it was . . . computer generated. It gave the address, and gave the street names of the bodies that we found there. Nothing else. First officers on the scene found a seventeen-year-old black male in the house. We don't believe he had anything to do with the killings . . . "

Back when he was on the streets, Elmore was considered one of the brightest investigators the department employed. Unlike some supervisors, he knew how to listen. He now applied those skills as Penn methodically explained the scene and presented the findings. Six dead black males with strong gang affiliations. Autopsies would have to confirm what the detectives suspected, but it appeared that each had first taken a gunshot to the legs to immobilize them so their hands could be bound behind their backs with stout electrical ties. Then their throats were slit. While they bled out, all six were stripped from the waist down . . . and castrated. Some, if not all, would have been conscious during the horrid ordeal. Finally, a bullet was fired point-blank in all twelve eye sockets, making just a terrible mess of the backside of six skulls.

"One might immediately suspect a rival gang," Elmore said thoughtfully.

"Always a possibility, but we don't think so," Penn continued. "The house was shit-full of heroin, cocaine, and meth. All found neatly stacked beside the victims. Along with four-hundred and fifty-two thousand in cash, stacked alongside all the drugs. No rival gang would have left the stash. Hell, it would have been their motive for being there."

"That is motherfucking strange," Elmore agreed.

"More motherfucking *very* strange to follow," Penn responded. "Forty-five long-caliber casings were left on the scene. These rounds are normally shot from revolvers, more specific, Single-Action Army types. Damn sure not the firearm of choice for street gangs. The casings were pristine. Carefully cleaned. We can only assume they were left as, well, a calling card of such. Also, we're not finding shit for evidence. It seems, that except for all the blood, the scene was cleaned by professionals. On top of all this, it's looking as if every security camera in at least a three mile radius was rendered inoperable. Finally, radio transmissions between communications and district cars suddenly became garbled… as if electronically jammed or something of the sorts."

"How the hell could they manage to do either?" Elmore blurted.

"We don't know," Penn answered.

Silence reigned for several stale seconds. Scully thought Penn did a good job of stumping the LT as much as the crime scene stumped the two detectives.

"The kid found on the scene. What's the deal with him?" Elmore asked.

"We think he kind of stumbled onto the scene. He goes by the name of P-Wac, won't give us anymore and won't provide the name of a guardian. So, we can't grill him. But, the punk was terrified. One of the street cops reported that he initially kept screaming, 'I didn't do it . . . it was the *outlaws.*' Have no idea what he meant. We're holding him in protective custody until we can get information on his guardian."

Ely Elmore took in a deep breath and let it out as a long sigh. "You have anything brilliant to add, Scully?"

Scully often felt Elmore didn't particularly care for him, considering him too brash for a younger detective, and Scully didn't care for the "brilliant" being added where it wasn't needed. Pride overruled common sense.

"I do, boss. I don't understand how any man can hold another man's balls in his hands, even to cut them off."

Elmore grinned, but ugliness flashed in his eyes. "I've been known to reach across this desk and shake subordinates like a rag doll.

But I know you're tired and frustrated, so I'll just let it go with . . . get the fuck out of my office, Scully."

Scully waited outside the office until Penn exited.

His partner spoke barely above a whisper. "Jesus Christ, Sean, have you lost your mind? The LT just came out of the closet a year ago. You know he's sensitive about that kind of shit."

Scully felt damned tired. Seen what humans should not have to see while wading in blood for too many hours, and he didn't need Penn on his ass.

"Yeah, it was stupid," he agreed. "But, fuck him. If he's that sensitive about being gay, he should have kept his ass in the closet."

They started down the hall for their cubicles as Penn pointed out, "He's still a damned good cop and boss."

"Never said he wasn't," Scully mumbled.

* * * *

Trey Remington stood practically in the middle of the monstrous and long-deserted warehouse watching *the team* load the Hummer into a semi-trailer. John Ledford stood some distance away in the shadows. Remington could only see the outline of his partner's hat and long duster. Had he stood closer, he would see the long and dark hair that fell to his shoulders. They'd been friends since childhood. He knew the man in the shadows like no one else ever would. He knew what he felt at the moment, and what ran through his mind.

In just a matter of minutes, support-team member Darren Weed approached Remington.

"We are ready for transport to the next staging area, Trey." the technician reported. "Your driver is two minutes out."

"Roger that, Darren. I'll go get him." he said, nodding toward Ledford. Before doing so he placed a hand on Weed's shoulder. "Your men did an amazing job tonight, dear friend. Glad to have you on the team."

Weed grinned, "Glad to be on the team, brother. Being a black man, I wouldn't wanted to be on the other side tonight."

Remington thought on the words for a few seconds, "You know, initially, we could be conceived as racists."

"Not all targets are going to be black, Trey." Weed said.

"True, but this is all about winning the hearts and the minds of the populace. Perception is everything."

"Trey, those who matter will know this isn't about skin color. But, both too early and too late to be bothered with such now. Best go get John. Time's dwindling."

Remington strode across the cement, his spurs reporting the pace with an echoing jingle.

"Time to go, John."

"I'm ready."

"Are you?"

"Just processing."

"We both know. It never gets easier. Just let me say . . ."

"Yeah. Know what you're going to say. 'It often takes good men acting evil to bring about true justice.'"

"No. Was going to say let's hurry. Sooner we get there, the sooner we eat. I'm starved."

* * * *

Detective Sergeant Marcus Jones went in early, found and read the intelligence update, and considered pulling up the supporting reports, but knew that would be damned stupid. Instead, he asked for the remainder of the day off. Probably not a real smart thing to do either. The next time, and he knew there would be a next time, he promised himself to do absolutely nothing to draw unnecessary attention. Jones left the office, went straight home, dismissed his daughter's caretaker, and poured a tall glass of bourbon.

He didn't give a shit about the time of morning. *Six people dead.* He had no idea, but what exactly did he expect? For one million dollars, should he have expected any less? Jones plopped into his recliner, lit a cigarette and took a hardy swig from the glass of whiskey.

I am not a bad man.

They were trash. How many had they killed? Certainly, more than six.

And I'm not a dirty cop. Just a cop with unusual and unfair circumstances.

Three ex-wives, and a grown child from each that wanted nothing to do with him. Not to mention the one still at home. Who could blame him? Just everyone who mattered. The Chicago Police Department would blame him. The district attorney would blame him. The courts would blame him. *The six dead would blame him.*

He lit a new cigarette from the butt of the previous one, and took another hit of whiskey. And another. Jones wished he'd asked more questions. Simple questions. Basic common-sense questions.

What will you do with the intelligence I provide?

How did you know of my unfair and unusual circumstances?

If it all goes to shit, how will you protect me?

But the man brought the two big briefcases to their initial meeting. Jones had never seen so much money. He'd never felt the heft of a million dollars. Until now, he'd never felt the weight of *six dead.*

"What have I done?" he asked aloud. "What the fuck have I done?"

And no answer came, but a voice did call out.

"Daddy? Daddy? Trisha made potty. Change Trisha's diaper, Daddy?"

Jones turned in his recliner to see his daughter standing in the tiny kitchen of the low-rent apartment.

"Go to your bedroom, baby. Daddy will be there soon."

He watched as she nodded before waddling away. If her hands were not so badly deformed, maybe the fifteen-year-old could change her own diaper, but then again, she had the mind of a three-year-old.

Marcus Jones finished off the whiskey, wiped away his tears, and took off on wobbly legs to change a shitty diaper.

TWO

Aspermont, Texas

Melinda Lollar wished she'd exited the feed store just one minute earlier. If so, she could have avoided Sheriff Jerry Ring. He approached with a strut, stopping only when close enough to touch her. Melinda knew he wouldn't dare do that. Instead, he propped his lanky frame against a stack of bargain dog food bags.

"You know, if you were my . . ." Ring started in lieu of a proper form of greeting.

Melinda turned to face him and waited for the rest of a disparaging comment.

". . . girl friend? Fiancé? Live-in lover . . . Uh, just exactly what are you to that man, Melinda?"

"I've never told you, Jerry?" Melinda smirked.

"No. No, you haven't, Melinda," he smirked back.

"Then I guess it's none of your damned business."

Ring chuckled, but it sounded fake. Melinda pulled in a deep breath of the thick Texas air and swatted a fly away from her face. She longed to so easily swat away the more persistent pest wearing a badge.

"Well, if you were my *woman,* I wouldn't let you out of my sight. I know what you're capable of when left unattended."

"You're a rude and bitter man, Jerry Ring. I would tell you to kiss my ass, but you'd really try to do it."

"That's clever," he scowled. "So, what's up with him? Where's he been? Haven't seen much of Trey Remington lately."

Melinda wished the stock boy would spend less energy sneaking peaks of her ass and put more effort toward loading the bags of horse feed into her truck. If loaded, she'd simply jump in and drive away, leaving Ring to stand on the curb alone with his bile.

"Trey's at the ranch. He doesn't like coming into the Stonewall county seat, Jerry. Imagine that."

"What I imagine, Melinda, is that he's up to no good. He's good at that."

Melinda smiled tauntingly. "A jury of his peers would disagree with your assumption. Oh, but that's already happened once, hasn't it?"

Ring pushed away from the bags of dog chow to stand upright. "Remington has no peers. Just loving admirers that buy into his bullshit hero image, Melinda. That Navy Seal bullshit in particular. Aw, I guess he has one peer, but let's not bring that asshole John Ledford into our pleasant little conversation." Ring paused to adjust the gun belt around his waist. "Shit, Melinda, you can do so much better than that man."

"Not a Navy Seal, Jerry. Army Special Forces. Do you even know the difference? And I could have a much better man? Like who?"

"Like me."

Melinda paused to watch an ancient pickup lumbering up Main Street, belching clouds of obnoxious fumes. The site provided her response. "I had you, Jerry. Or, don't you remember? You let me out of your sight."

Ring started to comment, but Melinda beat him to the punch. There'd been too many of these encounters over the past two years, and she increasingly resented being subjected to them. "Trey is a damned good man. Twice the man you can ever hope to be. You need to let the past be in the past. Let it go. And leave him alone. And leave me alone."

"Oh, the past is the past. It's the future I keep an eye on. It's just a matter of time before he fucks up again. The next time, I'll put him away. Save you from him."

The young man finished loading her truck, but Melinda stood in place for a final jabbing. "Better get him fast, your term in office expires in another year, Sheriff Ring. Talk has it that your chances of reelection are as hopeless as you ever having me back."

Ring didn't offer a comeback, but if looks could kill . . .

Melinda climbed into her truck. A blazing sun baked the streets and brick structures of Aspermont, but she still felt a chill. She only wished Trey could truly be found back at the ranch. If Ring knew of his absence, it could prove very unfortunate.

* * * *

West Chicago

Clinton almost stopped to watch the older boys play basketball at the community courts, but heeded his mother's words instead.

"You go straight to the grocery store, Clinton. Get the milk. Get the eggs. Get your ass back here. Don't you stop along the way. Not for nobody. Not for nothing. You understand?"

Clinton understood then, and still understood. He did not fear all the things she'd taught that could harm him on the streets, but Clinton did fear Mama. At eight-years-old, he surely loved his Mama and cared deeply about disappointing her, but he cared even more about getting an ass whipping. She didn't have to do it often, but when she did, she did it good. He understood that, too. She always told him that had she whipped his older brother's ass more often, Jason might still be alive today.

Jason chose the gangs over Mama. Clinton knew the terrible pain Jason caused her. Clinton lived daily with her pain. He would not do the same to her. She hurt enough already. He promised her all the time, and he meant it, that he would stay in school and out of the gangs. That's what Mama wanted, and what Clinton wanted Mama to have. And he didn't want his ass whipped.

Clinton picked up the pace, watching for the things Mama taught him to watch for. He made it to the small store without spotting any signs of danger. He bought the milk and eggs, and thanked Mr. Nguyen just like he'd been taught to do. He didn't understand all Mr. Nguyen said sometimes, but sure liked the way he talked.

Clinton only had a block to go when the stray cat walked out from between a row of houses. He loved all animals, and wanted a pet, but Mama wouldn't allow it. Standing in front of a house that looked no different than the others on the block, Clinton called out to the cat.

"Here kitty, kitty! Come here little, kitty. Come on, kitty. I just want to . . ."

He felt shoved, and real hard. His feet came off the ground. The milk went one way and the eggs another. Only then did he hear the terrible noises.

BANG-BANG-BANG-BANG-BANG-BANG-BANG-BANG
and shattering glass and tires squealing on pavement as an engine
accelerated.

Clinton landed on the concrete, and knew little else. He felt
confused. He became sleepy so fast, even though it seemed his back
and legs had been set on fire. It turned immediately dark, and Clinton
cried. Mama would whip his ass for being out after dark. His mouth
did not work well for some reason, but he struggled to call out to her.

"I'm sorry, Mama."

"I broke your eggs, Mama."

"*I . . . love . . . you . . . Mama.*"

Clinton continued to call to his mother until he couldn't. The
sleep overtook him, but just before it did, he wondered why his
mother never responded.

* * * *

Brujo sat alone in his safe place. He felt secure because few knew
of the house. Here he needed no bodyguard. Actually, Brujo seldom
felt the need for bodyguards. The streets bordering this place were his
streets. Everyone knew Brujo. Nobody fucked with Brujo. They knew
the ways he could fuck back. He picked up the disposable cell phone
next to his easy chair, and thumbed in a number.

"Did the muchachos do the deed?" He asked in his typically low
and menacing way he practiced since boyhood.

"Si☒Ese☒" the voice on the other end responded. "They sent the
message."

"Do we know of any unlucky ones?" Brujo asked.

"The house sustained much damage. Those inside...maybe so.
One chico negro got in the way. Very unfortunate for that small one."

Brujo chuckled in the devious way he'd perfected. "Awww, ese⊠ in our line of business, little niggers grow up to be big niggers. Fuck him."

Brujo punched the End button and leaned back in his easy chair. A message had been sent. Life was good. Except for some black mother.

"Fuck her, too," Brujo grinned while surrounded by walls that kept him safe.

* * * *

The slender woman with lovely green eyes extended her right hand, and Detective Sergeant Marcus Jones bent at the waist to shake it.

"Thank you for meeting me here," Jones said as he took a seat across the table from the woman. "I know it's very late. I apologize for any inconvenience, Ms. Myers. It's just that I have to be very careful considering . . ."

"I understand, Sergeant Jones," Marge Myers interrupted with a soft voice and warm smile. "And I'm the one who owes you gratitude for coming here. Could we start by you showing me your credentials?"

Jones expected the request, and looked around the small bar for a few seconds before pulling out the leather bi-fold that held his badge and identification card. He watched her pretty eyes quickly, but thoroughly, scan for authenticity.

"Thank you, Sergeant Jones. Why are you doing this?"

Jones gave the response he'd been informed to give. "I feel strongly that it's just something the public needs to be aware of. I've never done this before. You truly can promise to use me only as an anonymous source?"

"Absolutely. I promise. Why did you choose me?"

Jones didn't choose her, but presented the lie as instructed. "I did my research. I believe you to be one of the most competent reporters not only from your paper, but in the entire city. This must be handled in a manner in which you've proven most capable. What do you know about the deaths?"

"There's not much to know. A probable hit from an opposing gang. Very little released from the department. I considered it just more of the same . . . until you reached out to me."

"Exactly," Jones nodded as the waitress approached and asked for his order. He requested a double Johnnie Walker Red on the rocks, and hoped she'd promptly deliver.

When the waitress walked away, Jones leaned in close and spoke barely above a whisper. "There are no suspects, but unlikely a hit from another gang, and not an inside job. Vast amounts of dope and money were left with the bodies. The scene was professionally cleaned of all evidence before responding officers arrived. All victims were first immobilized, had their throats slit, were castrated, and each shot through both eyes. One source said it was perpetrated by *The Outlaws*. We believe it was a warning to gang kingpins . . . and that other such deaths will occur."

Jones could tell by the look in her eyes, and by her posture, that he gained her full attention, and she wanted more. His "handler" would be damned proud of him. Jones just wanted his whiskey.

* * * *

He did not know exactly when, but at some point Brujo fell asleep in his chair. Now, he awoke abruptly. The lights were out, and he knew he'd left them on.

What the fuck?

Brujo reached in the darkness to fumble with the switch of the lamp sitting on a table next to his chair. The bright light temporarily blurred his vision, but not enough to realize the S&W automatic he left on the table, was gone. He straightened to push from the chair, but froze in place at what his blurry vision told his groggy mind.

Vaqueros?

What the FUCK!

For a split second, Brujo thought he might still be asleep, and having a nightmare. What else could explain the two cowboys standing side-by-side just mere feet in front of him? He was sober, and had not smoked dope. He'd never hallucinated in his life. Maybe a vision? If so, surely not from God. The cowboys did not speak, and Brujo couldn't. Instead, he studied them much like they seemed to be studying him.

Black hats. Long black coats. Boots with . . . fucking spurs? Bandanas pulled up to conceal their faces, and each of their hands, hanging down to their sides, held long-barreled revolvers. It occurred then to Brujo it might be wise for him to ask a question.

"Habla Espanol?"

The cowboy to his right might very well be Hispanic. Dark hair fanned across his broad shoulders, and his eyes looked brown. But this one shook his head before speaking.

"Taco. Burrito. Chihuahua. That's about it, Senor."

Maybe a joke? If so, Brujo found no humor in the intrusion. "What the fuck are you doing here? Do you know who I am?"

As if on cue, both men raised a pistol and used the barrel to push down their bandanas. Not good. They felt no fear in revealing their faces. Not a good sign for Brujo.

The other cowboy spoke this time. "We know you go by the name, Brujo. We know what gang you lead, and that you lead it with an iron fist. We know that three weeks ago you got screwed out of a shipment of marijuana, and that just hours ago, you took revenge. We know you show no mercy. What are we doing here? We've come to send a message to the others like you. More to the point, we've come to cut off your balls, slit your throat, and shoot you through both eyeballs."

Brujo's eyes frantically scanned his safe place for the missing gun. Only then did he notice the other three figures standing behind the cowboys. What could be more unsettling than cowboys in Chicago? Very few things Brujo could think of, except people dressed in white biochemical suits from head to toe.

Cleaners.

With no other alternative coming to mind, Brujo let out a blood-curdling scream of rebellion and leapt from his chair. He didn't make it far before hearing the final words spoken.

"*Audios, Brujo.*"

* * * *

"Where the fuck you get this?" P-Wac asked while fixated on the flyer in his hand.

"Shit, P-Wac, they all over the streets," Nine Mil answered. "Fuck, man, they on light posts. On store windows. Everywhere. Is it for real? Do it look like they did?"

P-Wac had been lying low since the cops let him loose. He didn't fear the cops, they had nothing on him. He did fear the outlaws. The crazed bad-ass cowboys left an impression he could not shake.

"For real, Nine Mil. This some real shit." The flyer contained a close-up of D-Killa's badly distorted and dead face. Above the picture bold letters read, "DO NOT TAKE HIS PLACE." Below it read, "MORE TO COME."

"Shee-it, P-Wac. We need to find those cowboys and fuck 'em up. Hell, move up through the ranks, bro."

P-Wac stared hard at Nine Mil. "Don't you get it?" he asked before thrusting the flyer in his friend's face. "Movin' up means dyin', mutha-fucka. You wanna die this way?"

"Fuck, P-Wac, there's two of 'em. Just fuckin' two of 'em. How many of us they be? A hundred? Fuck, that many of us against just two?"

P-Wac exhaled hard and dropped his head. "You saw the mother fuckers. Fast as fuck with those guns. The way that one dude spun his pistols. Two at one time. Man, you saw them. Like they come from the past. And that Hummer? Fuckin' bullet-proof, Nine Mil. And look how they took out those niggas at D-Killa's pad. Believe me, man, those cowboys got some kind of magic shit. Like they fuckin' ghosts, man."

"Fuck this," Nine Mil groaned. "Don't tell me my main man is losin' his balls."

P-Wac sadly shook his head before turning and walking into the shadows. "What I tell you is this, bro," he called over his shoulder. "I fosho seen six fuckas that did."

* * * *

Sean Scully rolled over in bed mumbling profanities as he fumbled attempts to grab the ringing cell phone off his bedside table. Through the haze of deep sleep he finally managed to bring it to his ear.

"What do you want?" He growled.

"Get dressed. I'm on the way to pick you up. We have another one."

Scully could not help but recognize the voice of his partner, Mark Penn. All else seemed fuzzy.

"Another what?" he grumbled.

"Another body with no nuts, no eye-balls, and a sore throat," Penn grumbled back.

Scully pushed up in bed, and shook his head to clear it. "No shit? Where?"

"West side. We're being assigned out of district. I'll be there in ten minutes. Meet me outside."

Scully wasted no time in throwing on a suit, strapping on his gun, and making a tall cup of stout instant coffee. He stood waiting on the curb when Penn pulled up in the sedan.

"Did you say *a body?* Just one this time?" Scully asked as soon as his ass collided with the front passenger seat.

"Yup. Just one," Penn said as he gunned the car away from the curb. "Get your damned seat belt on."

Scully worked at strapping in and asked, "Another black gang leader?"

"Nope. Hispanic. One Juan Gonzales. Goes by the name of Brujo. Ring bells?"

"Hell yes, it does. He's a big-time player, known city-wide," Scully responded.

"Yup. Was. Can't play big no more. Has no balls," Penn chuckled, then added, "Someone must be planning one hell of a takeover."

Scully sipped the sorry excuse for early morning coffee and considered Penn's comment before rebutting. "Maybe not."

"What else could it be?" Penn asked while taking a corner so fast that it shoved Scully up against the door. "Could you slow down just a tad? Shit, made me slosh my coffee. Cocksucker is already dead. Can't get any deader."

"No fun being a big-city detective if you can't drive fast," Penn grinned. "Again I ask, what else could it be if not a power play?"

"Could be someone doing what we can't," Scully said. "Someone intent on cleaning up this shit hole of a city."

"A vigilante?" Penn questioned.

"Yeah, or an organization of vigilantes."

"That's a scary thought," Penn mumbled.

"Not really. Five key scum-bag players dead in this short of time? I say the killers deserve a commendation and a key to the city."

"Something like this could turn Chicago into a battle zone," Penn objected.

Starting to feel the effect of the caffeine, Scully laughed out loud. "Mark, Chicago's already a battle zone. Sad fact is though, until now, most of the casualties have been children, parents, and cops."

"Sean, if this continues, citizens could start arming themselves and join in on the fray," Penn said as he pulled to a stop behind three parked patrol cars.

Scully grabbed Penn's arm to hold him in the car a moment longer. "I wouldn't want you telling our illustrious mayor that I said so, Mark. But the thought of good people carrying guns and killing bad people, does not bother me in the least."

Penn nodded his head and replied, "The problem with that is, too often the lines get jagged between who is good and who is bad. It's a complicated topic."

"Okay. Let's say our suspects are vigilantes. Are they good or bad?"

Penn started out of the car. "Well so far, if that is the case, they've done a service to our city . . . in a most evil kind of way."

Scully got out of the car and looked over the top of the car at Penn. He knew his partner was one of very few who he could say this to. "If that is the case, I don't care how long they keep it up. I need the overtime."

* * * *

Kenneth Donning returned to his private suite of rooms after delivering the news to Charles Atkinson of another successful mission. He sat down behind his desk and loosened his tie. Sir Atkinson of course expressed delight and appreciation, and didn't say so, but Donning knew he wondered why his right-hand man did not express the same sentiments.

Donning's attitude over the matter had nothing to do with the fact that evil men were being murdered, or that the executions resulted from acts and orders he'd personally placed in motion. Donning had killed men in his day. He often thought he'd left his soul in the deep jungles of Vietnam long after the "official" war was over. As a result of the numerous special operations, many were left dead. Even now, he did not consider himself capable of caring that men deserving death were indeed being put to death. His only concerns were for Sir Atkinson.

Donning first met Atkinson in London after his operative missions in Vietnam. As a very young major he'd been assigned attaché duties at the American embassy, where Charles Atkinson served as an interim ambassador. The two men struck a very quick and close friendship. From the first, Donning had been deeply impressed by Atkinson. The man had something Donning lost: *his soul.* Atkinson truly cared for the plight of mankind. He gave more of himself than he requested in return. Because of his giving nature and undying care for the helpless, Atkinson was awarded an honorary knighthood from the Queen of England. Donning knew no other man more worthy of such an honor.

Donning and Atkinson remained close friends up to the time Donning retired from the army as a full colonel. Atkinson wasted no time in bringing Donning into his empire built from coal and oil ventures. Over the years, Donning worked his way up from chief of security to his personal assistant, a chief-of-staff of sorts and, more importantly, Atkinson's dearest friend.

Donning did not care that thugs were dying in Chicago. However, he did care deeply that Charles Atkinson, too, was dying. The rare cancer provided a prognosis of three to five years of life to live. Donning did not want this "operation" to end up in some way casting an evil nature on a very good man. The world would not understand, but Donning did. As a result, he promised himself that no blame could ever fall on Atkinson for what occurred in Chicago. If it all went wrong, Donning would take the blame. A hundred times over, he'd fall on his sword for Sir Atkinson.

* * * *

Sean Scully sat quietly as his partner finished briefing Lieutenant Ely Elmore on the murder scene.

"Just exactly like the murders on the south side," Elmore grumbled while rubbing at his temples.

"Yes," Penn agreed, "Except this time the call came in from Boston."

"First Detroit, and now Boston," Elmore seemed to say to himself. "I can't imagine where this is all leading."

"We think we do," Scully inserted, speaking for the first time.

Elmore turned a stern glare on Scully. "Oh, really?"

"Yes, sir. Want to hear it?"

"Why the fuck wouldn't I?"

Scully bit his tongue before continuing. "First, powerful black gang leaders were taken out. Now, one of the most prominent Hispanic leaders is in the morgue. That leaves only the white and Asian gang leaders. We think they are next to receive the message."

"The message?" Elmore barked. "What fucking message?"

Scully cleared his throat and glanced at Penn. Penn nodded for him to proceed. "The message that you don't want to be leading gangs in Chicago."

"That's a far reach," Elmore said.

"We suggest that surveillance teams be assigned to white and Asian kingpins, and that tactical units be on the standby," Scully offered.

"Oh yeah? And which kingpins? Just exactly how many of them? And where does the damned manpower and funding come from, Scully?" Elmore exploded.

This time Scully did not bite down so hard on his tongue. "That's not my problem, Lieutenant. Brass has to make that happen. You have to make that happen."

Elmore jumped up from behind his desk and turned to grab a newspaper from his credenza. "This is today's fucking Chicago Tribune. Have either of you seen it?"

"Been kind of busy, boss," Scully barked. "Didn't have time for my morning paper with coffee."

Penn elbowed him in the ribs before adding, "Haven't seen it either, Lieutenant."

Elmore fanned the paper in their faces. "This particular copy was presented to me earlier by the Chief of Detectives. Someone is leaking information to reporters on the south side case. The Chief is highly pissed. You two, of course, are the most informed. Have any idea who might be reaching out to a fucking reporter?"

"I don't appreciate the implication," Scully growled.

"I don't like the Chief eating on my ass, Scully!"

He'd be damned if he could help it. Sean Scully grinned, and arched his eyebrows knowingly.

Elmore grinned as he looked Scully straight in the eyes. "Make one more insinuation about my sexual orientation, Scully, and you will be writing parking tickets the rest of your career. That is unless you show up beaten to death in some ally."

The calm sincerity of the threat brought Scully to his senses. "I get the message loud and clear, boss."

"I am the goddamned boss. And as the boss, I'm telling you both. Get on top of these fucking murders. You probe, you dig, you come up with some damned solid suspects. Now, get the hell out of here."

The next thing Scully new, Penn had him by the arm, moving him out of the commander's office. In the hallway he sighed, "Sean, that is not a man you want as an enemy."

"You're right," Sean mumbled, "but he needs to develop a sense of humor."

"Oh, I'm sure he'd laugh his ass off while beating you to death in an ally."

THREE

C harles Atkinson placed the Chicago Tribune aside and took a sip of his tea. Donning picked up his cup as well. The two friends shared afternoon tea in the European fashion; a practice they adopted from their earlier years together in London.

"Two articles in three days' time," Atkinson smiled.

"And surely another to follow after tonight's mission," Donning nodded.

"A job well done, Colonel Donning. I particularly like how Ms. Myers has applied the moniker *The Outlaws* to our most effective duo."

"Yes, sir. It is most satisfying to see sprouts from a carefully planted seed," Donning said, gracing his comment with a coy smile.

"Indeed it is. The name will stick, and it will spread," Atkinson smiled again. He dabbed at his lips with a silk napkin before asking, "What we are having them do is most certainly outside the law. So, do you consider Ledford and Remington outlaws by nature, or as a product of necessity?"

Donning took another sip of tea as he carefully considered his answer. Atkinson simply loved discussing the two Texas ranchers. He could only know them through Donning, and Donning did not intend to cheat his best friend by leaving out the slightest detail.

"Well, sir. I do believe both would prefer living in peaceful anonymity on their vast ranch. Neither is of the nature to willingly seek the spotlight, but both are plagued with a strong sense of justice . . . no matter the means necessary to see it to fruition."

"The exact reason we chose them," Atkinson commented with an index finger in the air.

"Precisely, sir. More to the point of my answering your question, they are both outlaws because it is necessary for them to be such. However, I do believe that John Ledford, due to his heritage, possesses a streak of rebellion that I do not sense in Trey Remington."

Of course, Sir Atkinson followed with additional questions, and Donning provided the answers. Each and every time they discussed Ledford and Remington, Donning could not help but reflect on their initial meeting . . .

* * * *

. . . Donning gave considerable thought to his mode of transportation from the airport in Abilene, Texas, to the TRJL Ranch. He finally decided that his unannounced arrival should be as impressive as possible. As a result, he chose to rent a long black limousine to be driven by a highly trusted chauffeur who accompanied him from New York City in the private jet.

With a ranch of thousands of acres, Donning had anticipated a grand Hacienda. Or, at least, a decent house. He did not expect to pull up in front of two mobile homes separated by nearly fifty-yards of scrubby brush and weeds. For long seconds he simply sat in the back of the limousine and stared at the simple structures. He might have remained doing such longer if the slim woman had not stepped out of the trailer on the left.

The brunette clad in jeans, boots, and a plaid shirt stood on a wooden set of steps and stared out at the car. Donning took this as his cue to step from the car, and immediately wished he'd chosen a suit of lighter weight. The humidity assaulted him like a grip to the throat. Donning waved at the woman before calling out.

"My name is Kenneth Donning, ma'am. I'm here to see John Ledford and Trey Remington."

The woman cocked her head to the side. "And you came to see them in a limousine?" She called back.

"Well, uh, yes, ma'am."

The woman bounded down the steps and walked directly up to Donning. Her lovely dark blue eyes danced with mischievousness. "Well, they'll damn sure get a kick out of this," she said with a fetching smile. She stuck out a hand to be shaken.

"My name is Melinda Lollar. I'm Trey Remington's live-in maid, cook, clothes washer, and occasional horse handler. I prefer to be primarily a horse handler, but he only gives me the ones he can't manage."

Donning took the extended hand and the excessively strong grip surprised him more than her statement, of which, he did not know if she meant it as a joke, or the truth.

"Cops or reporters don't show up in limousines, so guess it's all right if you come with me. The boys have had their fill of cops and reporters, but don't think they'd object to a rich dude paying them a visit." Before moving, she looked down at his shoes.

"On the same topic, those look high-dollar."

Without the gift of gab or levity, Donning could only speak the truth. "I, uh, do not spend excessively on footwear, but do believe you get what you pay for."

"Ever had horseshit on them?"

"Uh . . . no, ma'am. That I haven't."

"Then best watch where you're stepping. Luckily for you, horseshit is easy to recognize. Can't always say the same for bullshit."

Donning followed Melinda between the two mobile homes and saw in the distance a large barn, which looked much statelier than the two dwellings. Fencing ran from both sides of the structure, and contained seven horses that Donning could see.

"What's your business with the boys?" Melinda said over her shoulder.

"Ma'am, I can only say that it is extremely urgent and highly confidential."

"Uh huh. Don't worry, if Trey don't tell me, I'll feed whiskey to the Indian. Whiskey always frees up the lips of John Ledford."

This time, although he could not once again tell, Donning seriously hoped Melinda Lollar was joking.

"I fear I might interrupt their working," Donning said out of a sudden need to say just anything.

"Don't bet on it," Melinda chuckled.

Melinda opened a door to the barn and motioned Donning through.

"After you, ma'am," Donning automatically responded.

Melinda chuckled again, "Damn, don't get me used to this kind of treatment. I might pack up and go home with you."

Donning followed Melinda into what he knew the locals called an indoor arena. No less than thirty feet in front of him stood two men dressed in western garb, leaning on an iron railing and staring at a saddled horse in front of them. The men exchanged words, but Donning could not determine if they talked among themselves, or to the horse. Both were solidly built, and although Donning stared up at few men, he thought he might find himself doing such to both.

Melinda announced their intrusion. "Hey, dead-asses, you have a visitor. He showed up in a by-God limousine!"

John Ledford and Trey Remington straightened and turned heads toward Donning at the announcement. Donning had studied enough footage to tell the two apart. Ledford would be the one with the long hair. Remington wore his cropped short in a military fashion.

Donning approached the men with his right hand extended. "Mr. Ledford, Mr. Remington, my name is Kenneth Donning."

Remington reached for his hand first, and then Ledford took his turn at shaking it. Both men possessed a strong grip, and Donning anticipated no less. The cowboys looked him up and down.

"Don't expect you're from these parts, Mr. Donning," Remington grinned. "What brings you to the TRJL?"

"A most urgent business matter, Mr. Remington," Donning started before being interrupted by Melinda.

"And a highly confidential business matter at that," She smiled.

Remington spoke up. "Mr. Donning, anything you have to say to me, you can say in front of my woman."

Donning cleared his throat. "Sir, I do believe you might want to protect Ms. Lollar from a proposition I've been dispatched to deliver. As a matter of fact, I've been instructed to talk to only you and Mr. Ledford."

Remington looked first at Melinda, and then turned his gaze on Ledford,

"What's your thinking on this, John?"

"Damn curious, Trey. And Melinda does have a big mouth," Ledford said dryly.

"Oh, hell, I don't have time to stand around and listen to silly man-talk anyway. I have real work to do." Melinda walked away, but stopped at the door and hollered back. "And you, John Ledford, can do without dinner tonight."

Ledford and Remington chuckled in unison over the comment.

At that point, Donning confirmed the men of his particular breed. Their lips could form a smile and emit laughter, but their eyes could not match any form of glee. Donning knew that meant the eyes he looked into had seen horrors unknown to typical men. Donning also knew a nerve of sorts stretched from their eyes to their hearts, and maybe even to their souls . . . if indeed the men still possessed such.

"I do hope she does not consider me rude," Donning said.

"Don't worry about it," Remington grinned. "If she'd wanted to stay, the three of us could not have done a darn thing about it. Now, Mr. Donning what is your business with us?"

Donning reached into the inner pocket of his suit and pulled out a wallet. He extracted a card and handed it to Remington.

"A retiree identification card," Remington observed, and then nodded his head as if impressed. "Dang, John, this isn't a Mr. Donning. This is Full-Bird Colonel Donning, U.S. Army, retired. Thank you for your service to our country, Colonel."

"And I thank you both for yours," Donning said with a slight bow. "In short, I am here to offer you yet another chance to serve."

Ledford shook his head defiantly. "Did two tours in Iraq and three in Afghanistan. Don't intend to do no more, Colonel."

"Oh, I'm certainly not here to re-enlist you into the armed service, gentlemen. I'm here to offer you a chance to right a terrible wrong in the country I'm sure you both love."

"Right a wrong?" Remington repeated. "Colonel, see that horse right there?"

"I do, sir."

"Well, that's one mean bastard that needs breaking. When you came in, we were discussing among ourselves which one of us should be the first to let that horse bust our ass or possibly break our neck. That decision has yet to be made, and we need to get to it."

"I understand, Mr. Remington, and . . ." Donning started.

"I can't speak for my partner here, Colonel, 'cause he can be a snooty sort of guy, but I'd be more comfortable with you calling me Trey."

Ledford displayed a middle finger to Remington before grumbling, "Never been a mister. Never cared to be. Call me John, Colonel."

Donning nodded his head. "Okay, Trey and John it is, and I understand the need to get to your business, but I can't just blurt the reason I'm here. If I did, you'd most definitely think I was insane."

"Well, Colonel, if it helps, there are people around here that think ol' John and me are crazy sons-of-bitches," Remington grinned while his eyes remained all too somber.

It did help, and Donning set about presenting the proposal.

* * * *

West Side of Chicago

"It's a good plan, Trey," Ledford said. "Stop fretting about it."

The two men sat across from each other at a folding table, cleaning their .45 caliber Colts. Trey Remington's soiled black hat lay

45

on the table next to him. Ledford preferred his on, but had it back on his head and tilted at a cocky angle.

"It isn't part of the operational plan. It's impromptu," Remington grumbled. "Like calling an audible when the coach has already sent in the best play. I wish I'd not come up with it."

Ledford put one of his pistols aside and picked up the other. "Donning has approved it. Why wouldn't he? The crew retrieved intel on a major drug buy from Brujo's apartment. He thinks your plan is a hell of a way to expedite getting the message out, and so do I. Besides, it gives a chance to eliminate Brujo's closest lieutenant. "

Remington pointed an unloaded revolver at an imaginary target and started cocking the hammer and pulling the trigger. "It's dangerous."

Ledford found no humor in the mission they performed, but could not help but laugh out loud. "Like the operations before this one have not been dangerous?"

"We put together a top-notched team of highly trained professionals. They reduced our risks. Not sure they can do the same with this mission."

Ledford nodded his head, but remained silent. He appreciated the fact that Donning had allowed them to select their support team, and had provided the great sum of money from a still un-disclosed source to pay for their services. Donning did at first seem skeptical that Ledford and Remington could find eight highly qualified men willing to take part in a felonious conspiracy, but then again, Donning had not known Donny Sparks . . .

* * * *

. . . Fifteen men were packed in the small briefing room. All bore long hair and scraggly beards along with the stench of days without showering. An Afghani major briefed the special operators huddled around the operational map spread on a long table.

"You understand a word this man is saying?" Ledford whispered to Remington.

"A bit here and there. Says he has a document to prove his point," Remington whispered back.

"This is some messed up shit," Ledford summed.

"Shut the fuck up, Ledford," Donny Sparks hissed into Ledford's ear. "We got to get what little we can get."

Ledford nodded his head. Donny was right, as usual. He'd been here longer and more times than the others. Being the team leader, he also out-ranked Ledford.

The Afghani mutilated the English language until interrupted by a CIA operative, who evidently understood more than Ledford could.

"Where is the document that supports this intel?" The operative asked.

For the first time since starting his briefing, the somber Afghani major offered a smile. He reached inside his camouflaged jacket and pulled out folded papers. He tossed them on the table. He put his hand back in the jacket just as the operative reached to get the first papers. This time the Afghani dropped a live grenade on the table.

"ALLAH AKBAR!"

Most in the room dove for cover. Donny Sparks flung himself across the table and over the grenade. Ledford, Remington, and two others put bullets in the major as Sparks took the brunt of the explosion. Blood splatter filled Ledford's eyes. It might have been Afghani blood, but more likely came from Spark's amputated legs, left arm, and tattered body cavity.

Ledford wiped at his eyes and joined in with those shouting curse words. Others rushed to give aid to a hero that somehow still managed to pull shallow breaths of air into badly damaged lungs . . .

* * * *

. . . Remington could tell Ledford's mind momentarily took a leave of absence. He playfully tapped his friend on the forehead with the barrel of his gun. "Did you hear me? I'm not sure our men can be of much help. We will be right out in the open. Just you and me."

"I heard you. Made me think about the men we selected, and that made me think of Donny Sparks," Ledford said softly.

Remington could not help but sigh. "Good to think about Donny from time to time. We might not be here if not for him. And we damned sure wouldn't have our team if not for him."

"Yeah, that's what I was thinking about," Ledford said as he went back to preparing his pistols.

Remington did the same, but now his thoughts also turned to Donny Sparks. For some reason on that distant day, God did what Remington thought he seldom did, he showed himself. He worked a miracle, and Sparks survived. He lived on to return to his home in the Bronx, but he lived a life confined to a wheel chair. Didn't slow Donny down. He got out and about, and was doing just that the day a young black teen pulled a gun on a store clerk, in a store Donny just happened to frequent. Right in front of Donny, the teen started to brutally pistol whip the clerk. Donny tried to talk the teen down. For his efforts, the young robber put his pistol to Donny's head and shot him three times, point blank. What dozens of Iraqis and Afghanis couldn't, the cowardly punk did. Later, the police determined the armed robbery served as a gang initiation for the teen. Now these years later, it proved a simple task to recruit men for a mission others might find despicable, or just too risky. Men whose lives Donny Sparks saved by pouncing on a grenade.

From the initial meeting with Colonel Donning, Remington and Ledford knew of others who would not deem his proposal ludicrous. Men, who like Remington and Ledford, had a score to settle, and would understand that what started in Chicago could spread to the Bronx in New York City.

Remington shook his head in order to bring his mind from the past to the here and now. "Go time is less than three hours away. You ready for this?"

"I am."

"You know, you've been following my screwed-up schemes for many years," Remington sighed. "If one of them ever gets you killed . . . Don't know how I'd live with myself."

Ledford picked up a gun in both hands and started spinning them in a manner to outdo any matinee dude cowboy. He grinned while doing so. "Don't be getting sentimental on me. We ain't never kissed, and I don't plan to start now."

* * * *

There were differences in the dialect, and some of the crew making the buy spoke only rudimentarily Spanish. Hernandez took his role of interpreter very seriously, and considered it a great opportunity to show loyalty to the man replacing the dreaded Brujo. "Hondo" Cortez, the new man in charge, possessed his own evil ways, but proved himself in the past to be a more sympathetic leader. However, Hernandez knew better than to disappoint Hondo.

Both crews were in place in the remote and vast parking lot of a vacated factory. Dealers stood across from buyers, a prearranged four from each gang organization. Hernandez drew close to Hondo as all gathered around the back of the van delivering the goods. Another of Hondo's men carried the suitcase with the great sum of cash.

Initially, all went well. Hernandez clarified a word here and there. They established from the start that the drugs were in the van, and the suitcase contained the money for the drugs. Hondo moved to confirm the shipment as the leader of the suppliers prepared to count the money. Suddenly a mixture of dialects along with exclamations in English rang out between both contingencies of men. Hernandez interpreted the clamor loosely as *what the fuck is that?*

The overall mood did not translate into fear or panic, but more simply as curiosity and wonder for what stood amongst some shadows just outside the soft glare of the few overhead lights in the parking lot. After all, why would so many armed men show fear or panic at the sight of two men, sitting side by side on . . . horses?

Both leaders shouted out for an explanation in their different forms of Spanish, but the two shadowy figures offered no response. Hernandez saw this as his opportunity to shine. He took the initiative to address the highly unusual intruders in English.

"Who the fuck are you and what the fuck do you want?"

One of the men on horseback immediately responded in a gruff but calm manner. "We want you to leave the drugs and money here, and get the hell gone. I think the word is *vamoose*."

Hernandez heard it, but could not believe the demand. He could do no more than translate it to those behind the van that did not understand. Those who spoke English were already laughing. When the others understood, they joined in.

Hondo stepped forward and called out in English, "And if we don't, hombres, what will you do? Stampede us?"

Hernandez repeated the words in Spanish, and all howled in laughter at the wit of Hondo Cortez. Then all laughter stopped as the two men on large horses reached beside their saddles and pulled long, old-fashioned rifles. The men did not aim the rifles, but held them upright with the barrels pointed to the heavens.

They should have aimed. Both buyers and sellers pulled guns. Two from the dealer's crew produced AK-47s that they did aim. And all hell broke loose. Two of Hondo's men let go with automatic handguns. The men on horseback separated and returned fire. To Hernandez's immediate surprise, the two with the AK's were the first to fall. Hernandez did not have a gun, but quickly wished he did.

Amongst heavy gunfire, the riders bore down upon the men on foot. Long black coats fanned at their backs like ominous capes. Neither man held their reigns, but instead used both hands to quickly cock levers and pull triggers, laying down accurate sheets of lead. Only as men started to drop to the left and right of Hernandez did he notice the black hats on the men's heads, and the bandanas that covered their faces. Hernandez knew the men around him were supported by superior weapons, but none proved to be as accurate as the cowboys. In a matter of brutal seconds, Hernandez stood alone. He considered grabbing a gun from a fallen comrade, but truthfully, he did not feel all that intent on dying. He stood in place as the men moved up close on suddenly tranquil horses.

This just did not seem real, but Hernandez knew the shit in his underwear felt damn real.

"Who are you?" His voice quaked.

Both men slipped rifles into long leather holders attached to their saddles. Their jackets had been blown back by the thrust of their

KEITH REMER

charge, and Hernandez observed both men carried pistols with butts forward in holsters from centuries past.

The man who spoke before spoke again now. "Around here, we've become known as the Outlaws. But we consider ourselves just concerned citizens of these United States. We're hoping others of a like mind will soon join us."

Hernandez opened his mouth to speak, but got out barely a word before the other man interrupted in a low but serious manner.

"Shut your mouth."

This man wore long and dark hair down on broad shoulders, and just the look in his dark eyes prompted Hernandez to obey.

"What is your name?" the other cowboy asked.

"Miguel Hernandez," he stammered back.

"Well, it comes to this, Senor Miguel Hernandez. Do you choose to live, or do you choose to die?"

"I want to live," Hernandez blurted.

"Then you will live. We'll grant that request, but would ask in return that you tell those you know who deal in drugs and belong to gangs, that they best find better ways to spend their time. Do you understand?"

"Yes . . . Sir." Hernandez could not remember the last time, if ever, that he used the title, but it now seemed damned appropriate.

"Okay. Start running and don't stop running until you get where you intend to be. And keep in mind, my partner here, if he can see you, he can drop you."

Hernandez only took time to nod, and then turned the rest over to his feet. He ran to where he needed to be, and kept on running from there.

* * * *

Sean Scully surveyed the apparent battlefield in the remote parking lot before turning to his partner.

"Why are we here, Mark? This does not fit the MO of our so-called Outlaws."

Penn shrugged his shoulders. "Don't know. But, look around. Dead bangers. Lots of drugs. A case full of money. All left here for us to find."

Scully reluctantly nodded his head. "Okay. I'll buy that." Sleep deprivation had apparently robbed him of his deductive powers. A detective lacking such proved as worthless as a diaper that couldn't hold shit.

Both detectives turned as a uniformed officer approached. "There were seven when we got here. Three were still breathing and were hauled off to Oaklawn Trauma Center," the uniform advised. "The four dead were all hit right between the eyeballs. Damn good shooting."

Scully followed Penn to observe the four dead. Two lay beside dropped AK-47s. Made sense to Scully. Those two needed put down effectively. The other two, Scully first thought, were just unlucky.

The uniformed officer pointed to one of the two Scully considered lacking luck. "That one we know," the officer said. "He goes by Hondo. Last name Cortez. He was Brujo's right-hand man."

It hit Scully like a brick. He nudged Penn and pointed at the third dead victim with the mangled forehead. "Betting whoever that is, he's a major league player as well."

"Wouldn't bet against you," Penn sighed. "But how did they know about this buy?"

"Proves what I've been saying all along, Mark," Scully grinned. "Our suspects are superheroes."

"Don't let Elmore hear you saying that shit," Penn grumbled.

"Fuck Elmore," Scully grumbled back. He didn't care to even hear the man's name. They'd both spent wasted time with the Lieutenant earlier in the day, and although Scully's attention should be on the crime scene at hand, he relived the meeting in his mind.

"Why the fuck would they do that?" Elmore questioned.

Scully didn't like the tone of voice, but he didn't want to widen the gap developing with his superior. He let Penn do the talking.

Penn replied with facts. "It's in the autopsy reports from both crime scenes. And we have a theory."

"So you are telling me," Elmore said, "That all victims were shot through the eyes first, and then, after they were dead, they were shot in the legs, had their throats slit, and only then had their balls cut off?"

"I'm telling you that is the finding of the coroners," Penn replied calmly.

"Why the fuck would they do that?"

"We think they want to send a message to the gang world. A message that says, you don't want us doing to you what we did to the others. It was meant to put fear in other top-level players. The word seems to be getting out, Lieutenant. Stats are already showing an unusual drop in gang-related crimes. It's not a significant drop, but the message might be working."

Scully tried, but just could not keep his mouth shut. "Also shows, LT, that our perps . . . aren't such horrible dudes after all."

Elmore bolted to his feet, and leaned over the desk to glare down at Scully. "You give me one more indication, Scully, that you find merit in what these murdering assholes are doing, and I'll jerk you off this case and put you to working property crimes."

The rebuke stung, and it still did, but this crime scene needed his undivided attention. And, he knew he best start viewing the suspects as no more than murdering assholes, at least while in the presence of Ely Elmore.

* * * *

Remington thanked God that the first part of his plan went extremely well. He also thanked God their adversaries couldn't shoot worth a damn. Had they been true marksmen, Remington would have no comments for God. He figured it would be hard to do so from hell.

Earlier, while a part of his team started sanitizing the scene, Remington and Ledford had retreated on the short route back to the waiting trailer. Horses and the big rig were far from the parking lot within ten minutes of the last bullet fired. In and out, smooth as possible. Thank God.

Now, with all tucked away in yet another secure warehouse, Remington turned his thoughts to the second part of the plan. The part Colonel Donning had called "marvelous."

He glanced to a darkened area some thirty feet away where John Ledford slowly paced back and forth. The two men possessed different means of decompressing. Ledford paced and struggled with demons, while Remington preferred slugging down whiskey and thanking a God that probably didn't really exist. Even if he did, he had more than likely long ago written Trey Remington off as a demented and hopeless case. If so, Remington could not blame him, and didn't give a shit. After all, if there was a God, it'd been him that allowed the messes Remington felt obsessed to clean up.

Remington took one more swig of whiskey from the bottle before standing and moving to a table laden with computers and audio and video equipment far too complex for him to operate.

Dan Hicks sat at the table applying only a smidgeon of his true technical genius. Hicks received his initial skills in the Army. After three deployments of waging cyber warfare, he'd used his GI Bill to help gain a degree from MIT. There existed few systems he could not hack, and Remington had yet to see an electrical component he couldn't manipulate.

"How's it coming, Dan?"

"It will be ready for delivery by 0900," the heavy-set technician replied without bothering to look up from his computer screen.

"Wow," Remington said with an impressed nod of his head.

"Told you before, Trey, this is mere child's play. Twelve-year-olds do this shit, man."

"I couldn't do it," Remington returned.

"Go figure," Hicks sighed.

Remington started away with a chuckle.

"But," Hicks said to stop him, "I can't knock off a gnat's nuts with a bb gun from twenty-yards away either, Trey."

"Aw, Dan, you sweet-talker, you exaggerate my skills," Remington laughed as he continued away. "But only a tad."

Remington grabbed his bottle on the way to an awaiting cot. He'd sip on it until going out. The practice proved to numb the tormenting nightmares.

FOUR

Marge Myers stepped into Candice Classen's office, and took the liberty to pull the door closed behind her. The attractive blonde sat at her desk, but stood and approached Marge with outstretched arms. Marge needed the sincere hug and hugged Candice back.

"Thanks for seeing me on such short notice," Marge said as the two women pulled apart.

"Don't be silly. You know my door is always open to you," Candice replied, flashing her smile of dazzling white teeth. She pointed at a chair and couch. "Please, have a seat."

"I should sit before I fall," Marge exhaled heavily.

"It's that big?" Candice asked as she escorted Marge to the couch.

"It's beyond big, Candi. It's amazingly phenomenal."

Candice selected the chair across from Marge. "Well, whatever it is, thanks for bringing it to me."

"You're the city's highest rated and most watched news personality, Candi. Who else would I bring it to?"

"You flatter me, and I'm curious as hell. What have you got?"

Marge took a moment to steady her breathing. It had been one hell of a morning and now, shortly after lunch, she still worked to calm her nerves. Little shook Marge Myers these days, but this was no small occurrence.

"I stopped this morning where I stop every morning for my special latte. I have to remove the keys from my ignition before the driver's door will open. At a certain distance away, the key fob automatically locks the doors. So, Candi, *I know* my car was locked tight. When I got back in the car . . ." Marge paused to reach into her purse and pulled out the item that rocked her day. ". . . this disc was lying on my passenger seat."

"What's on it?" Candice asked with apparent anticipation.

Marge stood and pointed at the television behind the newscaster's desk. "Best to see it. Words do it no justice." She handed the disc to Candice.

The petite blonde hurried the disc to a player positioned below the television.

"Be forewarned, Candi, it is shocking to say the least."

"I love shocking, Marge. It's what I do. It's in my blood."

Candice took a seat at her desk and worked a remote with her manicured thumbnail. Marge chose to stand, and knew soon enough, Candice would be on her feet as well. Marge had watched it over and over. At least a dozen times, but still she drew in a deep breath.

"Oh my God," Candice exclaimed. "What the hell, Marge? Men on horses?"

"Professionally miked-up, Candi . . . listen," Marge said quickly.

"We want you to leave the money and drugs here, and get the hell gone."

"OH MY GOD!" Candice this time squealed as she shot out of her chair.

"It's ugly, Candi," Marge warned.

"Your *Outlaws*!" Candice exclaimed.

"I have no doubt," Marge returned.

Marge remained silent as the video played on, while Candice emitted uncontrolled verbal upheavals. Marge certainly understood the reaction.

"We're hoping others of a like mind will soon join us."

After it ended, Marge practically had to pry the controls from Candice's hands. The newscaster collapsed into her desk chair. Marge waited until Candice found her voice.

"This is physical evidence," Candice finally muttered.

"It certainly is," Marge agreed.

"If we use it, the police will be pissed, Marge."

"Might even press charges for interfering in a murder case, Candi."

Long and tense seconds ticked by.

"Screw the police, Marge. I'm going to do my best to get this on the air tonight."

"I don't fear the police, Candi, but I am afraid."

Candice stood and took Marge's hand in hers. "Of what, Marge?"

Marge squeezed Candice's hands. "Those two," Marge nodded at the television. "They know who I am. They know my routine. They broke into my car. Who are these people? How are they doing this?"

"I don't know, Marge. But I want my viewers to be aware of it. However, I feel you have nothing to fear."

"Why not, Candi?"

"You know the answer, you're just too close to this. You don't push drugs, and you're not in a gang. Let them have full access to you."

Marge nodded her head. Candice made perfect sense. But then again, murderers where not familiar enough with Candice to know the kind of car she drove, or where she got her morning coffee.

* * * *

Detective Sergeant Marcus Jones felt the new phone vibrate inside the breast pocket of his sports coat. He could not answer it here, so he pushed away from his desk to find a private place from which to return the call. He did not have to guess who called. Only one person had the number, and that was the person who gave him the phone.

Marge Myers provided the phone so it couldn't be traced to Jones. It would only be used for their private conversations. He found a long stretch of a wide and little traveled hallway. Jones pulled out the phone and dialed Marge's number.

She answered on the first ring.

"Sergeant Jones, do you know anything about a disc being slipped into my locked car?"

The question baffled Jones. "Why, no ma'am, I don't. What's this about?"

"I didn't think you would know. How could you? But still, I had to ask. I just hoped it was you."

Jones listened carefully as Marge laid out the events of her day.

Once she finished, only two words came instinctively from Jones and out his mouth. "Mother fucker!" Then, he quickly apologized.

"No need to apologize," she sighed. "I've repeated the same words at least a dozen times today."

"I don't think you are in danger," He replied. She had expressed concern of how they pulled it off. Getting into the locked car. What

Jones knew, he could not share. The magnitude of the "Outlaws" network would astonish her, and probably frighten her even more. Jones didn't know the source, but tons of money backed their every move.

"So it airs tonight?" he asked.

"It does if Candice can make it happen. I'd be surprised if she can't."

"Big people in my line of work will be highly pissed," Jones admitted.

"What do you think they will do?"

Jones understood Chicago politics. They pampered the press. Needed them. Would not cross them. "They will make threats. They'll grumble. But in the end, they won't do a damned thing."

"Hey, uh, Sergeant Jones, would you care to meet for a drink tonight? It's, well, been a tough day for me."

Jones did not have a baby sitter . . . for a full-grown baby, but . . .

"Name the place and time. I'll be there."

. . . he could work that out.

* * * *

"We should have negotiated high-dollar call girls into the contract."

"I'm nearly a married man, John. Don't think Melinda would approve. I'd be forced to ask beforehand. I suspect permission would be denied."

"Most wives are that way," Ledford nodded. "You end up married long enough, she'll pay you to go have sex with someone else just so she don't have to."

Remington laughed out loud. "John, we've only been here eight days. You can wait a few more."

"Can. But don't want to. Too much war, Indian need love."

Remington knew absolutely that his partner did not enjoy killing, but he damned sure loved warfare. He lived for the battle. Remington could chalk that up to his Comanche blood, but Remington loved it just as much, and he had nothing but plain old white boy blood as far as he knew. No, some men were simply warriors by nature. Both Remington and Ledford snugly fit that mode. Remington had no doubt that if right now, Ledford could join in on a damn good bar fight, or have at some willing beauty, he'd fight first and love later.

"Indian should use hand," Remington grinned.

"Hey, watch it," Ledford said with an exaggerated scowl. "Only Indians can use the 'I' word."

Dan Hicks interrupted Remington's laughter.

"We got lucky, boys, our video is airing in just a few minutes."

Remington and Ledford walked over to Hick's arrangement of electronics.

"Damn if you ain't a technical whiz," Remington smiled. "How'd you find out it's on?"

Hicks looked up from his chair and grimaced. "I flipped through the news channels."

"Damn, if that ain't a stroke of genius," Remington smiled again.

Remington and Ledford pulled in tight behind Hicks to stare down at the monitor. After a commercial, cameras revealed a pretty blonde sitting behind a news desk.

"Good Evening Chicago, I am Candice Classen with this Channel 2 exclusive. For the longest time now, the streets of Chicago have been controlled by seemingly countless street gangs. Their ruthless and violent activities have inflicted on our communities far too many senseless deaths. These gangs are considered by many to be the reason Chicago leads the nation in most violent crime statistics.

"Police and courts have been ineffective in their efforts to control these street gangs. Residents of many communities have felt abandoned and defenseless against this onslaught of violence, with their only hope being that somehow, someone will come to their rescue. In the last eight days, a series of bizarre and brutal killings of seven known gang-leaders, and four additional gang members, seems to signify that a deadly vigilante force intends to, indeed, rescue citizens from their oppressors.

"In two recent articles, Marge Myers of the Chicago Tribune contributes that these actions are being carried out, phenomenally, by just two men, that she aptly dubbed, 'The Outlaws.' She reports from unknown sources that these vigilantes, oddly enough, utilize unsophisticated weapons from the American Wild West era.

"Now, for the first time, we will reveal visual proof of Martha Myer's seemingly outlandish reporting. Today, we obtained a videodisc that recorded a gun battle last night in a parking lot at 7739 South Halsted Street, which foiled an intended drug deal. Please be warned that although we have blurred out faces and some of the action, what I am about to show you is very graphic in nature and should not be viewed by children or those who might take offense at such terrible violence."

Remington, Ledford, and Hicks remained silent as they viewed the video along with no telling how many thousands of others. At the end, Remington mumbled, "Made me feel as if I was there."

Ledford and Hicks offered no response in return as Candice Classen's beautiful face once again dominated the screen.

"Let me clarify, that while this station does not in any way condone the actions of these two men, we felt it our obligation to share with our viewers the proof of their existence. We do consider it newsworthy that two men, on horseback, can wreak this kind of havoc on eight men with superior weaponry, utilizing tactics that our police, for obvious reasons, cannot.

"Let me also note, that although you heard what might be their plea for others to join in this battle against gang-warfare, we would sincerely hope the citizens of Chicago will leave this in the hands of our local law enforcement agencies…"

Ledford patted Hicks on the shoulder. "Good job, Dan, on production and placement."

"Not to mention," Remington butted in, "for bringing us the celebrity that will make this job just that much harder to pull off."

"Like it wasn't your idea," Hicks mumbled while punching keys and tweaking knobs.

"Oh, yeah, I forgot," Remington grinned.

"Yeah, well one thing is for sure," Ledford said. "Everyone that saw that video will be looking to get a glimpse at us."

Remington nodded his head and concluded, "Yeah, it's a pity, but the biggest percentage of those who do, will carry it into hell with them."

Ledford started away, but said over his shoulder. "Trey, does Arnold Schwarzenegger write lines for you?"

Remington fondly shot his best friend a finger. "You liked it didn't you, Dan?"

Hicks didn't look up, but did nod unenthusiastically. "Gave me goose bumps."

* * * *

At eight p.m., Sean Scully once again found himself sitting next to Mark Penn in front of Lieutenant Ely Elmore's desk. Scully resented the intrusion on his off hours, but relished the look on Elmore's face that was supported by an overall demeanor of weary shock.

"Since neither of you entered this office with a whirlwind of unbelievable outrage, I'm assuming neither of you caught Candice Classen's six o'clock report on Channel 2."

"I didn't," Penn responded.

"Me either," Scully grumbled.

"Upstanding and concerned citizens watch the evening news," Elmore said with little conviction.

"I watch another channel," Penn shrugged.

"I don't give a shit," Scully admitted.

Elmore turned weary eyes on Scully, and actually made an attempt to smile. "I didn't see it either. It was brought to my attention by the chief, who had it brought to his attention by the commissioner, who, more than likely, had it brought to his attention by the By-God mayor."

"What's going on, LT?" Penn asked.

"Oh, you can go on-line and watch for yourself on Channel 2's webpage. But, allow me to spare you the anguish. The shooting you worked last night at the parking lot, was somehow caught professionally on video. Our two suspects wore mics. It's a top-notch production, viewed by upstanding and concerned citizens all over this fucking city."

"Motherfucker," Scully exclaimed.

"Yeah, I heard that from the chief. Who heard it from the commissioner. Who no doubt heard it from the By-God mayor. Motherfucker. It's so applicable to the entire situation. Thousands of motherfuckers viewed tonight how two motherfuckers, dressed as cowboys, are cleaning up this motherfucking city. I might add that the two cowboy motherfuckers, are . . . motherfucking amazing."

"Uh, what do you want us to do?" Penn asked hesitantly.

"First, I want you to view the video. Then, somehow, which was not relayed to me by the chief, I want you to find the cowboys. And then, put together, let's say, a battalion of cops, and just try to arrest the amazing cowboys."

"That's it?" Scully mocked.

"Basically. Yeah, no big deal, but keep in mind, the video will point out, that our 'Outlaws' have called in reinforcements. Encouraging citizens to join in their vigilante onslaught. So, just go find them, and arrest them. If they don't want to be arrested, just kill them . . . and good luck with that."

"What charges will be brought against Channel 2?" Scully asked.

"What do you think?" Elmore half-heartedly chuckled.

"Absolutely none?" Scully scowled.

"Exactly. The commissioner's only demand is to obtain the original video. Also, at shift change tonight, every line-up will view the on-line version. Maybe some patrol officer will get lucky tonight and stumble across two gun-slinging cowboys. But if they do, may God be with them."

For the first time in days, Scully left Elmore's office without almost hating him.

* * * *

"Motherfucker," Penn hissed as he stared at the computer screen.

"That's rather redundant," Scully quipped.

"What in the hell are these two guys?" Penn said under his breath.

"Well, they are dressed like the outlaws and lawmen of the old West, but I feel safe in assuming they are not the ghosts of Bat Masterson and Jesse James," Scully mocked. "Therefore, a more reasonable explanation is they are simply superheroes."

"Screw that. They are flesh and blood."

"So is Batman."

"Batman isn't real. These bastards are *for real.*"

Scully strummed his fingertips on the desktop. "Okay. We know what they are. They are two highly trained and deadly individuals who just happen to dress like Wild Bill Hickok. What we don't know is who they are. More importantly, we don't know who provides their support."

"Support?"

"Why hell yes, Mark. These two are not in this alone. They know where and when to hit. They appear and they disappear. Who made this professional video? These two are just the tip of the spear. There has to be a support network prepping and then covering every move they make. Calls to report their actions are made from across the nation. The crime scenes are professionally cleaned, allowing us to find only what they want us to find. We've been over all this before."

"I know we have," Penn exhaled. "I just didn't want to buy into it."

"Why not?"

"Just seems too phenomenal. Too hard to grasp how big this really is."

"So, what are you thinking now?" Scully asked softly.

Penn took a second to shake his head and shrug his shoulders. "I'm thinking that I don't know what the hell to do with this."

"Finally," Scully grinned, "We are on the same page, partner."

"So, you have any suggestions whatsoever?" Penn asked.

"We investigate. We watch. We wait. Hopefully, they will sooner or later mess up, and we benefit from their mistake."

"And what if they don't mess up?" Penn smiled wearily.

"Then we continue to do what we can, and just force ourselves to be okay with the fact that they are ridding this city of assholes. It's kind of like this, Mark. We catch them, good. We don't catch them . . . even better."

* * * *

Marge Myers carefully studied Sergeant Jones' facial expressions as she asked, "So you watched the news exclusive tonight?"

"I did," he sighed.

She liked the features of his face, and the way he wore thick reddish hair closely cropped. His firm jaw line appeared clinched, but his eyes told their own story. They spoke of burdens that deeply plagued the slender man sitting across the booth from her.

"And what's your take on it, Sergeant?" Marge asked.

Jones took a deep swig of his whiskey before replying, "I wanted the people of Chicago to know. Now they do, Ms. Myers."

"Please, call me Marge."

"Only if you call me Marcus."

"So, that's it . . . Marcus? That's all you have to say about the video?"

Jones turned his troubled eyes on the tumbler of whiskey in his hands, and seemed to address the glass instead of her. "It's, uh, just unbelievable. Two cowboys, on horses, in the middle of Chicago. I can't wrap my mind around it."

"What do you think about what they are doing? The way they are doing it?"

It took him a long moment, but Jones looked up from his glass and into her eyes. "I can't condone it, if that's what you mean. I wear a badge. I take that very seriously . . . "

Something flashed in his eyes. Remorse? Maybe. A deeply held secret? More than likely. Marge intended to find out.

" . . . They are killing evil men. But they are killing nonetheless. It makes them no better than the men they kill."

Maybe if she could get him alone. "Marcus, would you like to follow me to my house? Have a few drinks? Maybe I could fix us a light meal?"

Marcus quickly looked from her eyes and into the glass in his hand. "I can't. I have a special needs child waiting at home for me."

Maybe that was it. Such would certainly be a burden that Martha could not relate to. "Oh, I'm sorry, Marcus."

"Maybe another time?" He asked in a sincere manner.

"Yes, another time. I'd like that."

When and if that time came, she intended to prod, and hoped she'd get what she wanted without causing the man additional anguish. He seemed to carry enough of that already.

* * * *

Sheriff Jerry Ring pulled his cruiser to the side of the gravel road that marked the northern boundary of Trey Remington and John Ledford's sprawling ranch. The Brazos River served as the southern boundary. Patrolling the boundaries of the ranch had become an obsession for Ring on the many late nights that he could not sleep. He stepped out of the car and brought a pair of binoculars to his eyes.

He looked for nothing in particular, but just hoped to observe anything that would give him probable cause to enter the interior of the ranch. Once there, Ring just knew he'd find some reason to put Remington and Ledford behind bars a second time. The time before, they'd ended up making him out to be a fool. That would not happen again.

Maybe this time it would be stolen equipment, or rustled livestock, maybe even marijuana fields or meth labs. Ring put nothing past two men capable of committing such a ruthless murder. Of course, Rudy Whitlock deserved death, but one determined by a jury and carried out by lethal injection. Ring also would not forget that their action prevented the Sheriff from enjoying the notoriety of a landmark case brought against the most notorious criminal in county history.

Instead he ended up arresting Remington and Ledford. In some twisted way, they ended up getting the media hoopla that Ring deserved. Out here in the dead of night, the memory of their arrest never failed to haunt him. Back then, Ring and three of his deputies encountered the two ranchers standing side by side at the bar in Little Joe's Tavern in Peacock, Texas, the closest drinking hole to their ranch. They'd not tried to flee the county, but instead got word to Ring where they could be found if, "*He thought he was man enough to take them in.*"

Ring and his three men stepped into the tavern to find themselves staring at the wide backs and shoulders of the two big cowboys.

"Remington! Ledford!" Ring called out from just inside the doorway. "Put your arms in the air and turn around. You are both under arrest for the murder of Rudy Whitlock."

It reminded Ring of a scene out of a B Western. Patrons dove under tables, and those at the bar with the suspects scurried to the left and right to clear themselves from the possibility of flying led. Remington and Ledford, however, did not move a muscle.

Ring took a deep breath and nodded his head. "Go get them," he ordered the deputies. They approached the bar with their service weapons pointed. One went to the right of the suspects, one to the left, while the third approached their turned backs.

Only when they were in position, did Remington and Ledford calmly turn to face Ring. They eyed him, but Remington addressed the deputy standing to his right.

"You really want to try getting this done, Bobby?" He asked calmly.

"Not really, Trey. Hell, we went to high school together," Bobby Johns started.

"It's our damned job, Trey," the deputy in the middle and directly in front of Remington interjected.

Ledford responded to this deputy, "Bryan Smith, you're dear old mama used to feed us cookies after little league games. Wouldn't she be proud of you now? It was your damned job to arrest Rudy Whitlock. It was all ya'alls' jobs, and ya' all refused to get it done."

"Arrest them!" Ring shouted from the door.

Deputy Manny Perry, standing closest to Ledford said, "Boys, you are under arrest."

Trey Ledford scanned the eyes of the three deputies, and then grinned. "Then, fellers, this would be the time for you to start shooting."

Perry moved for Ledford and Bobby Johns for Remington. Smith froze in place. It appeared to Ring that the scene quickly changed from a B Western to a Bruce Lee flick. Ledford used just his elbows and forearms, and Remington only the open palms of both hands.

A down chop of Ledford's right forearm dislodged Perry's pistol while at the same moment his left forearm came up to crash land beneath Perry's chin. Perry's head flew back, but Ledford stepped in and drove his right elbow into Perry's jaw. One deputy down and out.

Like a flash, Remington palmed Johns' gun with his right hand and a twist of his wrist sent it flying. Remington then buried the heel of his left palm beneath Johns' nose. His right palm careened into Johns' solar plexus. The coup de grace came in the form of the left palm exploding into Johns' right ear. Another one hit the floor.

Obviously in shock that it all went to shit in a blink of an eye, Smith took a step backwards, and Ledford executed a roundhouse kick that put the side of a size eleven cowboy boot into Smith's temple. Three down and three out.

Remington and Ledford started slowly and in an eerily calm fashion toward Jerry Ring.

Bar patrons between Ring and the two he wanted had not provided a clear shot, but he had one now. Ring pulled and pointed his service weapon. "Halt or I will shoot both you bastards!"

The two men did not halt, but pulled back jackets to reveal they were unarmed.

"Wouldn't look good for you, Sheriff. Would make you appear frightened and weak," Remington chuckled. "You got enough of that on your record already."

Ring lowered his gun, and Remington and Ledford stopped within an arm's reach.

Remington looked at Ledford. "John, if he lays hands on me are you going to jump in?"

"Don't see what for," Ledford grumbled.

"John, if he lays hands on you, you want me to jump in?"

"Don't see what for."

"There you have it, Sheriff Ring. Feel free to take on either one of us without the other lending a hand."

Ring considered his choices, and found they did not provide for his well-being. He tried to calm himself before speaking, but it didn't come off that way. "You're both still under arrest."

"You say so, then guess we are," Remington grinned. "John, you want to go to jail tonight?"

"Not tonight. Not in the mood."

"Okay, Sheriff, that's the way it be. When we get damned good and ready, we'll come and turn ourselves in," Remington advised.

Jerry Ring forced the memory out of his mind and drew in a ragged breath of the night air.

"Sorry sons of bitches," he whispered out loud. "Made me look foolish. No. *Made me look like a coward.* I swear to God, I'll make you pay."

FIVE

Clint "Sampson" Demont displayed the palm of a huge hand, signaling Thumper to stop talking.

"Let me get this straight," Sampson began. "Two white cowboys. They have killed a slew of niggers and spics, and now . . . you think they are coming for me?"

"Just saying, Sampson, it's all over the news. The dudes are taking out gang leaders," Thumper nodded.

"And you think they'd hit an Aryan brother?"

"Not figuring them to be white supremacists, Sampson. Not sure they had those around in the old west," Thumper shrugged.

Sampson threw back his large shaved head and laughed in his thunderous manner. "And what's the deal with them dressing up like cowboys? Who does that shit?"

"Real cowboys?" Thumper shrugged again.

"It's fucking weird man. Real cowboys in Chicago? From what you've explained, sounds like they are some type of superhero wannabees."

"They seem to appear out of nowhere. Do their killing, and disappear. Maybe they are superheroes," Thumper offered.

"Uh-hu. Like Batman Cowboy and Robin Cowboy. Ain't no such shit, Thumper."

"All right," Thumper sighed, "whatever they are, they could be coming for you, Sampson."

Thumper wanted his words to sink in, but just a look in his boss's eyes, told him it didn't. He watched as Sampson leaned in his recliner in the darkened room to casually reach for his cigarettes sitting on an end table.

"Well, fuck then, Thumper, let them bring their asses on," Sampson smiled as he lit a Marlboro.

Thumper moved around the clutter in the living room to get closer to Sampson. "Counted on that being your response, but I want you to watch this. It's all over the web." Thumper removed his i-Phone from a back pocket, thumbed up a video, and handed it to Sampson. "Got it ready to go. Just tap the play button."

Sampson watched the video, and seemed impressed. Thumper really believed the giant of a man had never experienced the emotion of fear. If so, he'd damned sure never expressed such.

"Now, that is some cool cowboys," Sampson smiled. "Motherfuckers sure can shoot."

"Exactly. I don't want them shooting at you, Sampson. They don't seem to miss."

Sampson handed the phone back to Thumper and pushed up from his chair. Thumper stood six feet tall. Sampson towered another six inches over him.

"Okay. We'll start preparing. Nothing wrong with being ready. Just in case they turn out to be cool . . . and stupid." Then he put a hand on Thumper's shoulder. "You know, with them already eliminating key competition, we take these assholes down, the city will be ripe for the taking. Make sure whatever you do, that it does not interrupt our baby bangers on the street pushing our dope. Any that get wind of this shit, and get cold feet, I want to deal with them personally."

Thumper nodded his head. He sure pitied any kid that contracted the cold feet virus.

* * * *

Melinda Lollar walked away from the laptop on the counter while trying not to grit her teeth. She picked up a pack of smokes and her lighter before stepping out on the trailer house's small porch. She plopped down on the first step and took a cigarette from the pack. As she stuck it between her lips, she thought the same thing she always did before lighting up.

Trey hates it when I smoke.

She lit the cigarette and drew smoke deep into her lungs before forcibly exhaling it. "Trey Remington can kiss my ass," she said out loud.

Some four months earlier she'd accepted the fact that Trey could not tell her the specifics of his "assignment." She had a difficult time admitting it right now, but she'd loved the idea of " . . . being rich beyond our wildest imagination." She wanted expensive jewelry and a luxurious house here on the ranch. What woman wouldn't? She could give a damn about fancy cars, but dreamed of the type of horses that rich-beyond-the-wildest-imagination could provide. When she met Trey, she'd been waiting tables. Being wildly rich meant she'd never have to return to taking food orders.

At the moment with a badly needed cigarette in hand, she couldn't care less about having money. Without Trey, all the money in the world could not make her happy. What the hell was he thinking? They had not discussed it, but he knew she assumed that this job would take him back to the Middle East. He'd been there so many times, and survived each tour. She trusted he could do it one more time. But from what she'd watched on the computer, she now knew, Trey was a lot damned closer to home than Iraq, Syria, or Afghanistan. He and John were right here in the good ol' United States of American playing cowboy and Indian side-kick in the hood *on the back of fucking horses.*

He knew what he was doing in the mountains and deserts of foreign countries, and counted among the very best at getting it done. But in Chicago, Illinois? Taking on and *murdering* gang-bangers? What was he thinking? Melinda felt confident that Trey could escape from the corrupt and inept police factions of, say, Somalia . . . but how would he fare against the Chicago Police Department? What about the FBI?

Jesus Christ, what was he thinking?

Over there, far over there, Melinda held no qualms with acts he might commit. No matter what he did in those foreign places, it would be difficult to call it a crime. But right here in the good ol' United States of America?

Criminals were not commonly hailed as heroes.

And *Outlaws* normally went to prison.

* * * *

Scully sat in the passenger seat of the unmarked car and waited until Penn tapped the "End" button on his cell.

"That did not sound encouraging, Mark," he said.

Penn kept his eyes on the street in front of him. "It wasn't," he hissed. "Channel 2 turned over the video. Our technicians can't tweak it. They can't enhance the faces of the outlaws. These assholes don't miss a beat. They seem to think of everything. They seem to be able to do the impossible."

Against his nature, Scully chose an encouraging word, "Well, hell, Mark, they were wearing bandanas. We'd just gotten a closer look at their eyes."

"That would be a hell of a lot more than we have right now," Penn shot back.

Sean Scully appreciated being a pessimist. When you didn't expect much, you weren't generally disappointed.

* * * *

"You know, this time last week, I wouldn't told a cop shit . . ."

Officer Gary Baker simply nodded his head, while looking around at the blood droplets on the sidewalk.

" . . . Didn't think anyone gave a shit. And didn't want any of those young hoodlums paying me a visit. Now because of them outlaws, I ain't so scared about keeping my mouth shut. Punk-assed kids been kind of scarce since them dudes been killing they leaders. These few here today, first I seen in a couple of days."

Baker looked up and into the dark eyes of the elderly black lady. "So, Mrs. Grey, you said there were four gang-bangers?"

"That's all I seen."

"And the men who came out with ball bats, they were older?"

"Some old enough to be granddaddies. I couldn't hear what they said, 'cause I was looking out my window, but I know they were telling the younger ones to get gone. Younger ones didn't have sense enough to get gone, so older ones went to pounding them with those bats."

Baker jotted notes on his pad. "The older men came out of houses here on the block, but you still don't want to give me names?"

"Nope. Why should I? Time well past that black *men* start acting like *men*. Just telling you what I have, to let you know those outlaws . . . they be doing some good."

Gary Baker thanked Mrs. Grey for her time, and started back to his patrol car. His partner, Jay Pierce, walked toward him from the opposite direction. Baker got in behind the wheel, and Pierce stooped to enter the passenger's side.

"Followed the blood trail just down the street. Looks like they got in a car and hauled ass. Damn, citizens taking on gang-bangers. That's sweet shit," Pierce chuckled.

"Yeah," Baker smiled. "Lady just up the street said some neighbor men engaged in a little batting practice."

"Well, Gary, no victim's names and no suspects. Case closed."

"Agreed partner," Baker nodded. He'd worked theses streets three years longer than Pierce, and had not once seen a time when the locals acted to curb gang violence.

"Let me ask you something, Jay," Baker said as he pondered the unusual situation. "If you looked up right now, and saw two cowboys, on horses, crossing that street up in front of us . . . what would you do?"

Jay Pierce chuckled. "I'd do one of two things. I'd either turn my head to look the other way, or . . . I'd jump out of this car . . . and salute them. And how about you?"

Satisfied that his inclinations did not make him a bad cop, Baker let the truth flow freely. "Well, I wouldn't want to interrupt their success to date. And I damned sure wouldn't want to try to take them on."

"Okay," Pierce smiled broadly. "We're supposed to be out looking for them. You want to look, or drink coffee?"

"Hell, Jay, I don't know where to find them. But I know where to find coffee."

* * * *

This shit ain't real. Ain't happening.

Oh, but it did happen. You lived it.

Don't want to relive it again. I drank the whiskey. I want to wake up and drink more.

Dream on.

Trey Remington tried to close his eyes. But knew they were already closed. He tried to turn his head, but he'd looked straightforward for so long now. Saw all the ugly the world had to offer . . . or thought he had.

"Is . . . she . . . dead?" he repeated night after night after night since *that night outside the barn.*

John held the tiny form in his arms. Tears streamed down John's cheeks. And John Ledford never cried.

"Alive when I found her. Dead now," John choked.

Yet she continued to bleed. From her face. From her torso. From places a baby girl of six, should not bleed.

"Where are her clothes? She has no clothes." Remington might have said those words on that night, or might have thought it, but whether he said it or not, he now dreamed that he did.

"Others are inside," John whispered.

Not others. Not others. Not others. Please, God, no others.

"How many?"

"Can't tell. All in pieces."

Even in his sleep, Remington knew dreams were no longer dreams when they strayed so far from reality that the recollection of unbelievably awful events, turned to unrealistic terror . . . the point where dreams transformed into nightmares.

The small head, hanging limp from the crook of Ledford's arm, suddenly straightened and swiveled to look Remington in the eyes.

"You knew what he was doing. Why didn't you come sooner?"

Remington screamed, and Ledford dropped the girl on the ground. All torn and broken, she could only writhe at their feet.

"NOOOOOOOOOOOOO! OH, DEAR GOD NOOOOOOOOOO!"

Ledford grabbed Remington with hands dripping blood and shook him, while somehow calmly calling his name to stop him from screaming.

"It's okay, Trey."

"NOOOOOOOOOOO!

Ledford shook him even harder. "Trey? Trey . . . It isn't real. Trey . . ."

* * * *

" . . . Trey! It isn't real. Not happening, man. Wake up, Trey!"

Remington shot upright in his cot, and gasped for air. Ledford let go of his shoulders, and took a step backwards. He'd done this before.

"Same one?" He asked softly.

Remington nodded his head, but did not speak. Ledford tried to show no reaction as his dearest friend swiped at the moisture on his cheeks.

"Same awful one," Remington moaned. "That shit is eating me alive, John. Just rips at me with sharp and ugly teeth."

Ledford certainly understood, and knew it did no good to say nonsense like, it will get better, or it will eventually go away. The life he'd led proved that some things never got better, and never went away. Not once they'd taken up residence in your soul.

"She spoke to you again?" he asked instead of spouting useless clichés.

"Said the same thing. Always says the same thing."

Ledford nodded his head.

"I wish we'd got there sooner, John."

Now Ledford shook his head. "We didn't, Trey. Simple as that."

Remington nodded and cleared his voice before looking away.

"Strike time is three hours out, Trey. You up for it?"

He took long seconds, but finally turned back to stare at Ledford. The look in his eyes warned Ledford of the words to follow.

"Yes. Absolutely. Killing worthless bastards deserving to die . . . just makes me feel better. God help me, John."

"God help us both, Trey."

* * * *

Sampson pulled his Harley into the alley, and observed Thumper's car straight ahead. It was running, but the lights were out. Sampson made out Thumper's form alongside the car, and noted the smaller figure squatting on his knees beside Thumper. Sampson idled his bike up the alley. Even at an idle, the loud pipes echoed off the surrounding buildings producing a sound like thunder. Sampson smiled at the mind-fucking the sound would provide for the kid Thumper held in place.

Sampson pulled up close, killed his engine, and crawled off the Harley. He took steps that positioned him to tower over the trembling youth, whose hands were bound behind his back.

"So, this is our slacker?" He asked Thumper.

"Yeah. Decided he no longer wants to live the glamorous life of crime," Thumper snarled.

Sampson nudged the boy with the toe of his heavy biker boots and spoke calmly just above a whisper. "You stopped selling dope? What in the world could convince you to make such a stupid decision?"

The boy dropped his head to shake it pathetically, but did not respond. Sampson reached down and gently applied two fingers beneath the kid's chin to slowly pull his head up. Tears now spilled from the captive's eyes and trickled down his cheeks.

"Do you want me to use my boot to grind your balls into the payment?" Sampson asked without malice.

The boy shook his head. "No. Please don't."

"Why did you stop pushing my product?" Sampson asked in a most kind manner.

This time the boy did not hesitate. "The Outlaws."

"Oh, you fear these . . . cowboys?"

"Yes."

"What's your name, boy?" Sampson asked as he took a step backwards and slowly started unbuttoning his shirt.

"Darrell."

Sampson made a production of removing his shirt and calmly arranging it neatly across the hood of Thumper's car. Darrell's eyes closely followed his every move. Sampson brought his arms up in a classic body-builder's pose, and flexed enormous biceps. He dropped them to his waist and tensed his massive chest before turning at the waist to exhibit deeply defined back muscles of great mass.

"Impressive isn't it, Darrell?" Sampson smiled.

Darrell's eyes were wide with fright. "Yes."

"Do you think those cowboys have such powerful muscles?"

Darrell shook his head no.

"How old are you, Darrell?"

"Fifteen."

"Good. That's very good. You are still young enough to learn. And I have a lesson to teach. I'm going to teach you, Darrell, something I learned in prison. I'm going to teach you how older much bigger inmates keep younger, more tender inmates in line."

Darrell started shaking his head and began to whimper. "I don't want to learn that."

Sampson looked at Thumper. "Put him belly down across the trunk of your car."

Darrell started screaming, until Thumper hit him hard in the back of the head with a closed fist. The blow dazed the boy and reduced his screams to terrorized muttering. Thumper jerked him to his feet and bent him across the trunk of his car.

"Get his pants down," Sampson growled, as he started undoing his own belt buckle and jeans.

Thumper held the boy in place, and Darrell let out a pitiful shriek when Sampson entered him. Sampson delivered brutal thrusts while Darrell's entire body convulsed as his knees buckled beneath him. When finished, Sampson slumped momentarily over the boy's back.

Upon catching his breath, Sampson reached his left hand over Darrell's head to grasp his forehead. Sampson pulled the boy's head up and back. Then he used the index finger of his right hand to open Darrell's right eyelid.

Sampson pulled a large hunting knife from a sheath on his belt with his right hand.

"Can you hear me, Darrell?"

The fifteen-year-old boy muttered a faint acknowledgment to the question.

"Good. You tell the others. Tell them what happens when someone disappoints me. Oh, you don't have to tell them about the butt fucking, but they'll ask about your eye. Tell them not to fear the *Outlaws*. Tell them to fear me. Do you understand, Darrell?"

The kid tried to nod his head.

Sampson raised his knife and was careful to only insert an inch of it into Darrell's eyeball. He gave it a slow twist.

Darrell let out a tortured scream before passing out. Sampson backed away and let the boy crumble to the ground.

"Dump him off at the entrance of the nearest emergency room," Sampson said in a relaxed manner as he buttoned his jeans and buckled his belt.

* * * *

Sheriff Jerry Ring took a sip from his first cup of early morning coffee when the phone on his desk started ringing.

"Sheriff Ring," he answered, curious who would be calling his office number at 6 a.m. Emergency calls went through dispatch, and Ring simply did not get an abundance of social calls.

"You need to watch the morning news on ABC," A male voice responded.

"Who is this?"

"Don't matter."

"It matters to me," Ring growled. He didn't appreciate having his morning alone time interrupted.

The voice on the other end laughed. "Okay. Let's just say I'm someone with information you'd be willing to pay for. But, I'm offering it for free."

"What kind of information?"

"First, watch the morning news."

"What the hell is this about?" Ring all but shouted.

More laughter. "It's about two of your favorite people. John Ledford and Trey Remington."

Ring straightened in his chair. "Okay. You have my attention."

"Watch the news. Then pay a visit to their ranch. They won't be there. You know why?"

"Why don't you tell me?"

No laughter this time, just a long pause that caused Ring to worry he'd lost the connection. He opened his mouth to speak, but didn't have to.

"Because they are in Chicago."

The unknown caller hung up, and Ring didn't immediately put two and two together.

* * * *

Ring heard someone enter the front office. "Who's out there?"

"Just me, Sheriff," A voice responded.

Of course, Ring recognized it. "Get in here, Smith."

Deputy Bryan Smith stuck his head in the door. "Do I have time to grab a cup of coffee?"

"Grab it fast." The sheriff had just turned on the television in his office and now fingered the remote to find the channel he wanted. Smith returned in a minute or less.

"Pull up a chair," Ring said.

Smith did as told. "What are we watching?"

Ring found the channel and adjusted the volume before tossing the remote on his desk. "Morning news. An anonymous caller instructed me to do so."

"No shit? Who?"

"Anonymous means unknown, dip shit," Ring grumbled.

Smith turned red and nodded, "Sorry. I know that. Just not used to watching television over coffee with my boss."

"Don't get used to it."

"Yes, sir."

The first segment updated war weary Americans on the situation in the Middle East. It included the President's two cents, that Ring wouldn't give a single penny to hear in person. Commercials followed. A fast talking clown pushing cars, a babe hawking furniture, and Ring lost count until . . .

"Early this morning, in Chicago, yet another brutal slaying of street gang leaders points to the growing notoriety of two men known first in Chicago, and now across the nation, as the Outlaws . . . "

"Oh, yeah," Smith interrupted, "You been keeping up with those two guys, Sheriff?"

Smith was vaguely familiar with the crimes and suspects, but truly could give a shit what happened in faraway Chicago. He raised a palm to mute Smith. He paid attention to learn more.

Dressed as Wild West cowboys. Rode horses. Drove a high-dollar super car. Appeared and disappeared. Killed gang-members in a horrific manner. Then the morning anchor cut to a video provided by the killers.

Ring watched only a split second before declaring, "Jesus Christ!"

"Amazing, right?" Smith blurted.

Ring grabbed the remote, turned the television off, and then laughed heartily before mumbling, "Horse shit."

"Uh, what's that, Boss?"

"Jesus Christ," Ring said again before adding, "The goofy son-of-a-bitch who called earlier, thinks those two are Remington and Ledford. I'd love to get my hands around his neck just to kick his ass for wasting my time."

"I wouldn't put it past Remington and Ledford. That's a vigilante situation they have going on up there, and those two are darn sure vigilantes," Smith offered.

"Yeah, Smith, I'm sure they drove that piece of shit old pick-up all the way to Chicago, and traded it for a Hummer. Or, maybe they rode their horses? Or, maybe, they simply have millions of dollars that we don't know about laying around that worthless ranch."

Smith again turned crimson from neck to forehead. "Didn't say they did it, Boss. Said I wouldn't put it past them. Besides, be kind of fun to see the looks on their faces if we accused them of doing it. You know, just to fool around with them?"

Ring shot out of his chair, and couldn't help but award his deputy with a grin. "I'll be damned. Of course. We have an anonymous tip accusing them of murder. That gives us every right to go out there and at least question them. Good thinking, Smith."

Smith stood up and returned the grin with a smile and a wink of his eye. "That last hit was barely four hours ago. Shit, Sheriff, no way they could already be back from Chicago."

Ring exhaled heavily. "Damn, Smith, you come up with a good idea, and then screw it up trying to be funny. Go get the car."

* * * *

Sean Scully rolled the disposable gloves off his hands, and placed them in the bio-hazard container. He raised his hands to rub at his eyes.

"Guess we've done about all we can here," Penn said from across the room.

Scully did not respond until standing next to Penn. "When we first got here, I just knew the responding officers made a mistake by having us called out."

"Yeah, I know," Penn nodded a clearly exhausted head. "Thought the same, until we discovered it's been sanitized like the others. Still, didn't go so well for your 'superheroes' this time."

Scully glanced around once again at all the bullet holes in the walls. "Yeah, the Asians were much better armed than previous victims, and apparently more prepared as well."

"Yeah, as if they anticipated the hit. But of course, they should have, considering all the news coverage," Penn said before emitting a well-deserved yawn.

"Whites will be next," Scully yawned in return.

"Right, just like we told Elmore. At least we've been right about one thing."

"How does the saying go? 'Even a broken clock gets the time right twice a day?'"

"Not a digital one," Penn smiled.

"You need some sleep," Scully smiled back.

"We both do. All this blood, and we're smiling."

"Crying takes too much effort and makes homicide detectives look silly," Scully grumbled.

Penn snorted a brief chuckle, but then seemingly fell into perplexed thinking mode. After a few seconds, he asked, "How do we determine what white gang they'll go after?"

Scully took another few seconds to ponder the question. "Whites don't control that many gangs, comparatively speaking, but enough that all we can do is make a wild-assed guess."

"I can only think of three really prominent white gang-leaders," Penn mumbled.

"At this point, I can only think of going to bed. Let's discuss this tomorrow."

Penn agreed, and Scully followed him to the door, imitating his steps to prevent stepping in puddles of blood.

SIX

Sheriff Ring sent Deputy Smith up to knock on the door of the shabby mobile home. Ring remained at the bottom of the steps. The rickety porch didn't appear capable of withstanding the weight of two men. It irked Ring that Melinda Lollar lived in such a dump. He could have done much better for her than this shithole.

Smith rapped on the aluminum door with a closed fist. A few seconds later, he called down to Ring. "Someone peaked through the curtain."

"Saw that," Ring nodded. If Melinda, or the bum she lived with decided not to open the door, Ring would have no choice but to leave.

"Knock again," he ordered Smith.

Before the deputy could obey, the door opened, and Melinda stood in the doorway.

"What business do you have here?" She asked Smith, acting as if she didn't see Ring.

But Ring gave the response. "Official business, Melinda. We need to see Remington."

He knew the woman well, or once did. They'd lived together for nearly two years. Even now, he knew her well enough to note a sudden worried look on her lovely face that she quickly brought under control.

"What official business?" She asked calmly enough.

"Is he in there or not, Melinda? My business is with him and only him."

Melinda stiffened. "I'll need a moment," she said before abruptly shutting the door.

"What do you want me to do, Sheriff?" Smith asked.

"Just stand there with your finger up your ass like you been doing," Ring barked.

Surprisingly, it did only take a moment for the door to reopen. This time Trey Remington hulked in the doorway.

"What's your business with me, Ring?"

"Come on down here, Smith," Ring said. Only once Smith retreated did Ring address Remington.

"Your buddy, Ledford, is he over in that other palace on wheels?"

Remington grinned down. "John's a grown man. I don't baby sit him. You want to know, send your deputy over to find out."

Ring did not appreciate Remington telling him what to do, but he held it inside. "See if he's there, Smith. If so, get him over here."

Remington chuckled, "Hey, Bryan, just keep in mind what happened the last time you stood too close to ol' John."

"I'd shoot his ass before taking another kick to the head," Smith replied.

"Shut the hell up and do what I told you to do, Smith," Ring growled.

Smith stomped away, and Ring looked back up at Remington. "Why don't you come on down here? I have a few questions to ask you and Ledford."

"Thanks for the invite, Ring, but think I'll stand right here and see if Bryan returns with John."

Ring gritted his teeth and fought back the urge to kick at the ground because he had no choice other than accepting that Remington knew his rights. He would just love having Ring trample on them. Both men just stood glaring at each other, until, to Ring's surprise, Ledford walked up with Smith following from a safe distance behind.

"This better be good," Ledford said.

Remington started down the steps. "It better be legal."

"Oh, it's legal," Ring said once Remington stood on the ground in front of him. "You've both been accused of a very serious crime. I not only have the legal right, but also the legal obligation to investigate."

"I guess you intend to advise us of our legal rights?" Remington grinned.

"It's not come to that yet, Remington," Ring forced himself to grin back. "For now, I'm simply going to advise you of the accusation. If I then decide to take you into custody, I'll apply the Miranda warning prior to questioning."

"I'm all ears, Ring," Remington smiled. "How about you, John?"

"I'm tingly with anticipation," Ledford deadpanned.

Ring nodded his head. "I will assume you two are familiar with the vigilante executions being carried out in Chicago."

"By those two cowboys?" Remington asked with a sly smile.

"The ones they call the Outlaws?" Ledford asked.

Ring let his eyes roam between the two men for a few seconds. "Yeah, those vigilantes."

"Who hasn't heard about those two ol' boys, Jerry? It's all over the news," Remington chuckled.

Ring decided it time to drop his bomb, and couldn't wait to see their reactions. "You two have been accused of perpetrating those murders."

Trey Remington threw back his head and erupted in laughter. His dear friend did the same. Ring could not recall ever hearing laughter come from the mouth of John Ledford. This was not the response he anticipated.

"This is serious business, boys," he hissed.

"Why, hell, Ring, morning news reported they killed some Asians just mere hours ago. Ain't that right?" Remington asked.

"That's what I understand," Ring reluctantly replied.

Remington threw his hands high in the air. "Dog-gone-it, Sheriff, if you didn't catch us red-handed. Yes, sir, after killing those Asians a few hours back, John and I jumped in our private Lear jet and flew right back here to Texas."

Ledford laughed again.

Remington continued. "We were just getting ready to break into our piggy banks for another couple of million so we could fly right back to Chicago to pull off a couple more murders that only two ol' Texas cowboys like us could mastermind. I'll be damned if you ain't for sure the Sherlock Holmes of Stonewall county!"

Ring could not prevent his face from reddening.

"Do we need to lawyer up, Sheriff?" Ledford asked in typically dry fashion.

Jerry Ring pursed his lips, and then ran a tongue around the inside of a suddenly dry mouth. He'd never grown accustomed to the taste of crow, but had no choice than to chew some now. He drew in a deep breath and let it out as a sigh before faking a smile.

"Well, fellers, had to do my duty. Of course I knew it was bullshit, but I never miss an opportunity to visit with my favorite boys down on the Brazos."

Remington stepped up close. "Sheriff, we can't afford trips back and forth to Chicago, but we can hire an attorney on a contingency basis. You ever harass us like this again, we'll set about owning this entire county, along with your badge."

Ring drew in a deep and painful breath before taking the only official action available to him.

"Smith, get your ass in the car."

* * * *

"That was ballsy beyond total stupidity," Melinda Lollar bellowed.

Trey had just stepped back into the trailer and shut the door behind him.

"You were listening?"

"Why hell yes, I was listening!" She wanted to strangle him before the law showed up. Now she wanted to hang, stab, and shoot him first.

"I intended to make him feel foolish for coming here."

"Make him feel foolish for confronting you with the truth? And you admitting to it?"

Trey smiled at her. He excelled in smiling. Had all kinds of different smiles for a myriad of occasions. This was his sweet and loving smile. She did not doubt the sincerity of it, but it riled her even more.

"You're not surprised that I know?" She nearly screamed. He'd only been home little over an hour when Ring showed up. She'd wanted an opportune moment to confront him with her knowledge, and this was about as opportune as it could get.

"Melinda. I couldn't tell you, but I knew you would figure it out."

"You made me think you were going overseas, asshole!"

Another sweet smile. "No. I never mentioned a word about overseas."

"But I did, and you didn't bother to correct me. That's the same as lying."

"Not even close to the same, Melinda. I simply let you think what you wanted to think. I didn't take any actions to prevent you from discovering the truth on your own."

"And what kind of actions could you have taken, big shot?"

"Like the action taken here today. What you heard, what you observed, was initiated in the master planning from the very beginning. "

Trey reached for her hands with both of his. Melinda offered only slight resistance before giving into his tender grasp. He used his hands to sit her down on the couch. He took a seat next to her.

"We knew we couldn't afford letting Ring come to the same conclusion on his own. Eventually, he might have done so. The flight back here in the private jet immediately after last night's mission, the anonymous call to Ring, every bit of this, was preplanned to happen just like it did. And it doesn't end there.

"Tomorrow, within an hour of us flying back to Chicago, two men will arrive here. From a distance, they will very much resemble John and me. They will be decoys. Anyone viewing from a long way off, even with binoculars, will believe they are us."

Melinda could not remain on the couch another second. She got up and started to pace. Trey settled back into apparent comfort.

"Oh, my God, this is all too . . . just too . . . "

"Hard to come up with the exact word," Trey interrupted. "I understand. I think three words sum it up best, Melinda. *Very, very, big.* The true complexity of this operation would totally boggle your mind. I don't want your mind boggled, baby. I want to keep you as untangled from this as possible."

"Who is making this happen, Trey? Who has that kind of resources? That kind of power?"

"We've only met Donning. He is deeply loyal to the source. John and I have had to accept that it doesn't matter who wants this done. It matters only that we do it. Whoever this person is, we share the same values."

Melinda took long moments to process. She first started to slowly nod her head, but then stopped, and emitted a cleansing sigh before she began to shake it.

"Values, Trey? These are capital crimes. You are *murdering* Americans."

It took several seconds, but Trey calmly replied, "I am."

"So is John."

"He is. I am. We are."

"And you are okay with that?" Melinda could not hold back tears a moment longer.

"Melinda, I've seen so many wounded men, that could only survive if a large chunk of their bodies were cut off and tossed away. I've known men that lost multiple limbs because the doctors removed them. It was necessary that mangled flesh and bone be carved away in order for the body to live."

Trey stood up and drew close to Melinda. He used a slight touch of his fingertips to wipe at her tears. "This world is greatly in need of rescuing, and we are citizens of the only nation that can offer hope.

However, our nation is severely wounded. The wounds are festering. Immune systems are terribly weakened, and other diseases are setting in. Honestly, Melinda, sick and damaged parts need carved out. Cut off. Discarded . . . I am okay with doing that."

She allowed him to pull her tightly into his arms. She listened as he whispered into her ear. "I've served in ancient and once grand cities and regions that have fallen to ruin and corruption, and mayhem rules. All that came about, because bad people did what they wanted, while good people stood by and did nothing. I'm no good, Melinda, at doing nothing."

"Your ways of doing *something* have been so brutal," Melinda said, while fighting back the urge to sob.

"That's what we wanted certain people to believe. The castrating and throat slitting happened after the victims were dead. What has been leaked to the media was meant to dissuade others from taking leadership roles. So far, it seems to be working. All died very quickly, shown mercy they did not deserve. Except last night."

Melinda pulled her head back to look up at Trey. "What happened last night?"

"Things got out of hand. You don't want to know more."

Melinda reburied her head into his chest. Moments later, he gently raised her head and looked into her eyes.

"Melinda, you knew what we intended to do with Rudy Whitlock when and if we found him. We found him and we did it. You had no qualms with that."

"Whitlock was a monster," she whispered.

"The people we are taking down, are only slightly better, Melinda. All have done horrible things."

Melinda remained silent to sort through her feelings and just enjoy the secure feeling of being in Trey Remington's strong arms. After moments of rearranging her emotions, she drew a conclusion.

"I just don't understand, Trey. Within these walls, in our bedroom, you are the most loving and tender man I've ever known."

It took Trey a few seconds, but he did offer an explanation.

"I just don't bring my work home with me, baby."

* * * *

Some minutes earlier, Ledford heard angry words coming from Melinda through the thin walls of his mobile home. He'd never heard the sweet woman raise her voice in anger, but knew her to be feisty enough to have such tendencies. He did not envy his dear brother, Trey.

"Better him than me, though," Ledford said out loud, and could not help but grin.

Ledford did not want a steady woman. He'd had one. She'd been his first true love, before taking her own life. He didn't figure on ever finding one to replace her, and he didn't care to try. Love proved fleeting. Hate lasted forever.

It felt good to grin. If for only a second. Ledford found little that amused him since the overnight debacle back in Chicago. It reminded him of movie scenes that plagued him from his youth.

Many times on television and at the movies, realistic or not, he'd viewed marauding cavalry troopers swooping into defenseless Indian encampments to slaughter people fleeing in fear for their lives. But never, until after last night, did it occur to him, that just maybe before the onslaught, troopers shouted promises of mercy that the Indians did not comprehend.

After all, the Asians had not understood.

Ledford would have delivered justice in a quick and merciful way. One shot through an eyeball, and it would have been over. He'd rubbed elbows with death enough times to believe that the end could come immediately with no pain.

The Asian gang leader and his two subordinates panicked. Ledford did not hold them at fault. They simply did not understand the commands.

Drop your weapons.

Get on your knees.

Death can come fast in a merciful way.

Instead, they opened fire. Rounds zinged past Ledford's head. He dove for cover, returning fire. Bullets ripped through Remington's duster, making Ledford fear his dearest ally might be struck. Remington managed to stand in place and return fire as well.

Too many rounds were fired. Too many struck parts of the body that could only produce pain. Ledford only had one round in his chamber when the last Asian slumped to the floor. Remington was already reloading a revolver.

"Damn it to hell!" Remington bellowed.

One gang member tried to struggle to his feet with a gun in his hand. Ledford placed his last bullet in the man's forehead. The others writhed in pain, badly wounded, but still conscious. Feeling pain Ledford did not intend them to feel.

"Are you okay?" he shouted at Remington.

"Fine. Is anyone hit?" Remington hollered to the support members of their crew.

Somehow, no member had taken one of the dozens of rounds fired by the opposition. Remington finished reloading a revolver before Ledford. It fell to him to complete the job at hand. Remington shot the two survivors in the forehead.

The support members went immediately to work on sanitizing the scene. Ledford stood alongside Remington. Both remained silent as they surveyed the scene and struggled with their thoughts. Remington finally broke the silence.

"We best get moving, John. Have a plane to catch."

Now Ledford glanced around his shabby abode, and concluded torturing his mind with two final thoughts.

Poor Indians of yesteryears.

Poor Asians of yesterday.

For a second time within the hour, someone knocked at his door. Ledford opened it to find Remington standing with a full bottle of whiskey in each hand.

"John, is it too early in the day for you to get just falling down drunk?"

"Probably," he grunted back. "But won't let it stand in my way."

* * * *

Kenneth Donning nodded his head at Charles Atkinson. "Yes, sir. That is the bad news. Last night's mission, unlike the others, was not perfect. However, it did prove successful."

"In that case, Ken, I don't consider that bad news. We both know that even the most perfect plans can and do go awry. No, not bad news at all. It certainly could have been much worse."

Donning nodded his head once again.

"Now, more importantly, what is the good news?" Atkinson smiled.

Donning picked up the sterling silver carafe of coffee and refilled first Atkinson's cup and then his own. "Last night in St. Louis, three middle-aged black men forced their way into a known gang-leader's house. They shot and killed the leader along with three other members of the gang. They found vast amounts of drugs and a large sum of money. They dumped it all over the bodies. Each of the three men wore cowboy hats."

Atkinson sighed long and hard. "I do regret that I must consider killing as good news. I truly wish there was another way."

"I know you do, Sir Atkinson."

"Still, I must focus on the positive. That is the third reporting of such activities. The one in Chicago. The one in Oakland. And now one from St. Louis. The process is taking hold. We have evidence of Americans starting to rid their communities of a dastardly plague. That can only be considered as a positive development."

Kenneth Donning nodded a final time, but felt a sense of dread. With such progression, the end grew nearer. In the end, Donning would have to initiate the final action. The act would be performed to solely protect Charles Atkinson, an act of which Atkinson could never know occurred. Donning alone would bare the weight.

* * * *

Marcus Jones had been stuck so long in the Intelligence Section of the Bureau of Organized Crime that he'd lost all hope of further advancement. Having done the same work for so long, he could perform his assigned duties in a deep sleep or drunken stupor. As a result, Jones stopped dwelling on his career with the CPD long ago. For that long period of time the detective worried only about ex-wives and a crippled daughter.

For the past four months, since selling his soul to the devil, Jones concentrated mostly on his fears of ending up in prison. For eight days now, he'd found Marge Myers to be a refreshing topic on which to dwell. Although closely related to his current dilemma, thinking about the lady took the edge off his fears.

How stupid am I?

Pretty damned stupid. Marcus Jones falling for Marge Myers? Damned stupid. Unless, by some great stretch of the imagination, she thought more of him than just a confidential informant.

She did invite me to her house.

For additional information. Yet, he wanted to consider it a starting point or view it as an opportunity. Centuries of relationships had developed under stranger circumstances.

With his pension and the money he'd traded his integrity for, Jones didn't necessarily have nothing to offer in the way of a life for Marge. A future with her could offer comfort for them both. All he'd have to provide beyond wealth would be love and happiness. Jones could certainly provide the love, but his record on making women happy proved far from successful. Happiness hinged on too many shifting variables. Say for instance, sharing life with a man and his handicapped adult child. Or, finding out the man she'd hooked up with could be bought for the right amount of money.

After more mental wrangling, it came down to taking one small and careful step at a time. He could not first go to Marge's house. She would have to come to his.

Marge Myers would have to initially experience what Jones hoped to share.

Good luck with that.

Having her there could serve another purpose as well. Jones thought he might have picked up on indications that Myers suspected his involvement with the Outlaws. Seeing how he lived just might suggest justification for a decision that made him an accomplice to numerous counts of murder.

* * * *

Sean Scully beat Mark Penn to the station, but not by much.

"Sleep well?" Scully grinned.

"About as well as you can for four hours," Penn grumbled.

Scully punched the elevator button. "Yeah, but this could prove worth giving up sleep."

The look on Penn's face didn't show much hope. "Do you know where they found him?"

"Hiding in some abandoned dump on the West side like a frightened rat."

"Can you blame him, Sean? I'd been in California by now."

"Me, too. But we're smart. He's a gang-banger. Says it all."

Sean followed Penn into the elevator and hit the third-floor button. The attending officer approached the elevator the moment the detectives stepped out.

"He ain't saying shit. Won't even give his name," the officer said in greeting. "But we know who he is. It's damn sure him. No doubt."

"You have the video ready to go?" Penn asked.

"All set up in the interrogation room. It's a copy of the original with nothing beeped or blurred out. All you have to do is hit the button, Detective."

The officer escorted them to the interrogation room. They peered through the one-way glass to observe a young Hispanic male sitting at a table with hands cuffed behind his back.

"Does not appear comfortable with the setting," Scully chuckled.

"Looks scared shitless," Penn agreed.

"I like them scared. Let's crack him like an egg."

"You take the lead?" Penn asked.

"My privilege."

Scully jerked the door open. As expected and hoped for, the sudden movement startled the kid. Scully strolled in casually, but with a stern look as he pulled a card from his pocket.

"You have the right to remain silent . . . " Scully began reading from the card. He concluded with, "Do you understand these rights?"

The kid never looked up from the table in front of him. "No comprende," he muttered.

"Oh, you do comprende, asshole. We have proof that you comprende," Scully growled. "As a matter of fact, we initially knew you as only 'The Interpreter.' Now, we know you are Miguel Hernandez. So, cut the shit, Miguel."

Hernandez lowered his head and shook it in response. "No comprende."

Scully looked at Penn. "Okay. He doesn't understand, Mark. So, let's fuck him up the ass."

Hernandez jerked his head up to look at Scully.

"You stupid, shit," Scully chuckled. "Tell you what we should do, Miguel. Let's watch a little television. You like television don't you?"

Hernandez still said nothing, but lowered his eyes to again stair at the table.

"Mark, could you get that going?"

Penn pushed some buttons, and the video jumped to life on the small screen.

Hernandez did not raise his head until hearing his own voice come from the television.

"Who the fuck are you, and what the fuck do you want?"

Penn hit the pause button. "Miguel, I'm simply a more believing man than my partner here, and I was starting to believe you. But that's your face clear as day, and that's some fine English you're speaking."

Hernandez's eyes were glued to the screen and he didn't move them. Penn hit the play button again. Scully watched Hernandez as all hell broke loose on the video. The kid seemed to be reliving it. The predominant emotion Scully observed could not be mistaken for anything but gripping fear. Penn let the video run uninterrupted to the end.

Scully stepped up close to the table. "Miguel to quote the cowboy, 'Well, it comes to this, Senior Hernandez, do you choose to live, or do you choose to die?'"

For the first time since entering the room, Hernandez looked Scully straight in the eyes with a definite look of concern.

"Let me explain, Miguel," Scully started. "Do you know how that video was released to the news media? We gave it to them. And they want us to give them more. If you don't start talking, we will give them more. We'll tell them how you turned yourself in for the patriotic duty of helping us find the Outlaws. You better believe those two are watching the news. They'll see it, and then they'll come looking to find you. You better give us something. Their faces were covered, but you could see their eyes. Tell us about their eyes."

Hernandez drew in a deep breath before clearing his throat. "You never want to look into those eyes."

"Awwww, he speaks," Scully said softly. "Why not, Miguel? Why would I not want to look into those eyes?"

"They are the eyes of demons."

"Give me colors. What color were their eyes?"

"I could not see colors. There was not enough light. But I could see the evil in the eyes."

Scully accepted that, and changed course. "Did you do as they requested? Did you spread the word?"

"To all who cared to listen."

"The horses they rode. Could you see a brand on them?"

"No."

"Did you notice any markings on the saddles, like a brand name, or initials?"

"No."

Scully leaned down to place his palms on the desk. "Give us something, Miguel. You told them you choose to live. Don't give up the opportunity to do so."

Hernandez looked around the room, as if searching the corners of his memory. He scratched at his forehead on the edge of the table. Finally, he looked up and displayed a look of hope.

"They were not alone."

"What do you mean?" Scully asked.

"When I first observed them, I saw movement outside the available light. They were close, but mostly hidden in the shadows."

Scully glanced at Penn, who nodded his head. "How many did you see?" Scully asked.

"Two, or maybe three."

"You don't know the difference between two and three?"

"Man, it was just movement. Like ghosts or something. Besides, I was mainly paying attention to two crazy-motherfuckers on horses."

"The ghosts," Scully scowled, "How were they dressed?"

"I didn't get that clear of a look at them. They didn't want to be seen, man."

Scully nodded his head. He believed Miguel. They wouldn't want to be seen. They were professionals. "Mark, you have any questions for Mr. Hernandez?"

Penn moved up to the table. "Miguel, did you set this up? Did you tell the Outlaws about the buy?"

"Are you fucking joking, man? Did you see the look on my face in that video? I don't even mind telling you, man, I shit my pants. Those mother fuckers aren't from this world."

Penn studied Hernandez for seconds before asking, "Miguel, if you see them again, we want to know about it."

Hernandez emitted a chuckle that held no glee. "Man, if I see those two again, I won't live to tell no mother fucker nothing."

Scully followed Penn out of the room, pulling the door shut behind him. Both detectives stepped in front of the one-way viewing glass.

"That was pretty much a waste of time," Penn grumbled.

"Not really, Mark. It confirmed what we knew had to be true. They're not in this alone. They have a team of professionals with them at all times. They set up transportation. They disable cameras. They provide the intelligence."

"Yeah, but we still have no clue who they are."

"No, but we also learned something else of value."

"Guess I missed that," Penn scoffed.

"We learned we don't want to look into their eyes."

Penn laughed. "I'd already made up my mind, partner . . ." Penn said as he pointed a finger to inside the room. "Only place I want to meet those two, is in a room just like that one."

"No shit," Scully agreed.

SEVEN

M elinda stared at the nondescript box van while wishing with all her heart that Trey would not be climbing up into the back of it in mere minutes. She didn't dare burden him with her emotions. He needed to be clear headed, and not worrying about her.

"Not very fancy wheels for a couple of famous outlaws," She said, trying to make light of a dark moment in her life.

Trey and John stood side by side. John responded to her comment. "Yeah, just a temporary inconvenience. You ought to see the jet. Attendants are all naked."

Melinda giggled and winked at John, and then turned a fake scowl on Trey. "You best keep your hands in your pockets, big boy."

"Don't worry your pretty head, baby," Trey grinned. "The attendants are all males."

Her pretty head was already worried, but with far greater fears. She pushed them aside as she stepped up to give John a hug. "You be safe, John Ledford."

John hugged her back and kissed her cheek. "No worries, sweet Melinda," John grunted.

Yeah, right.

She watched and remained silent until John disappeared into the back of the van. Suddenly, she could not hold all of it in.

"What this mission entails, you know, the things we discussed like you going to prison, are the least of my worries. I don't know what I'd do if you got killed." She let that out, but fought back the tears.

"I can't promise you I won't be, but I can promise you I'll do my damned level best to get back here to you."

"But, I still don't want you going to prison."

Something ugly flashed in her man's eyes. "I can promise you I will . . . *never* . . . go to prison."

She tensed even as the look in his eyes evaporated, and she sensed he'd said something he wished he hadn't. He flashed one of his many smiles. This one the jovial and light-hearted one.

"Oh, come on, baby. Haven't yet suffered even a scratch. And the cops are totally in the dark."

Melinda couldn't bring herself to dampen his attempt to make her feel better. She had to contribute to a farewell free of drama. "What are you going to do if I fall for the guy coming here to look like you?"

Trey laughed. "Believe me, you won't be tempted to fall for Buzz. On the other hand, I worry about Bingo. He's more your type."

"Buzz and Bingo? I can hardly wait," she chuckled.

"Old army buddies, baby. I'll feel better knowing they are here."

Then she was in his arms, and they kissed numerous times, and all too quickly Trey Remington joined John in the back of the van.

* * * *

Mark Penn handed the folder to Lieutenant Elmore. "We believe, LT, that one of these five white gang-leaders will be the Outlaws' next victim. The addresses on all are still good. We'd like each of the five to be placed under twenty-four hour surveillance starting as quickly as possible."

Sean Scully could see in Elmore's eyes that he didn't want to admit he'd been wrong, and they'd been right. Scully hoped for an opportunity to smear it in his face. But just enough to prevent totally pissing off his superior.

Elmore studied the files in the folder. "That's a lot of fucking man power."

"If we'd done it sooner," Scully said, "We might already have them in custody. Not to mention saving a life or two."

Elmore looked up from the file to glare at Scully. "Oh, I know, Detective, your heart bleeds for those Asian thugs."

"Just saying . . ."

"Don't say no more." Elmore turned back to the files.

After studying each for long minutes, he nodded his head. "I can pull from the budget someplace to cover it." He quickly looked to Scully. "How many Asians would we have had to camp out on?"

"Just guessing . . . probably six, LT."

"I can afford five. No way in hell could I have covered eleven. Because at the time we didn't know which they'd hit first, whites or Asians."

Scully didn't care to show it, but he did admire Elmore's attempt to cover his ass.

"Understood," Scully nodded.

Elmore reached to pick one file out of the folder. "If I were the Outlaws, this is the bastard I'd hit." Elmore showed them the most recent mug shot of Clint Demont.

"You're familiar with Sampson?" Penn asked.

"I am. Worked him when I was a violent crimes detective. Been around a long time. Should have been dead long ago. He's a sick and ruthless son of a bitch . . . Scully?"

"Yeah, boss?"

"You know him?"

"Never dealt with him."

"You'd like him. In contradiction to some alleged acts, he's a gay basher."

The comment took Scully by surprise, but he rebounded by placing a hand on Penn's shoulder. "LT, some of my best friends are gay."

"Fuck you, Scully," Elmore smiled.

Penn turned to look at Scully, "Yeah . . . uh . . . fuck you, Scully."

First, Scully said to Penn, "Fuck you back." Then to Elmore, "See, LT," Scully returned the smile. "Now, all of us are talking about fucking each other. How am I a gay basher?"

To Scully's surprise, Elmore genuinely laughed out loud before going forward.

"Okay, back to business. Anyway, if I were a betting man, I'd just place the asshole Demont under surveillance."

"Depends on what intelligence the Outlaws have," Penn said.

"Which brings us to another point, LT," Scully added.

"What's that, Sean?"

Sean?

Damn. Now they were chummy? He could accept that, until Elmore started sending him roses. "Intelligence, boss. Where are they getting it? We suspect they have a source within CPD."

Elmore took a second to consider the accusation. "History could certainly support such a theory, but it could also be coming from other agencies. I've considered the same. However, the last thing we need is a departmental witch hunt."

"But you can bring this to other's attention?" Penn asked.

"I can do that."

Elmore dismissed them. Once the office door closed behind them, Penn turned to Scully.

"I'll be damned if you don't have balls the size of grapefruit."

"What ever you do, dear friend," Scully grinned, "Don't leak that to Elmore."

"Do you honestly have a problem with him being gay?"

Scully gave the question sincere thought. "I don't have a problem with gays. I don't understand it, but, as they say, to each their own. I did have a problem with Elmore just being Elmore. Call it a personality clash. But I'll be damn if he isn't starting to grow on me."

"Guess you don't want me leaking that to him either?"

"No. Let him figure it out on his own."

* * * *

Melinda walked out of the house and down the steps to observe the return of the nondescript box van. First it took her man away. Now it returned with his "replacement." Melinda nodded at the same two men in the cab who made the earlier trip out to the ranch. The driver parked the van in the spot it'd previously occupied, aligning Melinda with the passenger side of the vehicle.

Both men got out of the cab, but only the passenger spoke to Melinda.

"Ma'am, I do pity you."

Before Melinda could ask why, unpleasant noises erupted from within the back of the van. The driver unlatched the double doors to the compartment, and stepped clear of the opening.

Melinda initially feared it was a Pomeranian pooch that came flying from the back of the van, until it landed with a splat instead of a bounce and a yelp. She looked to the van's passenger for an explanation.

"It's the one guy's wig," he grimaced.

"That guy?" she pointed when next a man tumbled from the van to land flat on his back.

"Nope. The one coming out next."

Melinda assumed the man on his back with the blondish hair and light complexion to be the make-believe Trey. The one who dove out after him, as if initiating a belly-buster into a body of water, would be John's fill in. She had no idea which one was Buzz or Bingo.

Make believe John landed right on top of make believe Trey, and started throwing blows that the man on his back tried to block from landing in his face. Both bellowed profanities.

"Aren't you going to stop them?" Melinda shouted at the driver.

"I've grown tired of trying to stop them," the man shouted back.

"They tire quickly," the passenger inserted.

Not quickly enough for Melinda. She stomped over to the combatants and used the sole of a western boot to remove the man on top. He rolled over on his back and simply lay still next to decoy Trey. Both suddenly appeared as if they'd simply plopped down for a side-by-side nap. Trey's replacement even placed the interlaced fingers of both hands beneath his head in a relaxed manner. Both men stared up into Melinda's eyes.

"What the hell is going on?" She asked, looking from one to the other.

The man she'd kicked from the other replied, "I'm Bingo."

The other responded, "I'm Buzz."

"Are you a couple of idiots?" she asked with sincere curiosity.

"We've been accused of such," Buzz grinned.

Melinda turned to the van operators for their input, but both were busy removing two large military duffle bags from the back. Both seemed in a hurry. They laid the bags next to the prone men before moving to the open doors of the cab. The driver gave her a wave as he climbed behind the wheel and called to her.

"Good luck, lady."

The passenger added once again, "Yes, ma'am, I sure pity you."

The van pulled away, while Buzz and Bingo remained on their backs just looking around the new settings.

"Are you just going to lay there?" Melinda scowled at the men.

"Pretty comfy," Buzz replied.

Bingo struggled to his feet and bent to pick up the wig. He placed it on his shaved head and adjusted it in place. Long dark hair now fell down on his shoulders.

"Do I look like John Ledford?"

Melinda shook her head, but only to clear it. This shit could not be real. Bingo obviously took the gesture as a "no." He turned and took off in a run away from Melinda. About seventy yards out, he turned back and cuffed hands around his mouth.

"How about from here?" he shouted.

Melinda looked down at Buzz, who stared up at her.

"If you nod your head yes, he'll come back. Which I guess you should do considering our mission. But kind of wish you'd shake it no. In that case, he'll just keep going further away."

Melinda drew in a deep and cleansing breath before nodding her head at Bingo. He started back at a trot. Buzz picked himself up off the ground.

"Bingo suffers from PTSD. He got blown off his feet two more times than I did in Afghanistan. Messed him up in the head. Didn't affect me. But, two more blasts might have jumbled my brains as well. That's the reason I take care of him. I'm kind of his guardian."

Melinda tried to stop her head from spinning in total disbelief. No other words came to her jumbled mind except, "Is he dangerous?"

"Only to me. You have no worries. We are here to protect you."

Jesus help me.

Bingo made it back to ask, "Is he talking about me?"

"Just telling her the truth," Buzz replied.

Bingo nodded his head at Melinda. "Okay, now you know it. I'm a bed wetter. Can't help it."

"I didn't tell her that part, Bingo."

Bingo responded by looking back and forth between the two battered mobile homes. "One of those is supposed to be where we stay. Which one is it?"

Melinda pointed at John Ledford's trailer.

"Wow. That's damned nice," Bingo nodded with enthusiasm, causing strands of hair to bounce about his shoulders.

Buzz spoke while Bingo nodded. "All right, Mrs. Remington, we'll settle in, and then get to work. Trey, said we should start by just driving around the ranch, but told us to stay far from the borders. What do we drive?"

Melinda pointed to one of three trucks in the dirt drive. A badly dented and decaying Ford nearly twenty years old.

"Wow, that's damned nice," Bingo's wig bobbed once again.

Instead of grabbing her head and screaming, Melinda decided on hospitality. What could she do but accept the arrangement?

"Have you two had anything to eat?"

Buzz pointed to one of the duffle bags. "We have MREs. That's Meals Ready to Eat. That's all we ever eat. It's quick and easy because they are ready to eat."

Melinda got it. She'd done her part.

"The key is in the ignition," she mumbled before turning to mope toward her trailer.

* * * *

Ten days earlier P-Wac had longed to cross this threshold. Although he'd dreaded the process, P-Wac knew it necessary to secure his right of passage. That was before all, too quickly, started changing in his world.

Like all young boys of his hood, he'd joined the gang for protection, primarily from the dangers posed by other gangs. The money to be had and the drugs made available just served as enticing perks of the trade.

Boof stepped up close to P-Wac. "You ready for this muthu fucka?" Boof hissed.

The five others pulled in close. Boof intended to perform the duties of the now dead D-Killa. Not that he'd stepped up to take command. None were showing interest in doing so. Boof wanted to be just enough of a big shot so as not to attract the attention that would get his balls cut off and his throat slit.

P-Wac reluctantly nodded his head. "Bring it on you bitch ass nigga."

The progression to higher status seemed so senseless now. The danger of opposing gangs proved the least of P-Wac's worries. Especially at this very moment. This would end though. But the Outlaws, and the suddenly concerned public they inspired, seemed here to stay.

Boof drove his closed fist directly into P-Wac's nose. P-Wac stumbled backwards, but managed to stay upright. Blood trickled from his nose into a mouth that held clenched teeth. He could not scream out in pain. One of the O.G.s behind P-Wac planted a punishing jab to his right kidney. P-Wac gasped, swallowing a mouth full of blood. His knees nearly buckled. Boof stepped in again and aimed the tip of his right shoe into P-Wac's balls.

At least I still have them.

He fought to stay on his feet. When he did go down, he hoped to be unconscious. Others told him it best to do so. That way the inductee did not feel what followed.

Someone struck him hard in the back of his head. Only fists and feet were allowed in the initiation into manhood, but P-Wac felt like he'd been struck by a hammer. His eyesight dimmed. A fist seemed to explode into his stomach, sending shrapnel to each vital organ. He bent double and suddenly could not breath. A viscous undercut caught him beneath the chin, straightening him upright, but only for a moment.

And all went black.

* * * *

"Route Alpha clear from CP 6 to CP 7."

Ledford pushed a button on the steering wheel. "Roger that."

Remington sat in the passenger seat closely scanning in all directions while marveling still at a source that could provide such a vehicle. Equipped with secure communication capabilities that would turn James Bond green with envy, the armored Hummer contained accessories surpassing that of even the presidential limousines.

Ledford pushed the button again. "Clearing CP 5."

Team Two crept ahead of the Hummer and in sight. Team 3 followed them from behind also maintaining visual contact. Team one worked far in advance, searching for the intended "Target of Opportunity." Team 3 would communicate only to issue a warning of danger. Team 1 would remain silent until hopefully locating a target. All monitored police frequencies. The mission objective was simply to make an impression.

"This time last night, we were at home," Remington mumbled.

"You were at home. I was at the bar."

"Oh, yeah, forgot to ask. Did you land a beauty?"

"She had beautiful talents."

"Congrats," Remington chuckled.

Remington continually hoped his buddy could find the woman to replace the one he lost. He still sorrowed over John's loss. But there was one consolation. The source that caused John's Karena to take her life, met a most horrific ending.

Don't do this now.

Any reference to Rudy Whitlock could possess Remington. He needed his mind crystal clear right now.

"Team 1 to Lead."

"Go to Lead," Ledford responded.

"Target in vicinity of CP 11. Standby for details."

* * * *

So far, Max Simms had only been shoved back and forth between the three younger men. Hell, he'd been pushed around before, and he'd put up with it. For that reason, he now refused to obey the demands of these thugs. Max was tired of putting up instead of standing up.

"I told you, old man, we been looking for someone like you. People suddenly spouting balls. One more time, Gramps. Take that mutha-fucking t-shirt off," Boss Thug threatened.

Max paid good money to have the embroidering done on his shirt. Back in the sixties, he'd worn the uniform of a United States Marine. The t-shirt paled in comparison, but still worked to remind Max of a time he stood proud.

"If you want this shirt, punk, you will have to take it off me."

Boss thug made a production of pulling his large knife from a pocket. The other two pulled knives as well.

"Was hoping you'd want it this way, old fuck. Of course, when we start cutting cloth, we gonna get some skin too. A lot of it."

Maybe I should just give them the shirt?

Nope. Been giving in too long.

Max brought his fists up in a fighting stance. "Well, then, get it on, bitch!"

Boss Thug bellowed in anger and brought the knife up high, just as a car turned the corner and crept in their direction. As if on patrol, but this was no police car.

Large.

Black.

Reverberating.

The Hummer.

"Uh-oh, Punks," Max chuckled. "You fucked!"

It certainly showed on all three faces. "Shit, man, what we do?" One thug asked Boss Thug.

The third punk offered his input. "We fucking run!"

"We don't run," Boss Thug, grunted. "But we do walk away quickly before those crazy mutha fuckas get out that Hummer."

An alley lie behind their backs, and all three turned that direction as the Hummer pulled to the curb. Boss Thug led the way in an exaggerated strut, but at top walking speed.

"And don't let me see your asses back on my street," Max hollered.

The three men, knives still in their hands, stopped in their tracks. Max glanced over his shoulder, hoping to see cowboys coming to his rescue. The doors were still closed. Max decided to start for the Hummer, but stopped at the sound of an unfamiliar voice.

"Going somewhere, fellers? Hell, the party is just beginning."

Max wheeled around to face the alley just as two tall figures stepped from the shadows just yards in front of the thugs. Max could only make out the long coats and wide-brimmed hats. The thugs started backing toward Max. The two men in front of them just took a few steps forward. Steps that put them beneath the glow of a streetlight. Max could now see the bandanas that covered their faces, and four holstered cowboy kind of guns.

"The Outlaws!" Max bellowed gleefully.

Boss Thug quickly glanced backwards at the idling Hummer. His voice stammered as he asked, "How the fuck . . . "

"It's magic man," the same cowboy spoke again.

The one with long hair then added, "Black magic."

One of the thugs dropped his knife.

"Oh, no," the long-haired one said. "Pick it back up."

Clearly shaking with fear, the thug did as told.

"Okay, bad-asses, here's how we're going to dance this dance," the first cowboy spoke again. "You run, we shoot to wound. Then we cut your nuts off. The only way out of here for you, is straight through us. Head-on."

"Ain't fair," the long-haired one seemed to object. "There's three of them and two of us."

The first cowboy nodded his head. "Right. Good point. Change of plans, bad-asses. My partner here is going to give me both his guns. To make it fair, I will sit this one out."

In a wink of an eye, the long-hair whipped out both pistols with butts pointed forward, kind of tossed them in the air, only to catch them before spinning and twirling them like nothing Max never saw before. He could not help but laugh and clap his hands.

Long-hair handed the pistols to his buddy, and stepped up close to the thugs. He raised his hands and used his fingers to motion the thugs forward.

"Come to poppa."

The three thugs rushed the lone cowboy with knives at the ready.

Shit!

My God!

Seeing, but not believin'!

Max loved Ninja movies. Long-hair moved like a Ninja. In a blinding speed of motion, he took hands bearing knives one at a time, and broke the arm holding them. Max heard the bones snapping. It all ended so quickly, leaving three thugs writhing on the ground screaming in pain.

First cowboy started nudging them with his boots. His spurs jingled. "You each have one good arm. Get up and get out of here before my friend decides to break three more. Or, I decide to just go ahead and saw off your balls."

Max stood as if in shock and watched the three assholes stumble down the alley and out of sight. The cowboys strolled right up to Max, and one at a time, they offered hands, concealed in tight black leather gloves, for Max to shake.

Max could not find words to speak.

The first cowboy pointed at the words on Max's t-shirt, and read them out loud. "Neighborhood Patrol. Gangsters beware." He nodded his head in apparent approval. "You, sir, are truly a hero."

In the next instance, both just seemed to fade into the shadows of the alley. Max heard the powerful engine behind him rev, and the pipes thunder. He turned and watched the Hummer pull away from the curb.

"Damn thing drives itself," he whispered aloud. "Outlaw magic!"

EIGHT

Thumper came in the door with the news, and Sampson peaked out a window for confirmation. "You're right, Thumper."

The unmarked car stood out like a turd in a fruit basket. Thumper never understood why plain-clothes cops used dark colored four-door sedans, but he appreciated their lack of imagination.

"I don't think they're out to get you, Sampson."

"Right. If they thought we stock-piled dope and guns here, they'd already kicked down the door and shoved a warrant up my ass." Sampson paused to shake his head and chuckle. "Fuckers are here to protect me."

"Not necessarily. But they are here to try and snag the Outlaws. Considering your run-ins with CPD, Sampson, I fear they would only swoop in once your throat is slit and your balls are gone."

Sampson chuckled at the truth. "In that case, I think I'll just mosey down and explain, respectfully, that I don't need their protection. That I want the Outlaws to find me, because I intend to fuck them cowboys up in order to become the true king of Chicago street gangs. Think they'd understand and go away?"

Thumper burst into laughter, and Sampson joined him.

"So, what are we really going to do?" Thumper asked, still smiling.

"Go out back. See if there is another one in the alley."

In his lieutenant's brief absence, Sampson formed a plan.

"None out back."

Sampson shook his head and snickered, "Stupid sons of bitches. Of course, works to our advantage. Thumper, I want you to leave. In exactly one hour, pull up in the alley to the back. Come in from the east so they don't see you. Meanwhile, I'm going to go out, smoke some cigarettes, and let them see I'm here."

* * * *

P-Wac lay in his bed, and tried not to move. Not a single part of his body did not ache. Most of it throbbed. He assumed they inflicted the most damage once he'd fallen unconscious to the ground.

"Can I get you anything, P-Wac?"

He moved only his eyes to get a glimpse of the pretty young face peeking through a slit in his bedroom door.

"No, I'm good, Charmane," he mumbled.

She stared silently for a long moment. "Was it worth it, P-Wac?"

P-Wac wanted to breathe deeply, but had tried earlier, and almost passed out. Thinking did not come easy, but his reply did. "Charmane, you stay away from the gang shit. You understand?"

"I do," she said before backing up and softly shutting his bedroom door.

At thirteen, Charmane had yet to show an interest in turning to the streets. She had no need to. P-Wac believed his young niece possessed a brilliant mind. She made nothing but A's in school, proving far better things awaited her than gang affiliation. She would never have to depend on such an association to protect her. Charmane had P-Wac. He deeply loved his niece, and vowed to do what her father could not. As long as P-Wac breathed air, he'd protect her from the ugliness of a fucked up world.

P-Wac's older brother, Jerome, fathered Charmane. He was seventeen at the time, and the streets took him before he could earn OG Status. Her mother, a crack whore, was most likely dead now as well. P-Wac's mom raised Charmane, and P-Wac did what he could do to help in the process. The most he had to offer was safety.

The thought of Jerome reminded P-Wac of how his older brother lived for the day he'd be an OG. So had P-Wac. Now he was one. He'd accomplished what his brother did not. Jerome would be proud.

P-Wac could give a fuck.

* * * *

Melinda spent the morning working with horses in the barn. Now on her way to the trailer to get a glass of iced tea, she saw the old Ford truck coming in from the range.

Oh shit.

She considered sprinting the remaining distance to her trailer just to avoid Buzz and Bingo. What sense did that make? They could end up being here a long while, and she couldn't dodge them forever. Besides, they were already up and gone before Melinda came out to do her morning chores. If they kept this up, she'd only have to endure them a couple of times a day.

She continued at a walk toward the house as Buzz parked the truck in its designated spot of gravel. Both men stood waiting for her as she approached the front porch.

"Howdy, boys," she said with a forced smile.

"Morning, Mrs. Remington," Buzz smiled back. His right eye looked puffy and just starting to swell. Recent damage.

"Hi," Bingo said, offering a slight wave of his hand. His wig looked askew on his head.

"Buzz, you need to know. I'm not married to Trey. Not yet anyway."

"Oh, okay," he nodded.

"So, uh, you guys need something this morning?"

Buzz grinned broadly, "Sure do, Mrs. Remington, we need a couple of cowboy hats. Figure Trey and John wear them out and about. And, we need to learn to ride horses. Surely, they ride around on horses out on all that land."

Before Melinda could process the request, much less speak, Bingo added to the want list.

"And guns. It'd be fun to shoot at shit."

She glanced quickly at Buzz's swelling eye and then looked back to Bingo. "Uh, I'm very concerned about what shit you might shoot."

"Awe, Mrs. Remington . . . " Buzz started.

"Buzz, did you not hear what I told you?"

"Yeah, you said you worry about what shit Bingo might shoot."

Melinda drew in a deep breath, and let it out slowly. What did it matter what he called her? Best she could do now, was learn to quickly disengage from this type of encounter. More were surely to follow.

"I got hats. No problem. And there are plenty of horses, but honestly, I'm not sure I have the patience to teach you two how to ride them."

"I'll be right back," Bingo said, as he took off in a trot toward Ledford's trailer. He seemed to trot about every place he went.

"What's he doing?" Melinda sighed out loud.

"Said he'd be right back," Buzz clarified.

Melinda just stood silently until Bingo actually came right back at a trot. He handed her a gold-plated oval piece of medal about the size of a cup saucer. Melinda read the engraving.

"Bingo, this is a championship bull riding buckle, and it has your name on it . . . Bobby "Bingo" Bonner." Melinda could not help but be impressed.

"That's me," Bingo beamed. "Tell you what Mrs. Remington, you just saddle up a couple of horses for us. See, I had some shit knocked out of my brains in the war. Like how to properly saddle a horse. But if you will do that part the first time, I think I can take the rest from there. All Buzz really needs to know is how to hang on."

Melinda studied the buckle a second longer. War sucked. Those who endured it, deserved tolerance for the results of inflicted damage.

"Okay, fellers, let's go saddle up some horses."

* * * *

It fell solely on Thumper to carry out the remaining elements of Sampson's plan. He paused at the opening of the alley. He would exit from the opposite direction from which he entered. But first he needed to be noticed. The two dicks in the unmarked car, if paying attention, had clear view of him and his car.

Thinking he'd given them ample opportunity, he pulled out of the alley and steered the car in a direction that would take him right past the cops. He slowly drove by the car without looking at the occupants. As expected, the cops did not follow. They knew who he was, but could give a shit. They'd not pull off as long as Sampson remained in his house. Still, Thumper paid close attention to his rear-view mirrors while being careful to observe all traffic laws.

He made it only two blocks away from Sampson's place before a marked CPD patrol car fell in behind him. It followed him three blocks before the uniforms flipped on their overhead lights. Thumper pulled to the curb at the first opportunity to do so. He watched in the rear-view as two cops got out of the car. A black cop approached the driver's side. The other, a young white cop, walked up to the passenger side.

"May I see your driver's license . . . *Sir,*" the black cop asked snidely.

Thumper longed to share with this one the roles he believed blacks should play, and the roles they should not. He doubted though that the cop would appreciate being told to go pick fucking cotton. Thumper calmly reached into his back pocket for his wallet while the white cop looked through the windows, paying particular attention to the back seat. The black cop took his license and went back to the patrol car. The white one stayed put, still looking for "probable cause" to extract Thumper from the driver's seat.

The black cop returned to his window. "Well, *Mister* Bryan Stamps, you have no outstanding warrants. Would you consent to signing a waiver to allow us to search your car?"

"Give me a moment to consider it," Thumper smiled pleasantly before making a production of studying his face in the interior rear-view mirror. He turned back to the cop with a snarl. "Don't see 'dumb fuck' stamped on my head, *Officer.*"

The cop flung Thumper's license into his lap, and bent down close to look him face to face. "Just give me a reason . . . *Thumper* . . . to pull your bigot ass out of that car, and I promise you a long stay in the hospital."

Thumper smiled the pleasant smile once again. "What did you stop me for, Officer?"

The cop stood upright and chuckled. "Why, hell Thumper, just to compliment you on your impeccable driving skills."

Both cops retreated to their car and pulled away from the curb to go their merry way.

Thumper watched with a hateful scowl. "Be merry now mother fucker," he hissed, "Because after the great cleansing, you'll be one of my house niggers."

* * * *

J.D. Roach pulled up a chair across from Remington and Ledford. Remington extended his right hand. "Great job last night, J.D.," he said to their Chief of Operations. J.D. had selected the route, found Max Simms, and drove the Hummer to and from the target sight after dropping off Remington and Ledford at the alley.

J.D. accepted the handshake of appreciation, but shrugged his shoulders, "No big deal, Trey. Piece of cake."

"Bullshit," Ledford grinned.

Absolutely bullshit, Remington thought. J.D. was truly the brains behind the operations. Everything had so far gone as smooth as possible because of J.D.'s skills and the effort he put into planning and supporting the missions.

"What you got for us, J.D.?" Ledford asked.

"Both our primary and secondary targets of the final mission are under surveillance by CPD."

Remington, along with Ledford, nodded their heads. Remington addressed the snag. "Well, we expected that sooner or later. Just pleased it came later instead of sooner. I know you have it covered."

"We're tweaking the alternative plans we discussed at the outset of operations. Will brief you the moment they're firm."

J.D. left to go immediately to work.

"What would we do without him?" Ledford smiled fondly.

"Without him and the others, we wouldn't be here," Remington replied.

"Yeah, right, but J.D. in particular though, all he does, he manages to do it on two artificial legs," Ledford said softly.

Remington let his mind wonder momentarily to the past. "Damned roadside bombs."

"Damned assholes," Ledford grumbled. "The ones everywhere. The ones that make people like us necessary."

* * * *

P-Wac awoke to the gentle touch of a hand lightly stroking his shoulder. He looked up to find Charmane standing over him.

"I made you some soup, P-Wac. You need to eat."

Last thing P-Wac wanted to do, but he thanked her for her kindness. The girl had a heart of gold.

"And something else, P-Wac, in a few minutes, there's going to be a special report about the Outlaws on Channel 2. Would you like me to turn your television on?"

P-Wac struggled with his thoughts and emotions, but finally responded, "Sure . . . but, I'd like to watch it alone."

Charmane nodded her lovely head. "I'll watch it in the living room."

She turned on the television and found Channel 2. "Let me know if you need anything."

"I will, baby girl," P-Wac said, as he prepared himself for the special. He hoped not to see pictures of the Outlaws. He'd seen them once in person, and then on the video, and hoped to never see a likeness of them again.

A camera zoomed in on a close up of a pretty white woman. P-Wac didn't watch the news, never seen her before, but she introduced herself at the beginning of the program.

"Good Evening Chicago. This is Candice Classen and we begin our coverage tonight with an update on the now notorious vigilantes known as the Outlaws. Police still cannot identify the two men accused of a string of gang-land type murders of known gang leaders. However, we will present a Channel 2 exclusive that indicates the Outlaws might be shifting efforts from taking lives, to saving lives."

The camera panned back from the white woman, to reveal a fairly old black man sitting beside her. He didn't wear a suit, just a silly-assed t-shirt with words that read, "Neighborhood Patrol. Gangsters Beware."

Crazy old mother fucker. Trying to get your ass killed?

"I am pleased to have as my guest tonight, Mr. Max Simms, a resident of South Chicago. Good evening Mr. Simms and thank for being here tonight."

The older man smiled broadly. "Thank you Candice for having me here. I just appreciate you believing my story."

"Mr. Simms, could you please start by telling us about the shirt you are wearing?"

Simms positioned himself to really show off the bullshit on his shirt. Seemed to P-Wac that the old dude just dared someone to bash his head in.

"I got this idea from the Outlaws. They are here doing a job that people like me should have done a long time ago. But I will be honest with you. I just stood by and let the thugs ruin my neighborhood. I'm not standing by doing nothing for no longer."

"So, Mr. Simms, are you saying you condone the actions taken so far by the Outlaws?"

"I sure am. I wish I could put that in stronger words, but you'd have to bleep me."

"As a result of being in support of the Outlaws, you have now taken to patrolling your neighborhood?"

"I have and I will continue to do so. Especially after what happened last night."

"Will you please share with our viewers what you encountered while on patrol late last night?"

"I encountered three pieces of trash that meant to carve me up, and then I encountered two guardian angels . . . "

P-Wac listened intently as the man told his story. Others watching might believe the man's telling to be a gross exaggeration of facts, or even pure make believe. P-Wac took every word as the gospel.

"Just one of the Outlaws took on the three men with knives?" the blonde asked.

"Sure did. Never seen nothing like it. Looked like a long-haired Bruce Lee. Those three thugs were full grown men. He threw them around like rag dolls."

P-Wac would bet on it.

"They were wearing the bandanas pulled up over their face, but did you get a good look at their eyes, Mr. Simms?"

"Only enough to tell you this. They was the eyes of two white dudes, that cared what happened to one old black man. I know I'd be dead right now if they didn't care."

Damn sure was not the eyes P-Wac stared into. He would bet the OGs the one Outlaw fucked up, didn't see any caring eyes either. Still, how the old man said that, along with the actions of the Outlaws to save him, tended to prick at the thick protective coating that insulated P-Wac's heart.

The camera once again moved in for a close-up of the white woman. "There you have it. Two men in unusual costumes, with amazing fighting skills, that can appear or disappear out of thin air in their super vehicle . . . that can drive itself. One can't help but consider Chicago might be Gotham City, and we have found our Batman and Robin. In support of Mr. Simms' story, police are not releasing the names of three black men who entered area hospitals early this morning with broken arms . . ."

P-Wac wanted to just nod his head over and over, but it hurt too much to do so.

Yeah, the Dark Knight and his Boy Wonder. You mother fuckers just now getting it?

* * * *

Marge Myers understood cops didn't make all that much, but the neighborhood and complex Marcus Jones called home, repulsed her. She parked her car as close as possible to his apartment, and literally ran the distance from her car to his apartment door. She'd so tried to talk herself out of coming this evening for dinner. She knew the seed she selfishly planted, had bloomed. In his invite, Marcus' words hinted of a developing attraction. It might not be fair, but a woman had to do what a woman had to do to get all the information she could.

The moment Marcus opened the door, Marge thrust a bottle of wine in his hands and all but knocked him down to get in the apartment. The damned landing didn't even have a light. Marcus' face revealed his understanding.

"Rough neighborhood. Should have told you to call on arrival and I could have met you at your car."

"Oh, you'll be walking me back out to it later," Marge responded with a forced smile.

Marcus welcomed her as she stole quick glances of his abode. A small living room opened into a tiny kitchen with just enough room for a dinette. A hall lead off the living room, and Marge bet it provided access to two bedrooms and a single bath. She followed Marcus to the kitchen so he could open the bottle of wine. Behind his back, she looked closer. The place was dilapidated. The furniture old and shabby. But, the apartment looked clean and organized. No clutter. And something cooking provided an enticing aroma.

"Whatever you're preparing smells delightful," She said, while he opened the wine.

Marcus pulled two juice glasses out of a cabinet of mismatched cups and glasses.

"Don't have much opportunity to drink fine wine. This is the closest thing I have to wine glasses. It's just an alfredo sauce you smell. My mom's special recipe. We'll apply it over roasted chicken and spaghetti."

Marge accepted a glass of wine and raised it to make a point, "In that case, I guessed right in selecting a white."

Marcus brought his glass up to tap hers, "Cheers," he said in a solemn manner.

She repeated the word, and glanced around openly. "Is your daughter not joining us?"

"Trisha . . . that's her name. She's taking a nap."

"I look forward to meeting her," Marge lied. She'd never been comfortable around even the healthiest of children.

Marcus took a healthy swig of his wine. "Good stuff. Thanks for bringing it."

Marge nodded and smiled, "Thanks for inviting me."

Marcus glanced around his apartment, before taking another swig. "You must be appalled. The expenses of a special need kid and losing the rest to divorces . . . well, this is home sweet home."

Marge truly did not want to go there, and abruptly changed the topic. "Did you see Candice Classen's broadcast earlier this evening?"

Marcus flashed a look of apparent embarrassment. Probably for his last statement, along with the way Marge sidestepped it. "Yes. I saw it."

"That puts her one up on my reporting," Marge hoped to sound light-hearted, maybe even joking, but she wasn't.

Marcus drained his glass. He refreshed Marge's and refilled his own. At the rate he put it away, there would be little left for dinner.

"I have something else for you," he sighed.

"About the three with broken arms?"

"No. That's too hot right now. Will need to let that one sit for a while. Internal Affairs is investigating the leak. I have to be damned careful from this point forward."

"What then?" It sounded too abrupt. "I mean if what you have is safe enough for you to disclose."

Marcus looked her hard in the eyes. Maybe he wondered if she really gave a shit about his safety.

"Remember the kid found in D-Killa's safe house?"

"I do."

"He goes by the name of P-Wac." Marcus paused to reach into his shirt pocket. He pulled out a folded piece of paper and handed it to Marge. "I wrote down his real name and last known address."

Not wanting to act too anxious, Marge reached for her purse, and stuffed it inside without unfolding it. The act seemed to help Marcus relax just a tad.

"Anyway he was one of the gang-bangers that first encountered the Outlaws right after they murdered D-Killa and his crew. He was a juvenile at the time. You couldn't have used him as a source without obtaining a release from his mother. You wouldn't have gotten that. Don't need to now. He just turned eighteen."

Marge fought back a squeal of delight. "That is a wonderful lead, Marcus. I am so . . . ."

Her words were interrupted by a sudden grunting sound from beyond her back. Marcus looked over her shoulder and emitted a sigh. Marge turned, and felt overwhelmingly unprepared for what she viewed.

Trisha?

A very round and squatty figure swayed on badly bowed legs. Both arms curled forward, locking in place two gnarled hands. The terribly deformed face could only be explained as hideous, and this was no child.

"Martha, I'd like you to meet, Trisha."

No, thank you. I truly don't care to.

* * * *

Thumper drove, and Sampson gave him the directions. Sampson still ached from the initial part of this journey. He was just too damned big to stay crammed in the trunk of Thumper's car for a little over an hour. Once Thumper finally sprung him, the two kept out of sight at the house of a gang-member too insignificant to draw attention. They didn't leave until it was good and dark.

"Damn, this is a remote area," Thumper observed.

"About as remote as you can find within an hour of Chicago," Sampson beamed. He instructed Thumper to make one more turn. This time onto a rutted dirt drive. Thumper idled along until the house came into view.

"Shit, Sampson. That's big, and old . . . and creepy."

"Was an uncle's farm house. I have a shit for a cousin who stays here now. I called him, told him to get the fuck gone until I tell him he can come back."

"Always helps to know the right people," Thumper chuckled.

They were unloading the car when Thumper's cell started to ring. He took the call, and Sampson proceeded into the house with a load of clothing and other necessities.

Thumper was off the phone by the time Sampson made it out to grab a final load.

"Told you so," Thumper grinned.

"Yeah, about what?"

"The Outlaws were on the news again tonight. They are super-heroes. Seems that Hummer drives its ownself. News woman said something about them being the Batman and Robin of Chicago."

Sampson emitted thunderous laughter. "By the time I lure those pricks to this place, it will be a fortress. That'll make me the Joker. You can be the Bane."

"Bane's an ugly mother fucker, Sampson."

"Have you looked in the mirror lately, Thumper?"

* * * *

141

Autumn seemed to try shoving summer aside, if only temporarily. In the fall and winter, Melinda loved finishing her evenings by building a fire in the pit behind her home. On this evening, a fire would take the welcomed but unexpected chill out of the air. She'd certainly not invited them, but first Buzz and then Bingo found their way to her fire. Like insects drawn to the flame.

"No one told me we were having a campfire," Bingo sulked.

"Hell, I didn't know either, Bingo. I feared something else was on fire, and I just came over here to put it out. And there sat, Mrs. Remington."

Melinda took a deep breath, and chose to be pleasant. "I didn't know you boys had made it in yet. You're welcome to sit at my fire and enjoy the peace and quiet of the evening."

"I got back about an hour ago," Bingo replied.

"I just got back," Buzz added. "Had to walk. By the way, Mrs. Remington, my horse is still out there someplace."

"Are you shitting me, Buzz?" Melinda asked.

"No ma'am, it tossed me off and ran away. Actually, it was running when it tossed me. Bingo, well, he just ran off and left me to have to walk in."

Bingo jumped in, "Well, Mrs. Remington, I know of no better way to teach a man not to let his horse get away from him."

Melinda looked from one man to the next. What the hell, the horse would return. More pressing matters bugged her at the moment. "So, you two were Army Special Forces?"

Bingo threw back his head and laughed. "Special Forces? Hell, no, Mrs. Remington. The army let me and Buzz be truck drivers."

"We were good truck driver's, Mrs. Remington. Hell, we both made it to the rank of buck sergeant. We thought about going Special

Forces, but thought we might have hell with all the testing," Buzz grinned.

"You think?" Melinda asked. Finding an admiration she temporarily misplaced. If these two could be in the Special Forces, she'd join up tomorrow.

"Oh, he's right, Mrs. Remington," Bingo nodded like a mad man. "We fuck up all kind of tests."

"Bingo! Don't say fuck around Mrs. Remington!"

"Fuck you, Buzz!"

"Both of you shut the fuck up," Melinda bellowed.

They immediately obeyed. Melinda took a few deep breaths before asking another question. "So, Trey said you were army buddies. How could you have served together?"

"Oh, we didn't really serve together. We just kind of bumped into him and John. Became close friends after that," Bingo said.

"Yeah," Buzz nodded. "You seen those scars around their gut area? I mean, I assume you've seen Trey naked, you know you being his . . ."

"I've seen their scars," she interrupted.

"Well, then I'm sure you know that came from one hell of a firefight. They both got shot to shit. All the others on their team, they got killed. John and Trey helped each other move back toward the firebase, but they finally went down. Before that, they'd called for air evacuation. Just so happened, Bingo and me were driving in a convoy real close to the coordinates they called in. Our Lieutenant intercepted their radio call, and I'll be damn if we didn't hit the area before even a helicopter could."

"That's no shit, Mrs. Remington," Bingo did that special nodding again.

Buzz continued. "We spotted them, oh, about a hundred yards from the road. I was in the first truck, and Bingo was in the second. Shit, we started out for them in a run."

"Lieutenant screamed at us," Bingo jumped in. "'Hey you two idiots! That area has not been cleared of explosives!' Didn't stop me and Buzz. We don't let Americans lay bleeding."

"So, we made it to them," Buzz picked back up. "I scooped up John Ledford, and Bingo here cradled your Trey in his arms. We made it back that hundred yards without a scratch. But, on the way back, a small pack fell off Trey. Bingo thought it might contain personal items that no soldier would care to loose. So, he took back off for it, and he stepped on his last damn IED. It didn't function properly, but it worked enough to mess him up in the head."

"Yeah, I piss the bed now," Bingo said softly.

Melinda again looked from one man to the other. Thoughts of doubt, and fear of crying momentarily seized her tongue. Finally, she managed to whisper. "Is that a true story?"

Buzz nodded his head. "Yup, he damn sure pisses the bed."

"About the rescue?" she asked patiently.

Bingo jumped on the question. "Who would lie about something like that? Yeah, that LT had it right. We're a couple of idiots, but we ain't liars."

Tears streamed down Melinda's face. She stood and walked over to Bingo, and put her arms around him. She hugged him tightly. Buzz jumped up to be next in line. She hugged him too.

"Welcome to the TRJL Ranch, boys. You are now part of the family."

NINE

Trey cautioned Ledford about reviewing the file. Ledford didn't consider it an option. A true professional in their line of work needed any and all intelligence on the intended target. A skilled hunter took every opportunity to learn the traits of the prey. He knew Trey didn't intend to encourage him to be less prepared. Trey just meant to protect him from haunting memories.

Key characteristics of the target stuck in Ledford's mind. Charismatic. Jovial. Brutal. Sadistic. The criminal tendencies of the target taunted the deep ugly thing that hid in Ledford's heart. By all indications of actual charges and allegations never proven, Clint Demont was a sexual predator. This "Sampson" did not discriminate by sex, age, or means of penetration.

Just a regular all-around pervert.

He was tried as an adult at the age of sixteen for rape by instrumentation. He'd used the handle of a rubber mallet on a nineteen-year-old African-American girl. He committed the awful act to prove his allegiance to a Neo-Nazi group of asswipes. Sampson spent five years in prison for the crime.

Should have had the same handle stuck up his ass, and then beat to death by the mallet.

He'd last been charged almost two years ago to the date for first-degree rape of a sixteen-year-old he'd deemed a snitch. The girl had been nearly beaten to death, and he'd "allegedly" carved a swastika into her forehead with a butter knife. Sampson also "allegedly" penetrated her vaginally and anally, nearly ripping her apart. The girl was the state's only witness. Two weeks before the trial, she committed . . .

Suicide.

Now, Ledford paced back and forth in a newly selected command post within an underground bunker that once served as a bomb shelter of a Chicago tycoon. He paced in order to resist feeding the ugly thing lurking in his heart. It didn't work.

"Karena? Hey, Karena? Where are you, baby?"

Ledford didn't want to return now to the old and crumbling hunting lodge they called home. He never wanted to wander back, but time and time again for so long, he did. Once again he stood just inside the front door and called her name.

"Karena, I have surprise for you. Where are you?"

She'd wanted this particular horse for months.

She would be delighted. The horse might be the only thing that could lift her from a dark depression over yesterday's atrocity, which Karena deemed her fault.

Ledford started through the rambling lodge. At one point he heard the sound of running water. He followed the sound to a bathroom at the far corner of the lodge.

Karena also had a surprise for Ledford.

Water was seeping from beneath the locked door. The water spreading across the white tiled floor was tinged red. Ledford kicked the door nearly off its hinges.

Karena reclined within the tub. Bloody water poured over the edges. Ledford suddenly heard mournful screams, and did not immediately realize they came from his lips. Karena's mouth slowly opened and closed like a fish too long out of the water.

But Karena, you are in the water.

Her eyes lolled in the back of their sockets. Blood now just barely seeped from deep self-inflicted gashes in both wrists and her inner thighs. Ledford, still screaming, fell to his knees and gently lifted her naked body from the tub. Karena took her last breath while in his arms.

Ledford carried the limp form from the house and laid it carefully on the ground beside his truck. He returned to the house and grabbed a blanket he used to cover Karena's body. Ledford took only one additional item from the house. He no longer screamed, but tears blurred his vision.

Karena's wonderful surprise stood hitched to one of six sturdy cedar posts that supported the roof over the front porch. Ledford reached in the cab of his truck for a tool of his most recent trade. The one he'd applied in far off places with strange names. Ledford walked over to the horse, pointed the 9mm Beretta at its forehead, and pulled the trigger.

He thrust the automatic into the front of his jeans as he stomped back to the truck. He removed a red canister and walked back into the lodge to splash its contents on the floors. He flung the canister and flipped a lit match. He walked out the front door as an inferno erupted at his back.

Ledford stood beside the body of the only woman he'd ever loved, and watched the only structure on his and Trey's newly acquired ranch burn to the ground. Only then did he pull the gun from his jeans and place it to his head.

But then it occurred to him. First he must find the true source of Karena's death.

I found the bastard. Oh, did he pay.

Ledford took a deep breath and swiped at his eyes. He had returned to the here and now of the musty smelling cavern. He walked over to a nearby desk and glared down at the file on Clint Demont.

"I intend, dear Sampson, you perverted monster," he whispered, "to send you to hell with another of your type . . . Karena would expect no less."

* * * *

This time Candice Classen came to Marge Myers' office. A power play? Yes, but after all, Candice would be the one who truly profited. It took Marge hours to talk herself into doing the right thing, and urging Candice to meet her at her office.

"Candi, do you remember the kid found in D-Killa's safe house by the police?" Marge began once Candice selected a chair in front of her desk.

"I certainly do," Candice smiled.

"Well he's no longer a kid, but a full blown man of eighteen. He goes by the street name of P-Wac, but his real name is Randal Cunningham. Don't know if you know it, but he's the one who coined the name, 'The Outlaws.' I have his last known address."

Candice gave her a sidelong look. "And you're giving it to me?"

"I am."

"Very generous. But why?"

Marge chuckled. Her generosity would earn points to use in the future. "A simple matter of journalistic professionalism. I must bow to the most effective medium for informing the populace in this particular situation. See, Candi, all I can truly do is request an interview with our Mr. Cunningham. Chances are great that he will refuse with very colorful words. You, on the other hand, can ambush him with a camera crew. His reaction alone will be news worthy."

"Very smart," Candice said before turning to thought for long seconds. "Have you ever considered what just the two of us have done, Marge?"

"We've reported the news," Marge said, knowing the bigger picture, but allowing Candice to expound.

"We've promoted vigilantism across the nation, Marge. Detroit, St. Louis, Los Angeles, and just today, New York City. We've encouraged citizens to violently take their communities back from street gangs."

"We reported the news, Candice," Marge repeated. "We do not control how the citizens of the nation might react to it. Neither of us has suggested they turn to violence."

Candice nodded her head and again looked to delve deeply into thought. "Have you ever considered we might be pawns of some grand design to stomp out street gangs?"

"I would bet we are," Marge smiled. "If so, is that such a terrible role to play?"

"I don't know."

"Neither do I."

"Marge? Who is your source?"

Marge chuckled to emphasize the ridiculousness of the question. "You know I can't, and won't reveal my source."

Candice chuckled in return. "Of course I know. I just hoped for a generalization."

Marge understood. "Okay. It is a very kind and troubled person who deeply loves a child others might not."

Candice nodded and smiled. "I'll ambush Mr. Cunningham."

Marge repeated her gestures. "I never doubted that, Candi."

* * * *

Jerry Ring sat studying budgetary reports on his computer when Deputies Bryan Smith and Bobby Johns walked into his office.

"Hate to bother you, boss," Smith said, "but do you have time to hear something damn funny?"

Ring turned from the computer screen with a scowl. "Funny as in suspicious, or funny like this better be damned hilarious to bother me with?"

Smith took on a look of sudden doubt, if not dread. "Uh, I think you'll get a kick out of it."

"Okay. Best make me laugh."

"Think I'll go back on patrol," Bobby Johns said as turned toward the door.

"No, you stick around. The few times I actually laugh, I like being surrounded with people tasked to do greater things. Things like, uh, let's say . . . working. Get on with it Smith."

Smith cleared his throat. "We were out patrolling around the TRJL ranch. You know, like you want us to do anytime we're in the area? Anyway, we were pulled to the side of the road, scanning the ranch with our binoculars. Way out there, we saw Remington and Ledford. Too far to see really clear, but clear enough to know it was them. I mean who else could it be?"

"I should be giddy by now, Smith," Ring warned.

"Well, this is the funny part, Sheriff. You see, Ledford was just beating the shit out of Remington."

"All right, Smith, I'm liking this. What did you two do?"

"Do? Uh . . . we watched. And we laughed."

"Yeah," Johns butted in. "They whipped our asses once. You were there. It tickled us to see them turning on each other."

Ring stood up from his desk. "So, you watched, and you laughed, and then you . . . drove away?"

Smith and Johns looked wearily at each other before turning back to Ring.

Smith nodded his head with uncertainty. "Uh, yes sir. We, uh, drove back here."

Ring fought off the urge to grab the stapler off his desk to throw at Smith's head. "You witnessed an assault, possibly an aggravated assault, and you did nothing?"

"We'd had to cut their fence wires," Johns moaned.

Ring wanted to rant. He wanted to rage. He wanted to lay hands on both deputies. Instead, he looked toward the ceiling. "Dear Lord, you cursed Sheriff Andy Taylor with only one Barney Fife. Why the hell did you give me two?"

"I'm sorry, boss," Smith groaned.

Ring nodded his head. "You're both sorry. Sorry excuses for lawmen. I'd fire you both, but it'd take me a half a day to train two more to your standards. I don't have half a day. Either one of you idiots know why?"

Both deputies shook their heads.

"Because the three of us are going to now spend a half a day going back to the TRJL to do what you should have done when you were there."

Ring stomped out of his office with his deputies right on his heels. He looked over his shoulder and shouted at Bryan Smith. "Thanks for the laugh, asshole!"

* * * *

It'd not been easy forcing his ass out of the bed, but P-Wac knew he couldn't hide there forever. For over an hour, he'd moved gingerly about the small house. An ugly world awaited, and he could find no good reason not to let it have at him. Sunshine might actually do him some good.

P-Wac pulled the front door closed behind him before starting to carefully make his way down the porch steps. Both knees were swollen from evidently being stomped on a number of times. He believed two toes on his right foot were broken. Once at the bottom of the steps he turned right on the sidewalk to face a sudden blur of activity.

What the fuck?

It took him only a split second to recognize the pretty blonde that now blocked his pathway. She thrust a microphone toward his face. Two men with cameras arranged themselves beside her. All three had waited on him at the side of his house.

"Mr. Cunningham, I'm Candice Classen with Channel 2 news. We'd like to talk to you about the Outlaws."

"I ain't talking to you," he growled.

"We understand that you have a special connection to the two men accused of killing gang leaders, and that you actually named them the Outlaws."

"Fuck this bullshit," he bellowed before turning to start back up the stairs. He wished he could run.

"You go by the name P-Wac," the blonde said as she and the two assholes with cameras paced after him. "You appear to be injured, P-Wac. Your face is badly swollen. Did the Outlaws do this to you?"

P-Wac worked to get his key into the doorknob. The ballsy woman was coming up the steps behind him. Her continued pursuit pissed him off, and P-Wac turned in rage.

"You fucking don't want to know what I know about those two, bitch!"

Undaunted, she talked faster. "Do you know who the Outlaws are, Mr. Cunningham? Do you know where to find them? You were apparently the first to have contact with them the night after . . . "

P-Wac stumbled through the door and slammed it hard practically in Classen's damned beautiful face.

He fell back against the door, and took deep cleansing breaths. She continued to shout questions. He had only one response, and didn't care if she heard it through the door or not.

"You fucking white bitch, you probably just got me killed."

* * * *

Melinda stomped out of the barn door and nearly flung herself at Sheriff Ring. "What the hell are you doing here again, Jerry?" She shouted.

"Get out of my face, Melinda," Ring said through gritted teeth.

"I'm about to get in your ass, Ring," she practically screamed.

"You calm down, or you will be going to jail right along with Ledford."

Melinda gave into her instincts to back down. Every internal alarm warned her to be cool. Keep a level head. She took a second to compose herself.

"What do you have on Ledford? You have charges?"

"You know, I don't have to tell you a damned thing, Melinda. But since we were once . . . close . . . I'll show you professional courtesy."

She fought back the urge to say something ugly. "I'm all ears, Jerry."

Ring smiled lasciviously. "Oh, you are much more than ears, Melinda. Remember? I've seen it all."

Melinda forced her own smile. "And I know you will remember this, Jerry. You'll never, never, get to see it all again."

Touché

Pain showed through the ugly snarl on his face.

"We are here to question Ledford on an assault against your man. I'm doing you a service. Looking out for your loved one."

"What are you talking about?" Oh, she knew. One or all three had apparently seen Bingo showing Buzz some more love. These uniformed clowns with badges might think it a secret. But Trey, John, and she knew they kept a close eye on the ranch with binoculars.

"That's all I'm telling you. Where can I find Remington and Ledford?"

Try Chicago asshole.

The thought brought a smile to Melinda's lips, but she still planned on ringing Bingo's neck.

* * * *

Buzz and Bingo sat on their horses, hidden from view of the barn by a clump of trees.

"What do we do now, Buzz?"

Bingo always turned to him with the hard questions. Normally, Buzz did not have a good answer. It was not necessarily a compliment being the smartest of this duo. But this time, Buzz did not have to make up bullshit. The answer rested in his back pocket.

"We use the special phone, Bingo."

Bingo beamed a smile. "I done forgot about the phone."

"Do you remember what you had for breakfast this morning?"

"Duh, Buzz. I had an MRE. Do you remember me kicking your ass this morning?"

"I do, Bingo. Probably the reason they're here."

"That'd make me feel just awful."

"Don't let it, Bingo. Times like this is what we have the phone for."

"Which one of us is going to call them?"

Buzz turned weary eyes on Bingo. "Oh, I'll just let you make the call."

"Uh . . . I don't know what the crap to say, Buzz."

"Then why did you ask in the first place?"

"You want another ass kicking, Buzz?"

"Shit, Bingo," Buzz sighed. "I'll make the phone call."

* * * *

Jerry Ring's cell phone began to vibrate in his pocket. He pulled it out, and did not recognize the number.

"I'm going to take this, Melinda, but only to give you time to make up your mind. Tell us where they are, or go to jail for interfering with official process."

He gave her a smile before pushing the answer button. "This is Ring."

He could not in a thousand years mistake the voice.

"Where are you, Remington?"

"Use your keen investigative skills to find me, Ring," Remington snarled. "Or, just look to your right, dumbass."

Ring jerked his head to look. He could not keep the look of hate off his face. Remington and Ledford sat atop horses about a hundred yards out. Remington's right hand looked pressed to his ear.

"Get your asses down here," Ring snarled.

"Do you have a warrant?"

"My deputies observed your buddy stomping your ass."

"That ain't no warrant. And are you stupid enough to think I'd press charges on John? Besides, we were sparring. Jesus, do you ever grow weary of appearing like a complete fool?"

"You son of a bitch," Ring bellowed.

"Takes one to know one," Remington chuckled before hanging up on Ring.

Ring watched and seethed as the two riders calmly turned their horses and took off in a trot.

"Oh, I made up my mind, Jerry," Melinda smiled. "I'll tell you where they are." She turned and pointed. "There they are . . . And there they go!"

"We going after them, Sheriff?" Smith asked.

Ring gave him a bitter look. "Shut up, Smith."

* * * *

Melinda thanked God for the little knoll. Bingo and Buzz were able to ride down it and out of sight. Not a moment too soon either. Ring and his traveling circus barely pulled out of the drive, when a rider-less horse came barreling over the knoll, headed for home. The horse from a distance looked almost white. Ring would have identified it as the horse "Remington" sat upon. He would have known that no horse could throw the real Remington.

The horse made it up to Melinda before she observed Buzz top the knoll. He looked to be picking up rocks and throwing them as if they angered him. At a further distance out, she could now see Bingo, still mounted and heading the opposite direction.

She grabbed the horse's reigns and waited for Buzz to make the trek back. She watched, and could not help but giggle. Once he reached shouting distance, that's what he did.

"That sorry-assed horse hates me!"

Melinda laughed until he stood face to face. "I need some damned riding lessons. And a friend that just don't ride away and leave my ass lying on the ground."

Melinda laughed that one away, before getting down to important business.

"How the hell did you two pull that phone call off?"

Buzz reached into his pocket and pulled out a cell phone. "It's a special one. John and Trey gave it to us for emergencies only. Trey said one of them would always answer it, and Trey damn sure did today. Out there, I just acted like I was talking into this phone, but Trey called that Sheriff on another phone. I doubt this one is so special anymore. I landed right on it when I tumbled off this hateful horse."

Melinda didn't try hiding her envy. "How come I don't have a special damned phone to call him?"

"I know the answer to that because Trey told me when they gave it to me. This thing costs a hell of a lot of money. Calls can't be tapped or traced. These phones are very hard to come by. Now, Trey also told me, that if I had to use this before next Tuesday, go ahead and tell you he plans to call you on that day."

"Next Tuesday?"

"Yup, it's your birthday."

Damn if he wasn't right, and if Trey wasn't sweet. So sweet she practically felt like hugging his decoy, but instead gave him a smile.

"Let's go in the barn, Buzz, and work on your ability to stay in the saddle."

"About time."

As they walked toward the barn, she asked, "Where's Bingo going?"

"Looking for bigfoot. Swears he got a glimpse of it this morning. I hope it eats him."

* * * *

Nine Mil, Tink, and Slash loitered on their favorite little piece of territory.

"Damn, niggas, fuckin' ain't da same without P-Wac," Tink said.

Tink would be the next of their little group to turn eighteen, but Nine Mil did not intend to let him be the one to fill P-Wac's shoes.

"Yeah, I know you miss you man, Tink. Hell you always P-Wac's bitch," Nine Mil grinned.

"Make you my bitch . . . bitch," Tink shot back.

Yeah right. Nine Mil just offered taunting laughter at the remark. Tink didn't have the balls to take on Nine Mil. Damn sure didn't have the balls to lead. As soon as shit got hot, he'd turn to Nine Mil to scoop the shit and toss it away.

Slash, the youngest of the group pointed to the street. "Yeah, P-Wac solid, but sometimes too fuckin' careful, man. Shit those dudes come back right now in the Hummer, right there where they did before, the three of us just take they asses out."

"They be dead mutha fuckas fosho," Tink agreed.

Nine Mil scoffed at Tink. "Fuck, nigga, you didn't shoot at they asses last time. Slash here did, and I damn sure did. First to throw down on the silly dressin' bitches."

"Shit, Nine Mil," Tink said softly, "I just followed P-Wac's orders. He da man at da time."

At that time. Not no more. Nine Mil once respected P-Wac, but lost that respect since the coming of the cowboys. Shit, right now, if he were P-Wac, Nine Mil would be moving on the top spot. No one else wanted to fill it. Fucking pussies. As far as Nine Mil thought, P-Wac done turned pussy too. No amount of slit throats or testicles lying on the carpet would dissuade Nine Mil. All he wanted was a chance to prove it.

"By age, you now da man, Tink," Slash pointed out.

"The fuck he is," Nine Mil grumbled.

"It's mine to have, Nine Mil," Tink said without moving a muscle.

See, shit like that. A man says something is his, he needs to step forward and take hold of it. To prove the point, Nine Mil stepped forward to put his face right in front of Tink's.

"It's yours to take, Mutha fucka," Nine Mil hissed.

As Nine Mil expected, Tink took a step backwards. Enough said. Nine Mil nodded his head at Tink and then nodded it at Slash.

"Guess you da man, Nine Mil," Slash nodded back.

"I don't give a fuck," Tink mumbled.

Slash stormed at Tink, "And that's the m-o-t-h-e-r FUCKING problem. No fuckin' body in this gang gives a fuck. Tell you both now. I'm goin' to the top. Let me, and I will take you two niggas with me."

"You got me at your back, Nine Mil," Slash said.

Nine Mil turned a cold stare at Tink. It took long seconds, but Tink started nodding his head. He opened his mouth to speak, but words came from some other source.

"Hey! You kids there!"

All three heads turned in the direction of the voice. All three observed a group of men approaching them from a vacant lot between two dilapidated shacks. Nine Mil counted six. Each held something down alongside their legs. Wasn't much light in that area, but Nine Mil figured they were clubs. Too short to be ball bats. Maybe pipes. Not a fucking problem.

"You best go 'bout ya bidness, mutha fucka's," Nine Mil shouted.

"You punk-ass boys is our business," the same voice responded. It came from the man in the lead.

He stopped, and the others drew up on both sides of him and stopped as well.

"We tired of you being here. Selling dope to our children. Making women step around you to walk in the mud," the man said forcibly. "We tired of you spreading hate in our neighborhood. We just tired of you."

"Tired enough to do somethin' bout it, old timer?" P-Wac challenged. "Tired enough to shed some blood?"

"We hope it don't come to that," the man said. "We hope you will leave, and stay gone. If not, yeah, were willing to bleed with you."

Nine Mil did not believe in no Jesus. Hadn't seen him doing shit around here. Didn't stop his old lady from beating him with a chain when he was young. Did not keep his old man from going to prison. Yet, if there was a Jesus, Nine-Mil would thank him now. The time had come for Nine-Mil to make a name for himself that others would not soon forget. Only one group would bleed here tonight. Clubs didn't do shit against bullets. Nine Mil stepped in front of Slash and Tink, then reached under his shirt to pull out his name-sake.

The men raised their clubs . . . but only to waste level. Fuckers not serious enough to raise them over their heads and charge.

But serious enough.

Not clubs.

Sawed off shotguns.

Nine Mil got his guns out, and assumed Tink and Slash did as well. But that is all he did, maybe all Tink and Slash did as well, because the first volley came from the older men.

Maybe Nine Mil felt part of his flesh being ripped to pieces. Maybe he just imagined that. He did not imagine his face being on the ground, looking eyeball to eyeball with concrete. He did not imagine hearing Tink scream. He did not imagine someone falling on top of him. Dead weight. Nine Mil heard someone gasping for breath.

Calling out to a Jesus he did not believe in.

Last name Nine Mil ever called.

TEN

Over the years Sampson certainly assigned Thumper to some strange tasks, but this was the first time he ever told him to watch TV. Thumper preferred his regular role of serving as Sampson's enforcer, but eye-balling Candice Classen every evening on Channel 2, wasn't all that bad either.

Oh, my, but wouldn't I like to drag you deep into the woods.

This hot babe and Channel 2 did the best job of keeping up with the Outlaws. Of course, another chick, Marge something, wrote articles on them, but to tell the truth, Thumper couldn't read all that well. Sampson followed her articles. Hell, he'd obtained a bachelor's degree while in prison. He could read like a son of a bitch.

Thumper just tuned in, watched only the first few seconds, and hit the pause button. He shouted for Sampson.

"You're going to want to see this," he hollered.

Sampson finally appeared from one of the dark recesses of the creepy old farmhouse. "What is it?"

"The sexy blonde bitch. Says she has an exclusive with some gangster with close ties to the Outlaws."

"No, shit," Sampson said, expressing interest. He plopped down on the couch next to Thumper.

The video only lasted for mere seconds, and Thumper thought it of little value. Sampson, on the other hand evidently thought otherwise.

"Run it back to the last words the homeboy said."

"You (beep) don't want to know what I know about those two, (beep)."

"Oh, yeah," Sampson nodded and grinned. "Tell you what, Mr. P-Wac Cunningham . . . I damn sure want to know what you know about those two."

Sampson pushed off the couch and started to pace. "See, the fear in that boy's eyes, Thumper?"

"Dripped off of him, Sampson."

"Damn sure did." Sampson stopped and faced Thumper. "Use every resource you have, Thumper. Find that dude. For now, just watch him. Learn all you can about him. Somehow, I just got a gut feeling, he's the one that will bring the Outlaws right to our door step. And then we'll kill them."

* * * *

"Sampson has disappeared."

"What the fuck does that mean?" Lieutenant Elmore asked Mark Penn.

"Means he's no longer at his home sweet home," Sean Scully butted in.

"Yeah," Penn nodded. "The surveillance team obtained a warrant. Kicked in the door. No one there."

"But he'd been seen there earlier?"

"Yes, sir, they took pictures of him," Penn said.

"So the incompetent bastards just let him slip away?" Elmore asked.

"Apparently so," Penn agreed.

Elmore drew in a deep breath. "Any further developments? Any new evidence? Any good news at all?"

"Just an observation and a hunch," Scully said.

"Go ahead."

Scully started laying it out. "As you know, LT, the department public information folks have not wanted to release the fact the Outlaws are assisted by a team of professionals. They'd prefer the pubic think it's simply two supermen carrying out the hits. Don't really want it to look as big as it is. Their theory is, that if the public knows how extensive the operation is, it will encourage more citizens to join in on the movement."

"I can accept that," Elmore said.

"Yeah, but what we've realized as well, is whoever in law enforcement is leaking facts to the media, they're withholding information about the support team as well."

Elmore nodded his head, "Hmmm, you're right. But why?"

"Only thing we can figure, is that the Outlaws want the public to believe they solely pull off the crimes. Kind of a way of pointing out, 'if just two of us can do all this. What can entire neighborhoods do?'"

"Maybe the public information branch needs to reconsider its strategy?" Elmore asked.

"I just gave you the observations, LT. Now I'll tell you our hunch. We think Sampson slipped his net because he wants the Outlaws to find him. He's an arrogant bastard, and believes if he takes these two out, it will up his standing in the underworld. Most likely would, too. However, Sampson thinks he's just going up against two people, not an entire team of killers. If he knew, he might back down. He might even let us use him as bait to catch the entire Outlaw organization."

"I will run it up the chain of command," Elmore said. "But even if they agree to release the information about the support team . . . we still have to find Sampson."

Scully offered the LT his friendliest smile, "All shit stinks, but probably for different reasons. But, yes sir, that's the source of this shit stinking."

Elmore let out a long sigh. "I assume that is your philosophical way of saying Sampson is going to be damn hard to find?"

"Yes, sir. Fact is, we probably won't find him . . . until he's dead. Unless he figures this organization is too big to take on by himself. Then he might work with us. I know it's a long shot, but it's the only shot we have right now."

"You know Detective Scully, I've slowly come to the realization that you're a bright and funny guy," Elmore said before turning to wink at Penn. "I'm having a party at my house next Friday night. Just a bunch of guys getting together to do what guys sometimes do. You'd really add to the fun. Care to join us?"

The son of a bitch was really starting to grow on Scully, but damn sure not in that sort of way. Still, he could not help but laugh. "Aw, Sir, you're fucking with me, in a manner of speaking. Well, I currently do not have plans that would keep me from attending, but I damn sure intend to make some."

Elmore grinned. "Don't worry, Sean, you're really not my type."

"I've kind of sensed that all along, Boss," Scully grinned back.

* * * *

P-Wac disconnected from the call, and then threw the cell phone across the room. He didn't know the last time he'd cried, but he damn sure fought it off now. Instead of crying, he buried his head in his hands and screamed.

"Nooooooooo! FUCK! NOOOOOOOOO!"

Charmane ran into the living room. "P-Wac! Are you okay? What's wrong, P-Wac?"

P-Wac turned to face the lovely child and saw the fear in her eyes. He didn't bother to wipe at the tears filling his own.

"Slash, Nine Mil, Tink . . . they're all dead," he nearly sobbed.

"Oh no! How, P-Wac?"

P-Wac took a long moment to calm his breathing, and clear his head. "Neighborhood vigilantes. Gunned them down."

Charmane started to sob. Didn't surprise P-Wac. They'd all treated her like a little sister. But it did alarm him. He took Charmane in his arms.

"What are you going to do, P-Wac?" she cried.

His dear old mom had taken a terrible fall and broke her hip two weeks earlier. She had another week of rehab in the hospital. For the time being, he was the sole provider for Charmane.

"I'm going to go to the funerals, and I'm going to protect you."

She raised her head from his shoulder so he could see the panic in her eyes. "Am I in danger, P-Wac?"

"Oh, no, no, no, sweet baby. It's just that . . . you're all I have left to love. Don't you worry. This shit won't touch us. I promise you that."

She relaxed in his arms, and P-Wac wondered if he'd ever be able to relax again.

* * * *

167

"You sure she won't have bodyguards?" Ray "Slick" Ringling asked Thumper.

Thumper lowered the binoculars and turned his eyes from the parking lot he'd been watching to look at the man behind the wheel. "Fuck, Slick Ray, she's not the president. She's just a woman that reports the news. Also, if she does have bodyguards, they'll come out with her. Unless they are tiny little fucking bodyguards she carries in her purse."

Thumper had given considerable thought on how to find the P-Wac piece of shit. He could roust black junkies. He could pay informants. He could use the drunken CPD street cop they kept on the books. Or, he could go directly to the source.

"Still seems damn risky to me, Thumper," Slick Ray groaned.

"Bull shit," Thumper chuckled. "We're simply going to do the last thing she'd expect someone to do." He turned his attention and binoculars back on the parking lot reserved for employees of Channel 2.

"If you say so, Thumper."

"I do fucking say so, Slick Ray. We just need a little luck and the right location. It won't take five minutes, if that long."

It remained quiet in the car until Thumper informed Slick Ray, "There she is. Headed for a four door Mercedes. Call Hawk."

"Already dialing," Slick Ray said. Then, "Hawk, she should be pulling out in a four door Mercedes. Remember, stay on the line, and Thumper will tell you when to make your move."

"It's a black one," Thumper said.

"It's black, Hawk," Slick Ray relayed. "Do you see it? Good."

The Mercedes pulled out of the security gate, and could only turn right on the one-way street. Thumper didn't have to tell Slick Ray when to pull out behind her. The man made a name for himself long ago as being one of the very best at tailing another vehicle. Thumper didn't have to worry about Hawk's skills either. He'd done what would be required many times in the past. Thumper took the cell phone from Slick Ray.

"Hawk, you see an opportunity I miss, just do it. We'll follow your lead."

Four blocks later, the Mercedes turned onto a major thoroughfare. "Come on sweet sexy, Candice," Thumper smiled, "Turn us out on a quiet residential street."

It took six miles of tailing her, but Candice eventually did just that. Thumper handed the phone to Slick Ray, and pulled the ski mask down from the crown of his head to cover his face. He hurriedly put on the pair of leather gloves that he'd held between his legs. Then Thumper reached to pick up the hammer lying in the floorboard.

"Now!" he yelled.

"Take her, Hawk," Slick Ray blurted into the phone.

In the next instance, a fast moving Mustang shot around Thumper and Slick Ray, and then went around the Mercedes. When the Mustang's brake lights came on, Thumper pushed open the passenger door. Three sets of braking tires screeched, and the Mercedes was hemmed in.

Thumper pulled the hunting knife on the run. The front passenger window shattered with only one blow of the hammer. Thumper reached in to unlock the door, and a second later held the knife to Candice Classen's lovely throat. She was already screaming, and pushing buttons on a cell. Thumper slapped the phone out of her hands.

"If you want to live, bitch, drive!"

It took only pressing the knife deeper into flesh to get her to shut up.

"Drive! Now!"

The Mustang had already sped away. The woman pushed down on the accelerator.

"Mrs. Classen, do as told, and you will not be harmed."

The calling of her name caused her to cut frightened eyes at Thumper.

"But do anything stupid, and I'll cut your tits off. Do you believe me?"

She nodded her head.

"I want one thing, and I'll be gone in the next second. But don't lie to me. If I can get you once, I can get you again. Police will protect you at first, but I'm a patient man. Do you understand?"

This time she nodded and spoke, "Yes, yes, I understand. Please don't hurt me."

"Turn here to the left," Thumper ordered.

She did as told.

"You obeyed. At this very second, you are in no danger whatsoever. Now, give me the address of P-Wac Cunningham."

She jerked her eyes off the road to glance at him.

"What tit you want me start on, Candice?"

She nearly screamed out an address.

"Pull over here."

Before getting out of the car, Thumper leaned in close to her face with the knife still at her throat. "I belong to an organization of hundreds. Mostly murderers and rapists. I would bet you have children. Many of them have a sick sort of thing for little ones. You call the police, you speak a word of this . . . and we will find you . . . and we will find your children, too. Did you give me the correct address?"

Candice Classen had sobbed all along, now she did so as if about to lose her mind. And all the while, over and over, she repeated one single word. "Yes."

Thumper jumped out of the car and sprinted for the darkness while pushing buttons on his phone. Slick Ray would be not more than a block away.

* * * *

Remington motioned for Chief of Operations J.D. Roach to pull up a folding chair. "Take a load off, J.D.," Remington grinned.

"I lose a load, I lose my edge," J.D. grinned back, as he took a seat.

Remington, Ledford, and Roach now sat in a tight little circle. Remington couldn't think of any circle he'd be more secure with.

"Something new, J.D.?" Ledford asked.

"Yes. The CPD surveillance team served a warrant on our man Sampson's residence. They walked out empty handed. We entered later and found exactly what they found. Not a damned thing."

Remington could not help but frown. "The piece of trash slipped the noose?"

"He did," Roach confirmed.

"He's a smart one," Ledford said. "Had to know he was under CPD surveillance. But what I wonder, J.D., is it possible he knows we have dibs on him?"

"Very likely so. Smart one or not, it doesn't take much brains to figure two plus two equals four. We hit blacks. We hit Hispanics. We hit Asians. White is number four, and he has to know he's a prime target."

"Your math is rather faulty, J.D.," Remington smiled.

"I manipulated it, Trey, to reach the number four and make a point," Roach smiled back. "But now, the question is, do we waste time to find target number one, or do we turn our efforts on target number two?"

"As they say, J.D., time is of the essence. I say we switch to number two," Remington replied.

"On, no. Hold on, Trey," Ledford blurted. "I want that bastard."

Remington drew in a deep breath. "John, I warned you about reading his file."

"I ignored the warning, Trey."

"John, I knew you might take this hit a little personal."

"I take all hits personal."

"John, damn it, listen to me . . . "

Roach started to clap his hands. "Excellent! I must admit guys, I've always wanted to watch you two just go one on one. No weapons. Just feet and hands. Always wanted to see which one would remain standing."

Remington very much appreciated the interruption to calm his emotions. He first grinned and then broke into laughter.

"J.D., first time John and I met, as adolescents, we fought. He whipped me. Over the years, for various reasons, we fought another three times. All three times, he whipped me," Remington stopped talking, jerked his head quickly to the right, stiffened, threw up a pointing finger and nearly screamed, "WHAT THE HELL?"

Ledford jerked his head in the pointed direction, whipped out a revolver, and was moving to his feet, when Remington again gave into laughter. Of course, he'd pointed at nothing.

"Oh, that's a good one," Ledford chuckled.

Remington bowed to his dearest friend, and turned his head back towards Roach. "He is truly the brawns of the two, J. D. The only reason he keeps me around, is that I am the brains."

"And I'm about to give you your fourth ass whipping," Ledford out and out laughed.

"Very entertaining," Roach scowled, "but what do we do? You want Sampson, or do you want the next in line?"

Remington turned to look Ledford deep in the eyes, and he saw what others would not. "Find Sampson."

* * * *

"Mother fuck, Thumper," Sampson grumbled, "that was damned risky."

"It damned sure was, Sampson. But now, we have eyes on Cunningham's house. And I'm sure it's the right one. Same porch and front door Classen videoed during the interview with the nigger."

Sampson drew in a deep breath and released it in laughter. "Well that is goddamned fast work. Don't want to say it, but good job."

Thumper thanked him.

But from this point, Sampson would keep a tighter leash on Thumper. He trusted his second in charge as much as one criminal could trust another, but that shit could have gone real bad and real fast. The cops damned well knew the relationship between Sampson and Thumper. Abduction, assault with a dangerous weapon, and kidnapping were serious charges with damn serious jail time. Like life without parole serious. The cops would have bent over backwards to reduce charges on Thumper for information where Sampson could be found. If roles were reversed, Sampson would have given up

Thumper, and as loyal as he was in good times, Sampson feared Thumper would do the same.

Going forward, Sampson would approve any action before Thumper initiated it, but would do so cunningly. He could not afford alienating his right hand man. With that in mind, Sampson almost put off the next order for a later day, but he had no way of knowing how fast things would move when all the pieces started falling in place.

"I have another job for you, Thumper. A damn big one."

"Lay it on me,"

"I want you to find out who the lead detectives are on the Outlaw shootings. I want to know where they live."

"Fuck, Samson, you talkin' some heavy shit here. What do you have in mind?"

"When it gets really heavy, I won't involve you. Let's just say right now, that some lucky subordinates looking to advance, will be given a golden opportunity to earn their stripes in the biggest way possible."

* * * *

Sir Atkinson did not seem concerned about the delay in Chicago. Donning knew he'd grown to have the upmost trust in the abilities of Remington, Ledford, and their team. As did Donning, however, when J.D. Roach provided the Situational Report, or SITREP, Donning had to fight off the urge to speak directly to Remington or Ledford over the secure line of communications. So far, Donning had received all SITREPs from Roach, which followed protocol because Roach did serve as the Chief of Operations. Donning did not have the inclination to talk to one of the leaders because he questioned their call. Had that been the case, he would have made the request. Donning was simply growing anxious to conclude the last of the strategic operations of this mission.

After all, the mission could already be considered a success. The overall objective was being carried out now in large cities from the east coast to the west. Citizens were working together to take back their neighborhoods. Nationwide, street-gang related crime statistics were falling. More importantly, state and national politicians from nearly every state were feverishly writing bills to put teeth in laws to alleviate street gang activities. These representatives and senators feared that national citizenry, thanks to the actions of "The Outlaws," were on the verge of anarchy.

Donning surely wanted closure for the sake of his beloved employer. Secondary to protecting Sir Atkinson, Donning wanted to initiate the final action. Not because he relished the thought of doing so, but because he wanted the repulsive act to be done and over with. He greatly desired the last execution to be swift, painless, and part of the past.

* * * *

Marge Myers had already turned in for the night when she received the frantic call. After giving her address and hanging up, she'd thrown on some clothes and started a pot of coffee. She had been given so little information, but enough to make her pace around the living room until the doorbell rang. Carelessly, she didn't even bother looking through the peephole, but hurriedly jerked the door open.

"Candi! Oh, my God, come in. Please come in."

The beautiful anchorwoman looked a mess. Tears had smeared her make-up, streaking it down her face.

"My ex has the children," Candice said as she pushed into the living room. "I didn't want to go home alone."

Candice said so little over the phone. Most of what she said had been drowned out by hysterical sobbing. Marge only knew "they" had done something awful to Candice in her car. Candice no longer cried, but her eyes were still wide with fright.

Marge shut and double locked the door before leading Candice to a couch.

"Candi, what happened?" Marge asked, hoping to sound soothing.

"Remember how you felt when you found the disc in your car?"

How could she forget? "It frightened me," she admitted.

"Imagine finding one of *them* in your car."

"Them? Who? One of the Outlaws?" Marge fought off gasping.

"I don't know if it was one of them. He wore a mask, but he was white. I could see skin around the eyeholes of the mask. He put a knife to my throat. He threatened to do . . . awful things to me . . . and my children." Tears started to flow, and Candice began sobbing again.

"I'm going to grab some tissues and a cup of coffee for you," Marge said before heading to the kitchen.

"Put something in the coffee, please. Something strong," Candice sobbed.

Marge poured two cups of coffee, and added Irish whiskey to both. She hurried back to Candice with the coffee and tissues. She handed Candice a cup and a box, and sat down beside her.

"Please, Candi, start at the beginning and tell me everything."

Marge relived the terror with Candice. Unimaginable? Shocking? Horrific? No single word could explain the occurrence.

"If it wasn't one of the Outlaws, he certainly worked for them. They sent him," Candice concluded after blowing her nose into a fifth tissue.

"I do believe they could want to know where to find P-Wac for a number of reasons, Candi, but it doesn't fit their MO."

"Who else would be that desperate to find him?" Candice asked.

Marge paused to think, and finally came up with an answer. "I don't know. But I do know who to ask."

Candice bolted off the couch. "Marge, I believe your source must be within the CPD. I don't want the police involved. I believed every word that man said."

Marge stood up and wrapped her arms around Candice. "Honey, I don't believe my source is in any position to be filing reports on this. Trust me."

ELEVEN

S ampson was lying on the couch smoking a joint when Thumper came in the front door of the farmhouse.

"Three different fucking cops stopped me in the city, Sampson. Man, they sure want to know where you are. I guess every uniform in CPD has my car description. Anyhow, I didn't tell them where you are."

Thumper clearly poked at Sampson with the last remark, and it made Sampson chuckle. "Mighty white of you, Thumper."

"Well, I could have brought you one hell of a nice surprise if you hadn't clipped my wings."

"I didn't clip your damned wings, man," Sampson chuckled again. Marijuana tended to make him giddy. "Fuck, dude, it's just that we are getting down to the real shit. Every move must be closely orchestrated. What kind of surprise?"

"Tell you for exchange for the rest of that joint, maestro," Thumper grumbled.

Orchestra. Maestro. Funny shit. Sampson giggled while handing the joint over to Thumper, "What kind of surprise?"

Thumper took a deep hit off the shit before replying, "A sweet, young, nice-looking, but rather plump little piece of black ass."

Oh, but Sampson did like plump young ass of any color, but he had scruples. The chick had to be at least over the age of ten. Damn if that wasn't funny. "What's the deal? Who is she?"

"I'm guessing she's that P-Wac's younger sister."

Sampson swung his legs off the couch to sit upright. "No shit? Saw her at his house?"

"Our boys did. Along with P-Wac. Said he looks damned protective of her. Seems to mean something to him. Hell, maybe his boo. Might like them young like you do."

Sampson shook his head to clear it. This could be very damned helpful. "So, you're thinking if we had her, he'd be more talkative?"

"Yeah, that's what I'm thinking . . . but what the fuck do I know?" Thumper grimaced before offering the joint back to Sampson.

"Huh-uh. Keep it. Need to think straight."

Thumper finished off the marijuana while Sampson thought long and hard. "Okay. Nab her ass. Bring her to me."

"You want the boys to grab her up, or do you want me to drive my ass way back to the city, get stopped no matter how many times by fucking cops, and do what I should have done without asking for your permission?"

"That shit's getting old, Thumper," Sampson said without chuckling.

"Okay, boss," Thumper nodded.

"Come with me. Want to show you something," Sampson said in a lighter tone of voice.

He led Thumper through the house to a door in the kitchen. The door opened to a set of stairs leading down to a damp and musky basement. He showed Thumper to yet another door deep within the cavernous basement. Sampson opened the door to reveal a small and dimly lit room with a single bed.

"Nice place to keep . . . and enjoy. . . some young black ass. Don't you agree, Thumper?"

"Fuck, Sampson, what was your dear old uncle into?"

Sampson erupted into laughter. "Don't know, bro, but maybe it runs in the family."

"I'll bring her back to you, Sampson,"

"Get a different car, Thumper."

* * * *

Sergeant Marcus Jones went to his safe place to return the call on his "Marge" phone. Maybe she called to simply tell him how much she enjoyed the evening at his dingy low-rent apartment. Or maybe, she desired to spend more time getting to know his daughter, Trisha.

Pull your gun and just shoot yourself in your pathetic brain.

He honestly could not tell what repulsed her the most that evening, his abode, or his offspring. Yet, he tapped the redial button.

Fuck her.

No. Make love to her.

Yeah, right.

"What do you need, Marge?" It came out harsher than he intended. Or maybe not. Confusion sucked, and Marge did not immediately respond.

"Uh, how are you, Marcus?"

Does it matter, came immediately to mind, but Jones fought off the impulse. "Peachy, Marge, and you?"

Another pause. "Something terrible happened to Candice Classen. I would appreciate your guidance."

Guidance? Yeah, let me guide you all the way to prison with me, Marge.

"What happened to her?"

Marge talked, and Jones all but heaved up breakfast. He longed for a heart attack. The killing kind.

"Do you think they had something to do with it, Marcus? Really? The Outlaws?"

She thought she knew what Jones didn't want her to know. Actually, she did know, but he dammed sure wouldn't admit it.

"Marge, I only know what the department knows about the Outlaws."

Another long pause.

"Marcus. I want to talk face to face about this."

Not going to happen.

"If you want my professional opinion, Marge. I agree with you. It does not fit their way of doing business. But that is all I have to offer."

"Will you meet with me, Marcus?"

This time, for whatever reason, Jones did his thinking out loud. "Marge, I am very much attracted to you, and I no longer trust my judgment in dealing with you."

Jones disconnected the call.

* * * *

"And she thinks we did it?" Ledford frowned.

"Yup. Or thinks we had someone else do it," Remington replied. He'd just gotten the report from J.D. Roach, who'd gotten the information from their CPD contact.

"I thought we had a better reputation than that," Ledford grumbled.

"Yeah, well, at least she won't be reporting on it anytime too soon. Whoever the son of bitch is, he has her scared half to death."

"So, who did it? Who would want P-Wac enough to pull something that daring?"

"J.D. has no idea. He suggested it might be another copy-cat Outlaw. We've had at least a dozen reports now of other copy cats across the nation claiming to be us."

"Uh huh," Ledford nodded. "But so far they've done nothing to sully our image."

"No, just killed a bunch of people," Remington snorted.

"At least they've been the type of people we would kill. We need to find this bastard. All in all, upstanding folks are sympathetic to the cause. We don't need them thinking we assault innocent women."

"Well, J.D. and Donning are all over it. Right now, we can only leave damage control in their capable hands"

"Right, but when we do find the one who did that to Ms. Classen, I'll be cutting off *one of his tits.*"

Remington chuckled for the first time during the conversation. "Tit for tat?"

* * * *

Charmane knew P-Wac didn't like her walking home from school alone. She normally travelled the six blocks with three other girls, but Michelle left early for a doctor's appointment, and Kristen and Coleen stayed to work on a school project. Charmane could have stayed too, but wanted to get home and study for tomorrow's algebra test. She didn't like disappointing P-Wac, but what could just this one time hurt?

It didn't hurt anything so far. Three blocks more and she'd be home. And a uniformed cop stood just up the block at the small opening between two old buildings that had long been abandoned to rot. The white cop turned to look her way, but gave her only a glance. Charmane took a step past him when it donned on her that she'd never seen a CPD uniformed officer wearing a shaggy goatee.

Then the hand reached to cover her mouth, and an arm closed around her neck. Charmane gave into hysterics, but the hand muffled her screams. She kicked and clawed, but the arm tightened around her throat, cutting off her wind. The fake cop dragged her backwards into the opening between the buildings. She could not breath. Just adrenaline and stark fear kept her from passing out. At the very least, she knew he intended to rape her. But then what would he do? Dozens of terrifying possibilities assaulted her mind in mere seconds.

The man said nothing. He just kept on dragging her. Then she heard a voice.

"Hold her tight, Hawk."

Another white man stepped in front of her with a roll of tape in his hands. The one dressed like a cop dropped the hand clamped to her mouth, and the other man slapped the tape across her mouth, and started running it around and around the back of her head. Charmane wanted to kick, but long moments with so little oxygen left her legs limp. The only thing holding her upright was the squeezing arm around her neck.

With her mouth securely taped shut, they spun Charmane around and she saw the awaiting car with both back doors standing open. Another man sat behind the wheel and had the engine running. One of the two men holding her, bent her forward and aimed her head toward the floorboard behind the front seat. The one in the uniform ran around the other side of the car, jumped in the backseat and grabbed a handful of hair at the top of her head. While the man behind her shoved, this one used her hair to pull her into the car and cram her face down in the floorboard.

Doors slammed shut, and the car started to move. One of the men had her hands behind her back, and roughly applied the tape to her wrists. Two feet were placed on her back to hold her in place.

Then the laughter began.

"Smooth as shit, motherfucker," a voice bragged.

"Hey, Thumper," another giggled. "Can I just pull her jeans down? Man, I want to look at this ass!"

"Fuck no you can't, Hawk," a rough voice responded.

Giving Charmane just a sliver of hope.

"Sampson will want to be the first to have at that ass. We'll all eventually get our turn."

Charmane started to heave and struggled not to strangle on the vomit.

* * * *

Thumper pulled the car over less than a mile away from the scene of the abduction, and parked alongside another newly acquired car. He got out of the car, and Hawk took his place behind the wheel. Slick Ray sat in the back with his feet resting on the girl's back. Thumper pulled open Slick Ray's door, and whipped out a cell phone.

"Pull her head up," Thumper ordered.

Slick Ray grabbed a handful of hair and obeyed the order. Thumper took one hell of a pic. The stark terror that filled her eyes would make a great impression. He slammed Slick Ray's door and stepped up to Hawk's window.

"You know what to do," Thumper said.

"Oh, we'll get her there. Don't worry," Hawk said.

Slick Ray rolled down his window in the back. "Sure you want to do this alone, Thumper? Fuck man, you deep within hostile territory."

"I got it, Slick Ray. No big deal. I'll be in and out."

Thumper unlocked the door of the awaiting car and crawled inside as Hawk pulled away. He grabbed a hoodie from the passenger seat and pulled it on over his t-shirt. Thumper then removed a nearly black piece of panty hose from his pocket and tugged it down over his head. He reached for the hood on the back of his shoulders and brought it up over the back of his head. Thumper adjusted the rearview mirror to take a peek at his disguise.

"Shit! From a distance, I'll look just like one of the fucking monkeys."

* * * *

"This will be a total waste of our time," Sean Scully grumbled as Mark Penn pulled up and parked behind the patrol car.

"The reporting officer said the guy is fairly convincing," Penn shrugged.

Scully stared out the window at the reporting officer. "Looks like he's fourteen. Probably been on the streets no more than a year."

"Young cops nowadays learn a lot on these streets in one year, Sean," Penn said before pushing open the door and swinging out of the car.

"Yeah, like how to totally waste my precious time," Scully said as he got out.

The young officer approached Penn and handed him a driver's license.

"He just walked up to me, Detective. Said he wanted to turn himself in."

Scully read the patrol officer's nametag. "How long you been on the job, Rhynes?"

"Three years, Detective."

"Jeez. I must be getting old," Scully mumbled.

Penn studied the driver's license. "Saul Kobalty, Sean. Ring any bells?"

"None."

"I ran him, Detectives. No warrants and no priors. Says he's served as a Navy Seal," Rhynes informed them.

Penn leaned down and looked at the man hand-cuffed in the back seat of the patrol car. "Big guy. Shoulder length hair," he observed. "Go ahead and get him out, Officer Rhynes."

Rhynes obeyed the command, and Penn read the suspect his rights. Scully shot off the first question.

"What kind of special idiot are you, Kobalty?"

"I'm no idiot. I'm one of the two Outlaws."

Sean looked from Kobalty to share a grimace with Penn.

"Why are you turning yourself in?" Penn asked.

"God told me to. Said my part of the job is done."

"What rank were you in the navy?" Scully asked

Kobalty raised his chin with pride, "A sergeant."

Penn ducked his head and mumbled, "Oh, shit."

"And God talks to you?" Scully asked.

"He does. He sent me on this mission to begin with."

"God's a smart dude, Kobalty," Scully scowled. "I'm sure he would have told you the navy doesn't have sergeants, you goofy bastard."

"I was one of a kind."

Scully looked long and hard at Officer Rhynes. "Did you have any conversation at all with him prior to calling us out?"

Rhynes' face turned bright red in color. "Uh, no, sir. Didn't want to mess anything up. Told him to remain silent."

Scully turned and started back to the car.

"Hey!" Kobalty called after him. "The killing won't stop. My partner is still out there. He's an android. Won't listen to God!"

Before getting in the car, Scully wasted just a little more time by showing his middle finger to Kobalty. At that moment a couple of skinheads slowly passed the detective cruiser in a pick-up truck, and both looked in at Scully. He showed them his middle finger as well.

* * * *

P-Wac pushed open the front door to his house, and immediately noticed the absence of lighting. He stepped inside and hit a switch.

"Charmane? Where are you girl?"

She should certainly be here by now, and it was far too early for her to have gone to bed. P-Wac searched his mind as he walked toward the kitchen. Did she have plans? A school functions? If so, she would have left a note on the kitchen table.

He rummaged through papers on the table. No note. Then he felt what could only be a gun being pressed to the back of his head.

"Be cool, nigger," a rough voice warned.

He could spin in place. Go for the gun. Most likely be shot in the head, and what would happen to Charmane then?

What had already happened to her?

"Where is my niece, mutha fucka?" P-Wac hissed.

"I'm going to take a step back. You turn around nice and slow."

The pressure disappeared from the back of his head, and P-Wac spun in place. Before he could do more, a heavy automatic landed on the side of his head, knocking him to the ground face up. A white dude, shaved head, stepped up and kicked him between the legs. P-Wac already felt like half his brain had been knocked away. Now he curled into a ball and wretched.

"Don't ever call me *mutha fucka*, motherfucker," the white trash thundered.

The man delivered another kick to P-Wac's exposed back. A kidney blow. P-Wac bellowed in pain. In the next instance the man had him on his stomach with a knee in his back. P-Wac already suffered too much damage to keep the man from using tape to bind his wrists behind his back. The man got off of him, and used a boot to flip him over on his back.

"Your niece, huh? We thought it was your little sister," the man chuckled.

"Where is she?" P-Wac moaned.

"You know in the movies, how the bad dude says, 'Don't worry she's safe for now?' Well, this bad dud ain't going to say that. She's anything but safe, little black boy."

"Skin-head mutha fucka!" P-Wac shouted.

The man wagged a finger at him. "Done told you about that shit."

He kicked P-Wac square in the mouth. Blood splattered his face.

"Now let me get to the introductions. My name is Thumper. I work for a man named Clint Demont. You most likely know him simply as Sampson."

P-Wac's guts clinched, and not because of the damage to his head, balls, kidney, lips, and teeth. Sampson ran the largest white crew in the city. One racist and sadistic bastard from what P-Wac always heard.

"Why you doing this?" P-Wac moaned. "Where is Charmane?"

"She's on her way to meet Sampson. She will be his house guest, in a manner of speaking."

"Why? What the fuck!" P-Wac cried out. Charmane in the hands of that animal? Possibilities assaulted P-Wac's brain and ripped at his heart.

"Guess it is time to get to the point. Sampson wanted her so you would talk to him."

"About what?" Made no sense to P-Wac. What could he have that Sampson wanted, now that he had Charmane? There was damned sure nothing more precious he could take from P-Wac.

"About the Outlaws."

P-Wac rattled off a litany of profanity before concluding with, "I don't know shit about them motherfuckers! Whatever you think, whatever you heard, it's bullshit, man."

"We knew you'd say just that. Thought taking the bitch would loosen your tongue, P-Wac. Guess we'll just give her back . . . one little bloody piece at a time."

"What the fuck do you want me to do?" P-Wac screamed, spewing blood with his words.

"Damn sure don't want you to go to the cops. Would be very ugly for the little fine piece of black ass. But we do expect you to save her, P-Wac."

"How? How can I do that?"

"Reach out to the Outlaws. Send them to save her. Of course, we're going to kill them. But we'll let the girl go."

"Are you fucking crazy, man?" P-Wac moaned.

"Yeah. Crazy about ass fucking little black bitches."

"Okay! Okay! I'll do it. Please. Just don't hurt her. I'll get you the Outlaws."

"Good. Then I'm going to leave you with a gift."

P-Wac watched as Thumper reached beneath his hoody and pulled out a cell phone.

"From Sampson to you. Your own private line to the man. He will be calling soon." Thumper placed the phone on the table. "Also, just in case you start thinking stupid thoughts. There's a picture on there for you. I took it. Fuck around, we'll be sending more. Oh, I lightly taped your hands together. You'll get them free. But damned sure better not do it until you think I'm long gone."

Soon after, P-Wac heard the back door open and then close. He didn't even make an effort to get his hands free. Instead, he just cried. To save his lovely Charmane, all he had to do was find the Outlaws. Just had to do what even the CPD couldn't. P-Wac cried, because Charmane was as good as dead.

* * * *

"Oh, my, my, my," Sampson cooed as he circled the girl. "Take the tape off her mouth, Slick Ray. Do it gently. Don't want to harm her lips. Scabs on lips can irritate the tender parts of a man."

The girl's wide eyes followed his every move as far as her neck could crane. Sampson found the look in the eyes so sexy. Some dudes needed that little purple pill. But all Sampson needed was a terrified child.

The very second Slick Ray removed the last of the tape from her mouth, the girl started screaming. Hawk stepped in to shut her up, but Sampson stopped him.

"Let her scream, Hawk." It was music to Sampson's ear, and his crotch. He stood in front of her and laughed while she screamed, clapping his hands to show his glee.

The girl too quickly screamed herself out, and turned instead to sobbing.

"What's your name?" Sampson asked in his most tender voice.

The girl sobbed it out in syllables. "Cha . . . r . . . mane."

"Oh, I like that. Pretty name for a pretty girl," Sampson smiled sweetly. "How old are you, Charmane?" He asked in a soothing manner.

"Thir . . . teen."

"Thirteen-year-old Charmane," He said barely above a whisper. "Why, sweet Charmane, I'm old enough to be your daddy. Come to daddy, baby."

Sampson stepped up and gently took her face in his hands. She twitched and tried to resist as he tenderly brought her head to rest on his torso. He held her in place until she offered no resistance.

"Take the tape off her wrists and ankles," Sampson said.

Slick Ray stepped up to do the bidding. "We just taped her wrists at first, Sampson, but then she started kicking."

"She kicks and she screams," Sampson smiled. He liked them feisty. Love without a fight was no love at all. "You two can go now."

Hawk and Slick Ray said their so-longs and left immediately. Sampson stepped away from Charmane. She turned her head to the left and right, taking in her new surroundings.

"Creepy isn't it?" Sampson chuckled softly.

Charmane bolted, and Sampson just laughed. He knew which doors were locked and which were not. "Go ahead, sweet Charmane, we'll play hide and seek."

He calmly walked to the couch and sat down. He removed his boots first, and then all remaining clothing. He stood erect, in more ways than one.

"Okay, Charmane, ready or not . . . here daddy comes."

* * * *

P-Wac cried himself to his senses. With no little effort, he freed his hands, and pushed up off the floor. He stared at the cell phone on the table. For one thing, he wanted to be free should it start to ring. He did not yet care to even touch it. But he did need to place a call. He limped to the house phone, and picked up the directory next to it.

He could not recall the woman's name, but he'd read her articles. Only those Outlaws could turn P-Wac to reading a newspaper. How many ways had they now cursed his life?

He knew the woman had an unidentified source. Maybe it was the Outlaws themselves. Maybe it wasn't, but P-Wac knew no other direction to turn. Police? Fuck that. If they couldn't find two cowboys on horseback in Chicago, he damned sure didn't trust them to find Charmane before she started losing parts of her body.

P-Wac found the number and started pushing the buttons. He asked for the woman who wrote the articles on the Outlaws. He gave his name. Thanks to the other female reporter, it might carry some weight with this one. Funny how God provided miracles. He seemed to reach deep inside a person, and tug them out the person's ass.

* * * *

Marge Myers hurried to her purse to retrieve the ringing cell. She'd not been home long, and hoped for a call from Marcus Jones. She'd not attempted calling back after he hung up on her, but sure wanted to talk to him. She could not let him slip through her fingers. Seldom did a reporter get an informant of such value.

She looked at the number. Not Jones, but the Chicago Tribune's number. "This is Marge Myers," she answered.

"Ms. Myers, this is Mike in central communications. We received an urgent call for you. The caller left his name and number."

"What's the name?" Marge asked.

"He said his name is Randal Cunningham, but you might know him as P-Wac."

Marge all but gasped. "Mark I want you . . . "

"Mike, ma'am," he interrupted to correct her.

"Mike, Mark, I don't give a flip. Text me his number right away."

For some reason the man hung up without saying goodbye, but Marge had the number within minutes. She wasted no time in calling it.

"Yeah," a male voice answered.

"P-Wac?"

"Yeah."

"This is Marge Myers with the Chicago Tribune. I just got your message to call."

Marge heard what sounded like a pitiful sigh.

"I need your help. I don't know where else to go." The initially gruff voice now seemed close to crying.

"What is it, P-Wac? What can I do for you?"

"Motherfuckers took my niece. She's only thirteen. They will kill her. I know they will. I need to talk to the Outlaws."

Marge fought off jumbled thoughts. "P-Wac, I don't know the Outlaws. I have no idea how to . . . "

"You have a source. Maybe they know them."

Maybe he did. "P-Wac tell me everything. Leave nothing out. I need to know all before going to my source. I don't know if he can help, but you work with me, and I'll do my best to work him."

TWELVE

Sampson turned off the television when Thumper walked in the front door. Thumper said hello, and Sampson responded with grave concern.

"It's been five days since the Outlaws have made their presence known. I hope to hell they haven't left town."

"Maybe they are just damned busy trying to find you, Sampson."

Sampson nodded his head. "Maybe. It's for sure they've not taken out another white gang leader."

"Could be too," Thumper grinned, "they are simply our kind of people. They took out niggers, spics, and chinks. Maybe they never intended to take out a white dude."

"I doubt they're our kind of folk, Thumper. Remember, they helped out that old black man. Fuck, we'd have let him die. And laughed while he died."

"Shit, dude, you sure seem awfully down for a man with a new piece of young ass."

Sampson chuckled. "She's resting in her bedroom."

"Still in one piece?" Thumper asked.

"Oh, very much so."

"Okay, well I have something else that might brighten your day. The two violent crimes detectives working the Outlaws are named Penn and Scully. I already have their addresses."

Sampson released a bright smile. "Now that is some quick and fine work, my man."

"Yup. Now, what do you want with them, Sampson?"

Sampson got out of his recliner and started to pace around the living room. "They would naturally be the two most informed in the CPD about the Outlaws. We don't know how close they are on making an arrest. But, we can't allow them to get the Outlaws before we do."

"You're thinking about killing them, Sampson? Two cops?"

"Oh, I won't be killing them and neither will you. But, with them gone, it could slow down the investigation. Of course, for only a couple of days, but it might be a couple of days we very much need. Also, their deaths will eventually be blamed on our gang. It won't stick, but you add that kind of balls with killing the Outlaws, and the other street gangs in Chicago will bow at our feet. We'll rule any trade we decide to rule, guns, dope, whores. Maybe all of them."

"That'd damn sure make us the big shits of Chytown," Thumper chuckled.

"It sure would. Thumper, I want you to find us four members intent on being up and comers. Work with them. Get them ready. I want two on the one cop and two on the other. Equip them with AR-15s."

"I'll get on it."

"First though, go get the young lady and bring her up here. She's going to help me make a phone call."

* * * *

"Thanks for coming here. I knew you wouldn't meet in broad daylight in public," Marge Myers said.

Jones just nodded his head. No, he wouldn't have met in public. But, Marge invited him to her home. He very much wanted to resist, but just couldn't.

"You said it was extremely important. Not something we could talk about over the phone. What is it, Marge?"

"P-Wac Cunningham has a thirteen-year-old niece. She was abducted yesterday by members of a white supremacist gang. He called last . . . "

"What does that have to do with me . . . and you, Marge?" He suddenly felt very much the idiot. How could he have even hoped for something of a more personal nature?

"If you will allow me, I'll answer that."

"Go ahead," he sighed.

"P-Wac was later accosted in his home by one of the gang members. He called himself Thumper. This Thumper informed P-Wac that the only way the girl would be returned alive, is if he reached out to the Outlaws, and convinced them to save the girl. I'm guessing they are trying to set a trap for the Outlaws."

Jones now did not like where this was going. "So? Why are you bringing me into this?"

"In Candice Classen's brief interview with P-Wac, she gave the impression that he had ties to the Outlaws. Of course he doesn't. He'd read my articles and reached out to me, asking that I reach out to my source. That's you, Marcus."

"Are you confused, Marge? The information I provide you comes from police files and records." Jones wished for a time-out to prepare a better strategy, but knew all he could do now was bob and weave.

Marge turned away from him and took a few steps before turning back around. "I think there's more to it than that, Marcus."

"And what would that be, Marge?"

Marge took a deep breath and cleared her throat. "I believe you are working with the Outlaws."

"You have proof of that?"

"Just intuition. A gut-feeling. A wild-assed guess."

Marcus forced a chuckle. "Then you have to agree, the accusation sounds pretty ridiculous, doesn't it?"

"And a look in your eyes. The tone of your voice. Body language. Don't forget, I'm an investigative reporter."

The front door stood right at his back, and Jones turned to grab the knob. "I think I'm finished here."

A soft hand fell on his shoulder. "I don't judge you harshly for you being a part of it."

He spun around. "So, you wouldn't judge me harshly for being an accomplice to a slew of murders, Marge?"

She took seconds to think. Seconds that Jones could not help but keeping his eyes glued to her lovely face.

"I know you have your reasons . . . I've met one of them."

"I can't help you. I have to go."

Marge stepped up even closer. "Marcus, I believe you are the only one that can help. If you refuse to, a thirteen-year-old girl will be brutally slain. She's two years younger than Trisha."

Jones brought both hands up to rub at his forehead. "What does he want me to do?"

"He wants you to arrange a meeting between him and the Outlaws. The leader of the white gang goes by the name Sampson, and..."

Jones dropped his hands and gave a too obvious response to the name.

"You know this Sampson?"

"Please go on with what you were saying."

"Okay. Sampson is demanding that P-Wac act immediately."

This proved to be a game changer. Jones didn't want to say another word. He shrugged his shoulders, nodded his head, and walked out the door.

* * * *

P-Wac had never before found himself in a situation that dictated pacing. Never had he walked around and around the house like a caged animal. Neither had he ever stared at a telephone and just wished that it would ring, and at same time dreaded the moment it would.

He wanted to throw things. Kick things. Tear things up. Things he had access to that could take the place of the people he really wanted to throw, and kick, and tear up. People he wanted to kill. P-Wac also wanted to smoke a shit load of marijuana, but his head already felt fucked up enough. He fought to keep his thoughts as clear as possible. Charmane's life depended upon him doing so.

Finally, the phone started ringing. They blocked the calling number.

Be cool mutha fucka be cool mutha fucka be cool mutha fucka . . .

"This is P-Wac."

"P-Wac! My man!" A deep and jubilant sounding voice boomed.

P-Wac tried to control his breathing, and damn sure his rage. "Who is this?"

"Why fuck, man, this is your new friend Sampson!"

P-Wac bit his tongue. "I want to talk to Charmane."

"Oh, and she wants to talk to you too, and she will, after we chat a bit."

"All right," P-Wac said, hoping to sound calmer than he felt.

"So, little brother man, have you talked to the Outlaws?"

P-Wac spent the entire morning working on the lie. "Shit, Sampson, I don't talk directly to them. I have to go through a middleman. But I sent the message. I can't do no more now but wait."

"Who is this middleman?"

P-Wac had prepared for the obvious. "No. No. No. If you know my man, you don't need me. You don't need me . . . you don't need Charmane."

Laughter boomed over the phone. "Aw, just checking to see if you got a head on your shoulders, *boy.*"

P-Wac drew in a deep breath, and exhaled it slowly before speaking again. "I ain't no fuckin' idiot."

"So glad to hear that, P-Wac. See idiots do stupid things. Stupid things done by idiots, gets pretty little nigga gals all fucked up. In a lot of really *ugly* ways."

P-Wac shook his head. Couldn't bite the hand holding his niece. "Man, I know you got me by the balls, and I know you know you got me by the balls. I ain't doing nothing stupid. Can I *please* speak to Charmane?"

"Why fuck yes you can. She's excited to tell you what we did last night." More booming laughter.

P-Wac felt like he might gag up his heart.

"P-Wac?"

"Charmane! Are you okay, baby girl? Have they hurt you?"

"I'm scared, P-Wac. But they haven't hit me or anything."

She sounded close to crying, and that made tears spill down P-Wac's cheeks. "Listen to me, Charmane. I will get you home. You just . . ."

"P-Wac," she interrupted. "He wants me to tell you what we did last night."

P-Wac started to tremble. "Okay, baby girl."

"We played hide and seek."

She started to sob.

"It's a big scary house, and I tried to run and hide."

P-Wac did not want to hear the rest, but had to all the same.

"Sampson found me . . . and he was naked."

She started crying hard, and P-Wac heard a muffled but strong rebuke.

"Charmane! Did that motherfucker do any . . ."

"He let me go, so I could hide again."

"Did he touch you?" P-Wac groaned.

"No. But he made me touch him."

P-Wac started to sob.

"P-Wac, he wants me to tell you this. He told me to tell you that he has a very big dick."

The phone went dead.

P-Wac went crazy.

* * * *

Funny how it turned out. If he only had fewer worries, Marcus Jones might have even enjoyed a good laugh. But it wasn't really all that funny. More coincidental than funny. Jones did some checking. It turned out the "Thumper," was really Bryan Stamps, a very close associate of the illusive Sampson. Jones, some days earlier, passed on to his handler the information on Sampson, the next intended target of the Outlaws.

Then Sampson disappeared.

And now, he was hunting the Outlaws.

"Not really funny at all," Jones grumbled as he readied the secure communications device.

"Sergeant Jones, you've never initiated a call before. This must be big?"

"It is, Mr. Smith."

Upon their initial meeting, the man had said, "Since you're Jones, I'll just be Smith." Jones knew nothing more about the man. Except he must have tons of money.

"What do you have for me, Sergeant?"

Jones laid it all out for Smith.

"Very big indeed, Sergeant Jones. Splendid information. I will make all arrangements."

Jones didn't doubt that, and he didn't care. He just wanted this shit to be over with.

* * * *

"Just got word on Sampson," J.D. Roach beamed.

"Must be good," Remington said and then teased, "Didn't know you could smile."

"You found him, J.D.?" Ledford asked.

"Nope. Still looking." He turned his head back to Remington. "That's why I'm smiling, Trey. Turns out, he's looking for you two as well."

"Really?" Remington asked. The turn of events didn't exactly thrill him. Not part of the plan.

"Really. That's the reason he slipped the police. I'm guessing he wants to be the one that does away with the Outlaws. Probably figures that would up his standing in the community."

"Give us the particulars, J.D.," Ledford said.

"It involves P-Wac."

"Damn that kid pops up more than a fourteen-year-old penis," Remington grumbled.

"He's in a world of hurt now, boys," Roach said. "Evidently, Sampson's thugs kidnapped his thirteen-year-old niece. Sampson believes P-Wac can make contact with us. In a nutshell, Sampson wants to use the girl as bait to lure you two into his sights."

"Well, evidently P-Wac can contact us," Remington said.

"He went to Marge Myers. She went to Marcus Jones. He went to his handler, and it went to the top from there," Roach smiled again.

"What's Donning say about it?" Ledford asked.

"He wants me to arrange a meeting between you two and P-Wac. Seems if we don't, the girl is dead."

Soon after, Roach left the room, and Remington noted the dark and ugly thing in Ledford's eyes.

"Warned you about reading Sampson's file, John."

"Trey, he won't just kill that girl. By the time he's finished with her, she'll beg to be dead."

* * * *

"Looks like we have company, boys."

The three of them were sitting out front on lawn chairs, enjoying the cool temps of early evening.

"Who is it?" Bingo asked.

"Have no idea," Melinda answered.

"Why we can't jump and run now. They done seen us. Look like a couple of idiots just taking off at a run," Buzz said.

Bingo quickly grabbed for the wig at his feet.

"Hey, Bingo," Melinda grinned. "Too late for that too." She could not understand how he could bare to have it on his head in the first place. By now it had tangles and burrs, and probably flees as well. She made a mental note to wash it for him.

"So, we just going to sit here?" Buzz asked.

"Might as well. Can't dance," Melinda chuckled. She watched as a man pulled up in a car too long past new. The man got out of the car. He didn't look like a cop. Dressed more like a store clerk. He was tall, but slender as a pole.

"Are you Ms. Melinda Lollar?" he called while standing just outside the door of his car.

"Depends on whose asking," Melinda responded.

"Her name is Mrs. Remington," Buzz shouted out. "Who the hell are you?"

"Can I walk up closer to talk to you?" the man asked.

"You can. Two of us don't bite," she said.

The man made his way from the car to stand about fifteen-feet from the lawn chairs. "Melinda, I recognize you from the trial a while back. My name is Gary Jinks, and if I can right now see John Ledford and Trey Remington, I'll crawl back in my car and you'll never see me again."

"Well," Melinda chuckled. "That ain't going to happen."

"They're not here, are they?" the man smiled.

Melinda did not know where this was going, but felt relieved to have Buzz and Bingo at her side. "That's none of your business."

"I don't mean to be rude, Melinda, but it's my new line of business. See, I know they aren't here . . . because they are in Chicago."

"You don't know shit, dandy," Buzz said.

Jinks looked first at Buzz and then at Bingo. "Melinda, I would like to speak to you alone."

"Ain't going to happen Mr. Gary Jinks. I don't know you from Adam, but these fellers are close friends. Anything you got to say, you best get to it quickly. I'm starting to think I don't like you."

"Okay, Melinda. I am somewhat of an authority on Remington and Ledford. I didn't miss a minute of that trial. I read everything I could get my hands on about the death of Rudy Whitlock. I for one, believed Remington and Ledford killed him in that awful manner, but I was greatly relieved when they were found not guilty."

"So why are you here now, Jinks?" Melinda asked. She more than a little dreaded the answer.

"I've spent the same fervor researching what's going on in Chicago with those Outlaws. I am certain it is Remington and Ledford, and I can prove it to the authorities."

Melinda stood up. "Mister, time for you to go."

"But! I don't intend to involve the authorities. That's why I'm here. I have no problem with what the boys are doing in that corrupt city. But, I do have some personal problems. I have a wife and two small daughters. I haven't been able to find a decent job in two years. I'll just get to the point . . . "

"Since Mrs. Remington already told you to go," Buzz interrupted, "you best forget the getting to the point and get to your car instead." Buzz then pushed to his feet and Bingo followed his lead.

"Melinda!" Jinks said urgently. "I know the boys must be making millions on that job. All I want is five-hundred thousand dollars, and you will never see me again."

Melinda rarely found herself without a comeback, but an ugly cat named Panic now had her tongue. How the hell should she handle this? Buzz provided the answer.

"We can't have that kind of money until tomorrow, Jinks."

Jinks expression brightened. "I can wait that long."

"Uh, Buzz," Melinda hummed.

Buzz turned his back on Jinks and threw his arms in the air, and started giving her greatly exaggerated winks of his right eye. "Melinda! We don't have any other choice. We have got to get this man the money."

He turned back to Jinks. "But before we do anything. I want to see your driver's license."

"Well, I, uh, don't think I care to show it to you."

Buzz stepped up close to Jinks. "How the hell do we know who you really are? For all we know, you're a cop, and this is a set up."

"I'm certainly no cop."

"Then get out the license. That's all you got to do man to earn half a million bucks."

Jinks seemed to mull it over, and then started to nod his head. "Okay. I'll show you," he said as he pulled out his wallet. He handed the driver's license to Buzz.

Buzz studied it, and then walked back to hand it to Melinda. He strolled back to Jinks and said, "Step over here Bingo."

Jinks stiffened.

"Jinks, you won't be coming back here tomorrow. You know why?"

"I don't understand what you're…"

"You won't be coming back, Jinks, cause you're not leaving in the first place. Never. Bingo, knock him down."

Bingo knocked him down.

Melinda involuntarily shrieked.

Jinks wailed.

In an instant, Buzz straddled the man's chest and pulled a large hunting knife from a sheath on his belt. He thrust the knife to Jink's throat.

"Buzz!" Melinda screamed.

Buzz thrust his free hand into Jink's face, violently turning his head away from Melinda and holding it in place. Buzz looked to Melinda, and he grinned. Then he started the winking again.

"It's the only way, Melinda. We'll burn his body and bury him where no one will ever find him. We'll sink his car in the river."

Jinks started to beg for his life.

"You don't want your throat split?"

Jinks squealed a series of no's.

"Buzz!" Bingo hollered. "Before you kill him, can I have sex with him?"

Bingo quickly turned to Melinda, and blinked like he'd seen Buzz do.

Jinks screamed like a woman in labor.

"Bingo, you talking about head sex or bottom sex?"

"Both!" Bingo shouted.

"Jinks, I know you don't want to die, but you are going to have to. Should have thought about that before coming here. My knife isn't all that sharp. Will have to kind of saw your head off. But before you die, I'm going to let Bingo here sex you up."

Jinks simply went into hysterics. A wide wet spot spread across the front of his cheap trousers. Buzz crawled off his chest, and just stared down at him.

"Shut the hell up, Jinks. We aren't going to do a damn thing to you."

It took long seconds for it to sink in for Jinks, and even longer for him to manage some sense of composure. "You're not going to kill me?" his voice quaked.

Buzz reached down and helped the man to his feet. For a moment, Melinda thought he might just fall back on the ground, but he managed to stay upright.

"No. We are not going to kill you. Not this time. But I hope you now understand how easy it would be," Buzz said.

Jinks nodded his head as if to dislodge something from his throat.

"We also have your address, Jinks. And know you have a wife and two little ones. I'd hate to see something ugly happen to them."

"I promise. No, I swear you'll never . . . "

"Shut up," Buzz hissed.

Jinks immediately followed the command.

"See, Jinks, you don't know how big this thing is. You don't know the powers involved, and you don't want to. If it was to go to the very top about you coming here today, you and your family will disappear. They'll never find your bodies. We don't have to send it to the very top, but that depends on you. Think you can wrap your head around that?"

"I can," Jinks stuttered. "You will never hear another word from me."

"If we do, nobody will ever hear another word from you," Buzz said.

When told to do so, Jinks sprinted for his car, and sped away.

"Dear Lord Jesus Christ, Buzz," Melinda exclaimed. "That was . . . magnificent! But, do you think it will work?"

"The man pissed his pants, Melinda. Think he took me seriously enough," Buzz nodded.

"Hey, Buzz," Bingo said, "You couldn't see me, but I was winking at Melinda when I talked about sexing that man."

"Well, Bingo, it was a mighty fine touch," Buzz grinned.

Melinda had to agree. She'd first thought Trey pulled some warped joke by sending these two, but she certainly appreciated having them here today.

* * * *

P-Wac looked out a window to see who knocked at his door.

A white dude?

He damn sure did not belong in P-Wac's neighborhood. Casually dressed in thirty-something white dude clothing, he didn't look like a cop. He looked like a white golfer. P-Wac opened the door a few inches.

"Who are you and what do you want?"

"P-Wac, you can just call me J.D. Consider me the door you must go through to reach the Outlaws."

P-Wac nervously glanced up and down the street. The sun had not yet sunk out of sight, and plenty of light existed to illuminate a white man standing at his door. "Are you fucking for real? Coming here in the light of day?"

J. D. grinned. "Don't think that just the two eyes you see are the only eyes I have. Now, you want to do business here or inside?"

P-Wac hesitantly opened the door, stepped aside, and motioned for the man to enter. Once inside, J.D. produced a folded piece of paper and handed it to P-Wac.

"Tomorrow evening, at ten p.m. sharp, you be at the address on that piece of paper. Come alone. The Outlaws will meet you there."

This shit did not seem real. "It's that fucking easy?" he asked.

"Oh, believe me, it will be easy for you. Not so easy for us."

Us?

P-Wac sensed it best not to ask. "I'll be there."

"The Outlaws will give you further directions. Take everything they say to heart, P-Wac."

"You need to tell me that? My niece's life depends on them two."

J.D. grinned before turning for the door. "She could not depend on a more formidable force."

P-Wac damn sure had issues with the two cowboys, but he didn't doubt J.D.'s comment one little bit.

THIRTEEN

P-Wac slept little over night, and grabbed the phone on the first ring. He sat upright in bed.

"Sampson?"

"Who else, Sambo?" Sampson thundered with laughter. "You know the story of Little Black Sambo, don't you, P-Wac?"

"Heard of it." P-Wac didn't know what time it was, but too early to be fucked with. As if he had a choice.

Fuck with me now. Get fucked in the end.

"Talk about political correctness gone amuck. They don't print the book anymore. Took it off the shelves. And Little Black Sambo even triumphs over the tiger. Now, if the tiger ate his little black ass, I could understand it. Kind of. I mean, goddamn, how many Af-freak-ens have been eaten by tigers? Probably thousands. We need more tigers in America. Don't you think, P-Wac?"

P-Wac knew better than to express what he thought.

"I have a meeting set with the Outlaws. Tonight at ten."

The big mouth fell silent for long seconds.

"Where are you meeting them?"

"Thought we already had this discussion," P-Wac said, struggling to leave out mother fucker at the end of his sentence.

"Don't fuck this up," Sampson growled.

"I want to talk to Charmane."

"She's tied up. In the tub. I mean literally. Thumper is giving her a bath. You know how *you people* reek after a day without bathing."

P-Wac couldn't help it. "Mutha fucka! I swear to God, you white scum will . . ."

Sampson bellowed to interrupt. "SHUT THE FUCK UP, NIGGER!"

P-Wac doubled his fist and hit himself hard in the forehead. He mentally threatened to cram the fist down his throat if his mouth opened again.

"Okay. Okay. Sampson. You win man. I won't fuck the meeting up."

P-Wac could hear him taking deep breaths. When he spoke again, he started with calm laughter.

"Good boy. Now, I'm going to do something to show how special you are to me. So far, I've blocked this phone number. I will text to you in a few minutes. You call me as soon as that meeting is over. If I like what I hear, I'll let you talk to Charmane."

Sampson hung up, and P-Wac fought off tears of rage and fear.

* * * *

"The rotating teams we've assigned to Detectives Penn and Scully have paid off in a unusual way," J.D. Roach informed Remington.

Remington gazed across the room to watch Ledford going through the motions of practicing his own combinations of martial arts. He knew his partner needed this to help him deal with his obsession over getting to and killing Sampson. He turned his attention back to Roach. The four members, pulled from the team of eight, were assigned to surveillance of the detectives in order to provide advance warning of any unforeseeable leads that might lead to Remington and Ledford. Remington gave Roach his undivided attention.

"In what kind of unusual way, J.D.?"

"As you know, the teams are in place to protect you two. Now, they're serving to protect Penn and Scully."

Remington felt his face scrunch involuntarily. "How's that?"

"They are being watched. Followed. Looks like their tails work for Sampson. White. Skinheads. Doing a good job, I might add."

"Sampson is making a chess game out of this."

"Who would of guessed?" Roach asked.

"Good thing we don't have to guess," Remington smiled.

"Right. Will keep you appraised. Now, on tonight. I'll brief you two at six p.m. Currently, there are no bumps in the road."

Remington knew with Roach at the controls, bumps in the road, would most assuredly be smoothed. Now all he had to do, was keep John in hand. And keep his own demons at bay. Sampson proved to have the potential of touching them both in places they preferred not to be touched.

* * * *

Sampson bellowed laughter at Thumper's response.

"What the hell, Thumper? Where is your sense of fair play?"

"These are some dangerous mother fuckers, Sampson. I mean there are all kinds of people everywhere now that believe they have like super powers. Or super natural powers. Some even say they're ghosts. Man, we need every advantage we can get."

Sampson laughed ever harder. "I believe twelve against two is all the advantage we need. So, can you get the guns?"

"Shit, you know I can get them. That's not the issue," Thumper paused as if viewing a warning sign. "I just don't know how . . . smart it is."

Sampson didn't laugh this time. "You calling me stupid? A dumb fuck?"

Thumper put palms in the air. "You know I'm not. I'm not stupid either."

"Get the fucking guns."

"I will."

Sampson laughed again. "Oh, come on, Thumper, think about it. It will damn sure add to our reputation. The Outlaws use old-time guns. Any twelve men with AR-15s can take them out. Especially in the ambush we've planned. But it is some cool badass gangsters that can take them out with lever-action rifles. Don't you see? We'll not only destroy them, but we destroy them with their choice of weapons. That's badass."

"Okay. Okay, I see the point, Sampson. I said I'll get the guns, and you know I will. Now, I'd like to change the topic, and please don't get pissed, but when do I get my turn with the young black chick?"

"Once I've had my turn, of course."

"I know it's none of my business, but what are you waiting for?" Thumper asked.

"You're right. It's not your fucking business, but it's a fair question. Let's just say I'm keeping her pristine. Those two cowboys might not risk coming for damaged property. I'll use her well-being as a card up my sleeve. Also, if we need to say, up the ante, I might have to piss them off into coming for us with some home-videos. I want them to be able to tell by her reaction, that she's getting it for the first time."

Thumper started nodding his head. "Now, that makes perfect sense."

"Are you saying the lever-action rifles don't?" Sampson grimaced.

"Are you just looking for a reason to really tear into me, Sampson?"

Sampson thought it best to respond with only thunderous laughter.

* * * *

Detective Sean Scully sat at his desk simply reviewing reports on the Outlaws' crime spree. Mark Penn sat a few feet away at another desk doing the same.

Scully looked up and glanced at Penn. "I have grown bored with sitting here with thumbs up our asses."

"Want to switch to fingers?" Penn sighed.

"It's been six days since they've made a showing," Scully grumbled.

"You think they're on vacation?" Penn asked.

Scully gave it some thought. Made about as much sense as the rest of the investigation. "I hope that's not it, Mark. I hope they've been called back to the nineteenth century. You know? Kind of like Wild Bill needs them back in Deadwood?"

Penn turned in his chair to look directly as Scully. He held an unusual look in his eyes. "Funny you should say that, Sean. I think my wife honestly believes they come from the past."

"Is Martha off her meds?" Scully chuckled.

"You know how she can be," Penn chuckled in turn.

"Main reason I don't have a wife, Mark."

"She, uh . . . has an unhealthy fear about those two. She thinks they will eventually come for you and me. You know, just to keep us from finding them first."

"Hope you made her feel better, Mark. Hope you told her how damned far we're away from finding them first."

Penn stared down at his desk for several moments before turning his eyes back on Scully. "You know, she has this certain intuition. I know it sounds screwy, but she has been right on a few times. She woke up one morning and said she was worried about Fluffy, our cat. Next day, the cat got squished by a car."

"Jesus, think the Outlaws are going to squish us with their horses?"

"Go ahead, make fun. I just feel uneasy with her thinking we are in danger."

"I understand," Scully said before winking at his partner. "Right now, I feel I am in danger of being bored to death."

"She made me promise I'd be more careful than ever before."

"Well, you tell Martha, I promise to keep you safe," Scully grinned. "Like when I'm driving after we've just gotten coffee at McDonalds, I won't brake suddenly. That hot-assed coffee can sure do damage to a detective's crotch and thighs."

* * * *

P-Wac fought off pissing yet again. Why would the Outlaws choose to meet in the middle of a cemetery? He guessed they had no idea what P-Wac thought about being alone in a graveyard after dark. Especially one with such tall and ancient monuments. P-Wac did his best not to look again at the one being hugged by life-sized angels. These two damn sure did not look angelic. P-Wac would bet no blacks were buried in this place. Just rich and long dead white folks. Then he felt the soft touch of a hand being placed on his shoulder.

P-Wac let out a squeal as he spun and involuntarily swung a haymaker.

The fucking Indian cowboy. Hiding his face with a bandana.

The long-haired cowboy effortlessly blocked the blow with a forearm. P-Wac had not yet spent his fright, and swung again. The cowboy simply swatted his fist away with an open palm. Why stop now?

"Mutha fucka!" P-Wac bellowed as he leapt at the much bigger man.

The cowboy just spun him around and then placed a single arm around his chest to pull him in and hold him in place with his arms pinned to his side.

"Why are you fighting young man?" The cowboy spoke softly into his ear.

P-Wac let it out. "Cause you scared the fuck out of me! And cause you fucked my life up! And cause my niece is being held hostage cause of you bastards!"

The other cowboy stepped from behind the monument with the scary angels. A bandana concealed his face as well.

P-Wac let out a moan, and kind of went limp in the Indian Cowboy's grasp. "Jesus Christ, you dudes spook the fuck out of me," he sighed.

"Can he let you go now?" The whitest cowboy said as he leaned back against one of the angels.

"Yeah, man. I'm cool." Actually, he felt ice cold, and could not keep a tremor out of his words.

The one holding him let P-Wac go. The one relaxing against the angel shook his head. This one said, "See, P-Wac, one the greatest problems facing this nation nowadays is too many people try to blame their problems on somebody else. We didn't screw up your life. You made choices that screwed up your life. Now, we got to un screw it."

P-Wac didn't feel like arguing, and couldn't come up with a sensible argument any way. "You dudes know my name. What do I call you?"

The cowboy pushed away from the angel. "You can call me Wyatt. The big feller behind you, call him Doc."

"You mean like Wyatt Earp and Doc Holiday?" P-Wac snarled.

"Oh, you know your Wild West history?" Wyatt asked.

"I know enough to know they were good guys. Not outlaws."

Both cowboys chuckled. "Well, P-Wac, I think they were good at times, but mostly did bad things to combat what they thought were more evil men. You know, kind of like fighting fire with even hotter fire."

"And you think that's what you do?"

"We know it's what we do," Doc said from behind him. "And we're awfully good at it."

Another point made that P-Wac could not argue. "Are you two gonna to save my niece?"

"You can bet we are," Wyatt responded immediately.

"You're awfully sure of yourself. What if Sampson ends up killing you, or nearly killing you?"

Wyatt laughed with gusto. "You know, P-Wac, that's another problem with America today. We seemed obsessed with vulnerable heroes. Take the movies for example. It seems like the heroes always have to nearly get killed before they eventually get the super bad guy. Ol' Doc and I aren't those kind of heroes. See, we've both been nearly dead once . . . and don't intend to be nearly dead again. Or, killed by the super bad guy. No. When we make our move, Sampson won't stand a chance."

P-Wac thought it over before asking, "How you gonna to save Charmane?"

Wyatt reached within his long duster and pulled out a cell phone. "First things first. You get this phone to Sampson. We'll do the rest."

P-Wac truly sensed that both men would at least die trying.

* * * *

P-Wac knew Sampson stood anxious to get the phone, and thought his troll, Thumper, would be there right away. Nearly an hour had passed since he made the call to Sampson, and still no Thumper. How far away were they holding his Charmane? The question gave P-Wac chill bumps. Ten minutes later, a fist pounded at P-Wac's door.

He pulled the door open, and Thumper barreled in. "Where's the phone?"

P-Wac pointed toward the kitchen. "On the table."

Thumper strode for the table, turning his back on P-Wac. Ugly thoughts sped through P-Wac's mind. More like fantasies. What all he could do to Thumper behind his back. But anything he did do, could only put Charmane in greater harm.

Thumper grabbed the phone and examined it. "Wow, not just a regular cell. Some high-tech son of a bitch," he chuckled.

P-Wac didn't care to offer a response. Thumper shoved the phone into a pocket and walked back to P-Wac. "You did good, boy."

"I'm bout tired of bein' called boy," P-Wac said with a grimace.

Thumper got right up in his face. "Well, what are you going to do about it . . . *boy?*"

"Considerin' my circumstances, not a damn thing," P-Wac replied.

Thumper grinned. "Well, don't say I didn't give you a chance." In the next instance a gun filled his hand. He put the barrel to P-Wac's forehead.

"What the fuck?" P-Wac bellowed.

"Sampson said put you out of your misery. Didn't want you to go on worrying about what's going to happen to your niece. But, hell, I'll tell you just so you'll die thinking about it. She's going to be fucked everyway a black bitch can be fucked."

P-Wac only had a split second to consider grabbing at the gun stuck to his head before a flurry of motion took him by complete surprise.

And Thumper as well.

Both of them seemed to just come out of thin air. "Doc" grabbed the gun, dislodging it and nearly twisting Thumper's wrist off. He then used the gun to knock Thumper backwards into the arms of "Wyatt." Thumper was certainly no small man, but Wyatt handled him as such. To P-Wac it looked as if Wyatt twirled the white trash like a baton. Thumper landed hard on the floor face up, but laid there only a second before Doc jerked him to his feet and screwed one of his old guns into an eye socket.

"Well, don't say we didn't give you a chance," Doc hissed.

To P-Wac's delight, Thumper started to beg for his life. Doc buried a knee into his crotch.

"Shut your ugly mouth," Doc hissed.

Thumper would surely have fallen to the floor again, but Doc held him in place. He stopped begging and now only nodded.

"Let me kill the mutha fucka!" P-Wac shouted.

Wyatt stepped between him and the other two. "No. Sadly, P-Wac he won't die today. He needs to get that phone to the other bigot."

Wyatt slowly turned back to Doc and Thumper. P-Wac moved to the side for a better view.

"Let it be known, puke, that anything that happens to that girl, will be done to you and Sampson before we slowly put you out of *your misery*. Of course, we won't be using our man parts. We'll use a ball bat with the fat end whittled into a still fat, but spiked end. Do you understand me?"

"Yeah," Thumper groaned.

Wyatt grabbed Thumper from Doc and twirled him in the air again. This time when he hit the floor, Wyatt stomped down hard on his crotch. Thumper went crazy in pain, and P-Wac fought off the urge to giggle and clap like a kid at a circus.

"Yeah?" Wyatt mocked. "I want to hear a 'yes, sir,' bad ass."

Thumper tried immediately, but it took him seconds to repeat the two words. Once he did, Doc scooped him up again and shoved him toward the door. Thumper stumbled and fell. Doc picked him up and tossed him again. This action continued until Thumper was out the door and the door slammed shut behind him.

P-Wac wailed a string of obscenities in amazement and appreciation before asking, "Were you two here all the time? Just hiding away?"

Wyatt winked at him. "Maybe. Or maybe we were instantaneously transported here from the outlaw cave."

P-Wac wouldn't even doubt that about these two. He didn't care how they got to his house, but felt most lucky that they had.

Doc spoke this time. "Anything else we need to un-screw while we're here?"

P-Wac considered his response before replying, "No, sir."

Wyatt thrust something toward P-Wac. It was a phone like the one Thumper carried away. "Sampson's phone can only receive our calls," Wyatt smiled, "but yours can be used to call us when needed."

Both Outlaws started toward the back of the house. P-Wac called after them. "Hey, uh, Doc, Wyatt . . . Thanks."

Both nodded their heads, but Wyatt gave a response. "P-Wac, there's hope for you yet, son."

* * * *

It was two in the morning before Thumper returned to the farmhouse. Sampson knew the minute he laid eyes on him that Thumper experienced extreme difficulties. He limped into the house, and his upper lip was busted.

"P-Wac do that to you?"

"This?" Thumper grumbled, pointing to his lip. "No. The floor did it to me about the third time I crashed into it."

"What the fuck happened?"

Thumper all but collapsed on the couch. "The Outlaws happened."

Sampson's breath seemed to freeze in his lungs. "Get to talking, Thumper."

"Man, they just came out of no place. Like fucking ghosts. I was just getting ready to drop the hammer on P-Wac. The long-haired one was . . . was. . . just there, dude. He took my gun and they both did crazy Karate shit to me, man."

"P-Wac set your ass up?"

Thumper started shaking his head. "No. No, I don't think so. I was looking in his face. It surprised him as much as it did me. He didn't even know they were there, man."

"What did they say?" Sampson asked.

"One thing I remember, and won't forget, they told me that whatever we do to that bitch, they do the same to us with the fat end of a baseball bat, but they'll carve it into a spike first. The dude that said it, was talking about sticking it up our asses, Sampson."

"I got that," Sampson said through gritted teeth. It wanted to fuck with his mind. Just like they intended. Sampson shook it off.

"What are they like, Thumper?"

"Big dudes. Almost as big as you are. Strong too. That one flipped me in the air like a pizza crust. They were both wearing those bandanas. Couldn't see their faces, but could damn sure see their eyes, Sampson. Don't care to look into them again. One thing I remember, the first time I crashed to the floor, the long-haired one jerked me to my feet, and pulled one of those old guns so fucking quick. Like lightening, dude."

"So they're super humans? Is that what you're telling me?"

"You asked what they're like. I just told you the truth."

"So, you didn't kill P-Wac. I hope to hell you at least got the phone?"

Thumper leaned and pulled it from his jean's pocket. "It's the only reason they didn't kill me. They wanted to make sure you got it."

Sampson jerked it out of Thumper's hand and examined it. He fingered the keypad and quickly learned it would not make outside calls. It could only be used to receive calls from them.

He took a deep breath and exhaled it sharply. "So, the assholes played games with you, Thumper? Fuck them. Go get the girl."

Thumper limped off towards the basement door, and Sampson started stripping out of his clothes. He then walked naked into the kitchen and started rummaging through drawers until taking hold of the biggest butcher knife he could find.

* * * *

Remington turned to his computer guru, Dan Hicks. "We all set, Dan?"

"Ready when you are, Trey."

J. D. Roach and Ledford joined Remington at the table with all the high-tech gadgetry that only Hicks understood.

"Well, it's 0430 hours," Remington said. "Bet the asshole has been in bed just long enough to get good and asleep. Make the call, Dan."

Dan punched keys on a laptop computer, and the other three soon heard the ringing that would hopefully awaken Sampson. Remington knew the effects of being harassed by an enemy.

It took numerous rings before a groggy voice responded, "This is Sampson, asshole. Thanks for calling at a decent hour."

"You are certainly welcome, Sampson," Remington said. "I am one of the two men you seek. You can call me Wyatt."

Sampson coughed to evidently clear his throat. "Wyatt, is it? Would love to know your true identity."

"I'll make a promise to you, Sampson. My true name will be one of the last words you hear."

Sampson belted out loud laughter. "Can't wait, Wyatt. By the way, didn't appreciate you roughing up my main man, Thumper. That was not cool, dude. Forced me to take retaliatory measures. You know, on the girl?"

Remington paused to look into the eyes of Ledford and Roach. He wanted seconds to think, but could not show that weakness. "I hope your main man delivered our main message. Whatever you do to the girl, we do to you."

More laughter. "Well, then here is what you are going to have to do first, Wyatt. You're going to have to get naked. Then find the biggest knife you can find. Then you're going to have to threaten me with that knife until I remove my clothing in front of you. Then you are going to have me pose in the sexiest of positions while you masturbate, and finally, shoot your wad in my hair. But you can't touch me, because I didn't touch her."

Remington watched as Ledford formed his hands into fists, and his face contorted into unabashed rage. Remington raised a palm to hopefully keep Ledford quite. "Well, Sampson, when will I get the chance to do that?"

"I know I can't call you, Wyatt. You control the calls. But I control the time-line. You'll simply stand idle until I decide what date to kill you and your friend. Speaking of which, what do I call him?"

Remington again glanced at Ledford. "Allow me, Sampson, to borrow a well-used cliché. You can call him your worst nightmare. Tomorrow we will want to speak to Charmane. If we don't like what we hear from her, you won't get your chance to meet us face to face. Do you understand?"

"Do I understand?" Sampson bellowed. "Do you fucking understand that I hold all the cards, motherfucker?"

"I know you heard me, Sampson. We talk to her tomorrow. She better be safe and sound."

Sampson started raging, and Remington gave Hicks the signal to disconnect. The line went dead.

Ledford jumped in. "Did you get his location, Dan?"

"I got it, John."

All except Hicks breathed a sigh of relief.

"I'll forward it to you, J.D.," Hicks said.

"And I will make good use of it," Roach said to Remington and Ledford.

Remington put a hand on Ledford's shoulder. "I pushed his buttons, brother."

Ledford nodded. "I'm going to push things up his ass."

Remington forced a chuckle in an attempt to lighten Ledford's mood. "I fear he might just like that, John."

"I can promise you . . . he won't like anything I do to him."

FOURTEEN

Ledford woke at six a.m. to Remington's nightmare produced screams. Before he could roust himself from his cot to render comfort, the screams stopped. Ledford fell back on the cot, but his mind now churned.

It seemed funny how two men so much alike dealt differently on what happened with the ordeal involving Rudy Whitlock and the terrible aftermath. Ledford never dreamed about it, but it haunted his waking hours on nearly a daily basis, and he had no qualms in voicing his feelings on the haunting with Trey. Who on the other hand, never brought the subject up while wide-awake. Trey refused to discuss it.

Had to be the reason the dead girl accused him in his sleep.

Some things made the memories more unbearable for Ledford to face. *Things* that too closely resembled Rudy Whitlock and his demented cravings.

Things like the monster Sampson.

If at the very moment, Ledford could lay hands on Sampson to stop him and punish him, Ledford could ward off the haunting. For now, he could only wait. Waiting on such matters served only to send Remington back into the past . . .

* * * *

. . . He shook his head at hearing the latest news.

"Dear, God. Another one?" he moaned to Trey.

"Yup. Yet another grade-school girl is missing from Aspermont County. The sixth one in just nine months. And still, our numb-nutted Sheriff, Jerry Ring, sits around with his thumb up his ass," Trey hissed.

Ledford could not help but to initially think that Trey's dislike for Ring had a lot to do with Trey's new girlfriend, Melinda Lollar. She and Ring lived together once, and nearly married. Ring had it in his mind that Trey stole her away, and harsh words had been shared between the two men. However, the longer this crime-spree went unchecked, Ledford more and more held Ring to blame.

"I'm tired of his excuses, too," Ledford agreed.

"Yeah, not enough man power. Budget can't support overtime. But, still he won't call in the Texas Rangers. That's pride, John. He can't do the job, but doesn't want outside interference in fear that they will make an arrest. That would steel his spotlight."

"Politics and influence hold him back as well, Trey."

"Oh you bet. Hell, he won't admit what the county folk know. It's Rudy Whitlock taking those girls. But then again, up until lately, Whitlock was the most influential and wealthy preacher in the county."

"He disappeared a month ago. Seems Ring would now admit he is the prime suspect. Especially considering that parents of little girls from his own congregation are making accusations of sexual misconduct."

"Yeah, but Ring knows, that by the slim chance it's not Whitlock, that he loses a significant campaign donor."

The men mulled it over silently until Ledford took the discussion in a whole new direction. "We were discharged out of the army a little over a year ago. I miss the excitement. I miss the hunt for a bad guy . . . let's find Rudy Whitlock."

Trey looked as if giving it serous thought before asking, "And what do we do when we find him?"

"We'll let the situation dictate."

"What I'm thinking is, John, that his groping of little girls has escalated into something really ugly. I hear that sort of thing happens. What if we find out he's doing terrible things to them?"

Ledford looked Trey square in the eyes. "Well, then, the situation will dictate that we mess him up in a really awful manner, but we take him to the police. Now, would you back me on that?"

The expression on Trey's face proved evidence of more deep thinking. "You know, don't think I'd have a problem with that."

* * * *

For the next month, Ledford and Remington conducted their own investigation. They talked to witnesses, and poured over newspaper accounts of the disappearances. They delved deeply into Whitlock's personal life and history. The two went as far as to pay informants. They talked to enough people and snooped in so many places, that their efforts soon came to the attention of the county sheriff.

Trey and Ledford were having breakfast in a mom and pop joint in Peacock, Texas, just ten miles from their ranch, when Jerry Ring rudely interrupted their eggs and bacon.

"I've been looking for you boys," he said after marching through the door and directly to their booth.

"Congrats, Sheriff," Trey grimaced, "you found us."

"I don't like what I'm hearing about you two probing around the county for Rudy Whitlock."

"Is there a law against that?" Ledford growled.

"There is a law against interfering with a criminal investigation," Ring growled back.

Trey joined in. "Well there should be no problem with that, Ring. The whole county knows there is no investigation. In other words, you're not doing your job."

Ring rested his hands on their table and leaned across it. "You two don't want to make me angry. I don't give a damn what kind of war heroes you *were*."

That made Trey chuckle, and Ledford could not imagine why. It pissed him off.

"I don't understand your hostility," Trey continued to chuckle. "Seems you'd be thanking us for doing your job."

"You heard me," Ring emphasized with an ugly smile.

"What I heard was a threat," Ledford said without any smile at all. "If you're that bad, lawman, take that gun and badge off and step outside with either one of us."

Ring jolted upright from his leaning position.

Trey chuckled again. "Choose me, Sheriff. Please, I'm begging, choose me."

Ring grew red in the face and stepped back from the table. "First chance I get, I'll be putting you two in jail."

"Now, that's what you ought to be saying about Rudy Whitlock, Sheriff," Trey grinned.

"Fuck you. Fuck you both," Ring snarled in a near whisper.

"Those are fighting words, Ring" Ledford said with a straight face. "Well, I say again, take your pick of one of us."

Ring stomped away, and it took Ledford all he had to keep from following him out into the street to make him eat his badge.

* * * *

The evening of the very day Ledford and Remington decided to check court property records on Rudy Whitlock, Karena came through the front door of the old hunting lodge in complete hysterics. She cried. She screamed. She made no sense at all. Ledford tried to take his woman into his arms, but she struggled free, and ranted and raved.

Until Ledford bellowed, "Karena! WHAT HAPPENED?"

Karena's knees buckled and she fell to the floor. Only then did she scream two distinct words.

"Isla Belle!"

Her niece. Karena had watched her throughout the afternoon to give her sister a chance to do some shopping. Karena deeply loved the seven-year-old, and Isla Belle idolized her aunt. Ledford rushed to Karena and lifted her to her feet. She continued to act hysterical until he shook her to near senses.

"What happened to Isla Belle, Karena?" he asked forcibly. Ledford did not cherish using the same technique on his love as he had on shell-shocked soldiers. Karena now only sobbed.

"Went in to pay for gasoline . . . Left her in the car . . . She was gone when I got back."

"Police are looking for her?" he asked.

"Yes. Yes, we all looked. We didn't find her."

Ledford pulled her into his arms, and this time she did not resist. "We're not finished looking, sweetheart." He moved her to the couch, forced her to recline, and grabbed his cell phone to call Trey.

* * * *

The remainder of that night, Ledford, Trey, Melinda, Karena, and her sister, Katelyn, searched the surrounding areas around the gas station from which Isla Belle had disappeared. They found nothing to give them hope. At one point, Ledford pulled Remington aside.

"We know where to look, Trey. We got to go there."

The court records revealed that Rudy Whitlock owned a hundred acres and a second home. "But that's nearly seventy miles away. At the far end of the county, " Remington objected. Then he nodded at the women. "We can't take them there."

Ledford quickly understood. "No telling what we might find. Yeah, they can't see that."

"But, you and I, we go at daybreak," Remington said.

Ledford couldn't think of a better solution. Yes, they could alert Ring, but he knew they would be there quicker than he would act.

At daybreak, Katrina had grown worse off. She shivered and quaked in their bed, refusing to leave it. He dared not leave her for any extended time. Even when he suggested going to get Katelyn, she begged him to remain at her side. He obeyed her wishes until she finally gave into exhausted slumber.

He rushed to Katelyn's home, but she refused to go with him back to the ranch and the old hunting lodge. She wanted to remain at her home in case the police tried to contact her there. Knowing nothing else to do that might help Karena, Ledford bought the horse she'd longed for. He borrowed a trailer from the seller, and sped his truck and the trailer back to the ranch. When he got there . . .

He found Karena bathing.

He removed her body from the tub. He took the blanket to cover her . . . and *the* one other item out of the house. Ledford then killed the horse, and set the old hunting lodge on fire.

For the next two days, he grieved. On the third day, he buried Karena. On the fourth, Trey and he took off to find the other property owned by Rudy Whitlock.

* * * *

The luxurious log home sat practically in the middle of the hundred acres. A magnificent barn made of rock stood a football field's length behind the house. Ledford and Remington approached on foot after hiding their pick-up in the woods at the front of the property.

"No cars in the drive," Trey said.

"Yeah," Ledford nodded, "But the house has a three car garage."

They moved to the garage and peered into the windows at the tops of the garage doors. Trey felt his adrenalin spike. "That's Whitlock's Mercedes."

"Sure is. He's here, John," Trey said.

Ledford took a deep breath and leaned back against the wall of the house. "Something I better tell you."

Trey leaned back on the wall beside Ledford. "What's that?"

"If Isla Belle is here, and she, uh, ain't in just real good shape, I intend to kill the bastard. It will prove he's responsible for Karena's death."

Ledford heard Trey taking in calming breaths. "John, I understand how you could feel that way, but we didn't come here to kill him. If he's harmed Isla Belle, we'll get our pound of flesh, and I ain't got a problem with nearly killing him, but I'm not here to commit murder, and neither are you."

"You got to do what you got to do, Trey. And I have to do what I got to do. I won't make you no promises, but I'd ask that you not stand in my way."

It took Trey long moments to respond. "And I can't make you the promise I won't try to stop you."

"Fair enough," Ledford nodded. "How we do this?"

"I say one takes the front, and the other the back. We try to get him to the door first. If he doesn't open one of them, we kick them in."

Ledford took the liberty of selecting the front, and took off in that direction. Trey went the opposite way. Ledford tried the doorbell several times before starting to pound on the door. He could hear Trey doing the same in the distance. Whitlock didn't come to either door.

Ledford stepped back from the door and shouted, "I'm going in, Trey!" He didn't wait for a reply before he started applying viscous kicks to the door. The fourth one splintered the door jam, and Ledford threw the door open. He entered with a Colt .45 automatic at the ready.

The lavishly furnished home was quiet inside, and seemed deserted. Then Ledford heard Trey holler from the backside of the house.

"I'm in, John!"

"I am, too," he responded.

The two men carefully searched every nook and cranny on the ground floor, and could find no entrance to a basement. Once they were sure the downstairs was empty, Ledford pointed to the staircase. "He's up there."

They climbed the stairs with Ledford in the lead. John carried a Browning Hi-Power, and pointed it over Ledford's shoulder at the landing above. Ledford had his Colt ready as well. The upstairs looked to have four bedrooms. They located the master suite and went in it first.

Whitlock was neither in the bathroom nor under the bed. Ledford went to one side of what had to be the master closet, and Trey took the other side. They both grabbed their side of a double door and jerked it open.

Rudy Whitlock crouched in a far corner, and started to whimper.

"What is the meaning of this intrusion? I am a man of God!"

Ledford reached him first, and jerked him to his feet. Trey moved aside as Ledford flung the rotund and balding man out of the closet and to the bedroom floor.

"Where are the girls?" Ledford bellowed.

"Girls?" Whitlock screamed. "I don't know what you're talking about! I am a servant of the Lord Jesus Christ!"

Ledford once again jerked him to his feet and stuck his nose close to Whitlock's. "I do believe there is a God, although he and I seldom see eye to eye. I'd guess he don't much care for my ways, and I'd damn sure bet he don't count you as one of his own. I'll ask you one more time, before you start to bleed. Where are the girls?"

"I don't know what you're . . . " Whitlock started to sob.

Ledford brought his heavy Colt up and down across Whitlock's forehead. Blood spouted from a gash and trickled down into Whitlock's eyes. The man started to scream and tried to break loose. Ledford struck him again with the Colt, nearly taking off his right ear. He then let Whitlock fall to the floor. All the blood reminded him of the blood that Karena shed. He fought off the need to see Whitlock bleed even more.

"I'll check the other rooms," Trey advised.

Ledford stepped back away from Whitlock, and hoped he would just try to bolt.

"I haven't done anything," Whitlock cried.

Before Ledford could respond, Whitlock rolled on the floor and to his hands and knees. He scurried to the bedroom door and tried to reach behind the open door. Ledford kicked his hand aside, and then placed his boot in Whitlock's back to hold him to the floor. Ledford pulled the door toward him and saw the baseball bat propped against the door.

"I have a gun you idiot, and you're going for a baseball bat?"

Whitlock just lay on the floor and bawled like a baby. Remington returned seconds later.

"The other bedrooms are clear. No girls."

Ledford picked up the ball bat. "That leaves only the barn out back."

Whitlock squirmed beneath his boot. "I want to see a warrant!" he screamed.

Ledford stuck the Colt down in his belt before jerking Whitlock to his feet. He put the business end of the bat beneath Whitlock's substantial jowls.

"This is the only warrant we need, preacher man." He shoved him through the bedroom door, and led him toward the staircase by the scruff of his neck.

"You can't enter that barn without a warrant!" Whitlock screamed again.

"He's very protective of that barn, John," Trey commented.

"He sure is," Ledford agreed as he manhandled Whitlock down the stairs and toward the back door. Whitlock struggled against each step taken.

"You can't go in my barn! You have no legal right!"

Ledford paused just long enough to shake the man like a ragdoll. "We don't care about legal, you bastard. That's where you keep the girls, isn't it, you perverted scum?"

Whitlock suddenly grew silent, and said not another word as Ledford tugged him out the back door and across the yard to the barn. The main door to the structure was padlocked shut. Ledford shoved Whitlock toward Trey before pulling his Colt to fire rounds until the padlock flew to pieces.

"Keep the fat shit out here. I'll take the inside."

Ledford fumbled around in darkness until finding the appropriate light switches. It took him less time to find the cellar type door on the concrete floor of the barn. He used the Colt to destroy a second padlock. He started down the stairs beneath the door, fumbling once again in darkness. He groped at the bottom of the stairs until finally finding another light switch. When he flipped it on, the light only illuminated an unimaginable darkness.

* * * *

Remington stood over Ledford's cot. "Hey, John, you awake?"

Ledford pushed up from his cot. "Yeah, Trey, I'm awake. Your screams woke me up."

"Sorry, man," Remington said, "Had the dream again."

"I know. I understand," John said as he brought hands up to rub at his face. "Took me back in time, old buddy. Back to Whitlock's barn."

"We got business to attend to in the here and now." Remington hoped his partner would say no more, but knew better.

"In my mind, I'd just reached the bottom of the stairs in the barn basement, and found the light switch."

Remington drew in a deep breath in hopes that exhaling it would keep the memory at bay. It didn't work. "John, J.D., will brief us in an hour. This could be the most complicated mission to date."

"Yeah, I know that. I'll get my mind right."

Now, Remington would have to do the same. He returned to his own cot, and plopped down hard. John had sent him back to a place he didn't care to go . . .

* * * *

. . . Remington stood outside holding Whitlock by the throat. He heard the shots ring out.

Another padlock.

Although he quaked now more than ever, Whitlock grew defiant. "You two will regret this."

"Maybe so, Whitlock, but I'm thinking you will regret it long before we do."

Remington didn't expect John to be in the barn for this long of a time. Dread turned his stomach sour. Tired of holding on to Whitlock, he shoved him face down on the ground.

"Move an inch, and I will start breaking bones." Ledford had left him in charge of the ball bat.

A little over an eternity later, John stepped out of the barn, and not empty-handed. Trey's guts lurched when he recognized the small and still form John cradled in his arms.

Isla Belle. Bleeding from places a child should not bleed.

"Is . . . she . . . dead?" Remington's voice quaked.

Tears flowed from John's eyes and down the cheeks of his face. In all these years, through so many painful events, Remington had never seen the man shed a single tear. Not even at Karena's funeral.

"Barely alive when I found her. Dead now,"

Remington's shocked mind took over his tongue. "Where are her clothes? She has nothing on."

"Other kids are down in the basement, Trey."

"How many?"

"Can't tell. All in pieces."

A voice sounded at Remington's feet. "You have violated my civil rights . . . "

The bastard actually chuckled.

" . . . This will never even make it to the courts."

Remington landed a kick to the already damaged side of Whitlock's head.

Whitlock screamed out in pain, and Remington wanted more. He raised his boot, intending to stomp down hard on the wailing head.

"No!" John said sternly. "I want him conscious."

Remington watched as John carried the lifeless child a few yards away to gently lay her on the ground. He then walked back to Remington and took the bat from his hands. Once again, he walked back into the barn.

Remington could hear the faint sound of a power tool, and the guttural humming of wood being subjected to a table saw or lathe. Minutes later, John stepped out of the barn, welding a bat that no longer was rounded at the end, but carved into a spike. Remington took a step away from Whitlock to allow Ledford to jerk him to his feet.

Whitlock's eyes locked on the altered implement of recreation.

"What are you going to do with that?" he babbled.

John turned his now dry, but bloodshot eyes, on Remington. "You might want to wait out here."

Remington thought he might, but knew he couldn't. "If you intend to take him inside, Trey, I'm going with you."

"I hope not to try stopping me."

Remington shook his head. "Since we've returned from war, just seen too much wrong here at home, and too little being done about it. Isla Belle dead, other babies mutilated. No, John, this isn't something that lethal injection or years in a country club of a prison will revenge. Do what you need to do. I'll lend whatever hand you allow me."

Whitlock screamed and used both arms and legs to resist being bent over a table inside his cavernous barn. Remington held him in place as Ledford tugged down his trousers and boxer shorts. Then Ledford raised the bat and pointed it.

"Preacher man . . . do unto others . . ."

The brutal insertion of at least eight inches of wood left him all but unconscious. Ledford stepped back, leaving the bat in place, and reached beneath his jacket.

It did not surprise Remington what he removed from a sheath.

The knife Karena used to take her life.

Remington knew that it and the blanket John had used to cover Karena's body were the only items to escape the fire that destroyed the hunting lodge.

Ledford reached over the back of Whitlock's head with his free hand, and grasped his forehead. He lifted the head backwards, extending the neck. Remington expected John to slit Whitlock's throat. He didn't.

Instead, he forced the blade into the monster's mouth, and started jabbing it deep into the back of Whitlock's head. He didn't jab quickly, but methodically, and didn't stop until Whitlock stopped breathing.

* * * *

Remington let out a low moan as the memory of the event played to the end. He did not moan for Rudy Whitlock. He felt no remorse for the man's brutal death. He moaned instead for the remnants of the little ones that lay scattered and decaying beneath the floor that Whitlock deservedly bled out on.

Remington and Trey were already in jail by the time it took the authorities to process and identify the girls in the basement. Remington moaned because fourteen innocent babies died in that pit. But only after being raped in every way *unimaginable.*

And he moaned again because there were and would always be predators like Rudy Whitlock. And all he could do, was destroy the very few that crossed his path.

Soon, very soon, another would do just that.

FIFTEEN

Two days earlier, Sean Scully sat in his office bored to tears, and Mark Penn fretted over his wife's worries. Now, Scully guided the unmarked sedan down streets that would take them to an abandoned factory on the outskirts of Chicago, and felt anything but bored.

"You sure we shouldn't have a squad car on standby?" Penn asked.

"I think it's too risky," Scully once again defended his views on the situation. "You heard the man, they see any cars but this one, and the boy hauls ass. Shit, man, he's scared to death. Don't know who the hell to trust. We can't afford losing him and what he knows. I mean, if he knows what the caller said he knows."

"Still wish we'd had time to check on his residence personally," Penn said.

"We'll just have to rely on what the patrol officers said a few minutes ago. He didn't come to the door. They looked around, and don't believe he's in there."

"The caller sounded legit. I guess we're doing the right thing," Penn sighed.

"Under the circumstances, we're doing the only thing we can do. Worst case scenario, it turns out to be a prank, but my gut tells me the guy was legit."

"Well, guess we'll find out in about fifteen minutes, partner," Penn said with no signs of enthusiasm.

* * * *

Just a few minutes earlier, P-Wac did what any black dude in the hood would do when uniformed cops knocked at his door. He acted like he wasn't there, and stayed away from the windows. He had no idea what they wanted, but they didn't kick the door down, so they had no warrants. He fought off the urge to use the phone to once again call the Outlaws. But he'd evidently called one time too many already.

The last time he'd called to ask, "Why the fuck aren't you two doing something?" Wyatt had asked him in turn, "P-Wac are you needing a good old-fashioned ass whooping?" It was the last thing he needed. He'd had two just recently. But, *fuck,* it'd been four days since they'd promised to save Charmane. Wyatt did go on to tell him that Charmane was "relatively safe and relatively unmolested."

What the hell is relatively?

But P-Wac didn't ask that. Instead he asked, "How do you know that?"

Wyatt answered, "Son, you wouldn't believe me if I told you."

P-Wac even tried calling Sampson to talk to Charmane. Seemed the white asshole was very pissed over the fact P-Wac was not dead. Told P-Wac that Charmane, at that very moment, stood naked in front of him. P-Wac could hear her crying. P-Wac made horrible promises to Sampson he regrettably could not carry out, and the line went dead. He'd tried calling Sampson's number the next day but a message informed him that the number was no longer in service.

Now, he could only sit and wait. And trust the Outlaws. And wonder why cops had come to his door.

* * * *

"Turn here," Penn told Scully. "Only a few blocks ahead now."

Of course, they'd recorded the incoming call that brought them here, and both detectives listened to it numerous times. Enough times that Scully had it memorized.

" . . . I'm not another nutcase. Consider me to be P-Wac's representative. He does not want to die, and knows nowhere else to turn. I encouraged him to accompany me to your office for an interview, but he's simply too frightened. He chose the location I gave you. Believe me, he does have information on the Outlaws that you want, and, like I said, he knows they have a source within the CPD, and he knows who the source is. Honestly, he's just a young man in something way over his head, and he wants out of it."

The voice sounded white, and educated. That gave the caller credence, Scully had agreed with Penn. Not because the man sounded white or educated, but that a white man would have some link to a black street gang member. Scully suggested he might be an attorney, and Penn thought that it could be possible.

A grouping of deserted buildings was now in sight, and Scully slowed the car.

"We're looking for the building with a sign that reads 'office'," Penn said.

"Yeah, I know," Scully replied. Not meaning to be curt, but he felt anxious. He so hoped this would not be another dead end. He needed something to actually *happen.*

Penn spotted the building first and pointed it out to Scully.

"Thanks, Mark," he said in a kinder fashion. He pulled the car in front of the building and put it in park before killing the engine.

"Now, we sit in the car and wait," Penn said.

Scully noted the stress in his voice. "Yup, that's what the man said. But so what dear friend? We're good at waiting. Have been waiting for weeks."

* * * *

They had removed the bulb from her tiny room, and Charmane didn't know if it was night or day. She could only lie in the bed and wait. Wait without clothing. She'd lost track of time. Didn't know how long she'd been without clothing, or how many times she'd stood before them naked. Posing in positions that sickened her. And if she didn't? That monster had the big knife.

Sometimes it was just him. Other times he had the one he called Thumper. And a few times . . .

How many How many How many How many

. . . there had been a few more.

They never touched her. With their hands. But they touched their *things* and made her touch their *things.*

But only with her hands. Charmane was a virgin, but knew what boys could have women do with other than their hands. She had not yet gone totally insane, but if the other things did happen, she knew she would.

And Sampson had, and Thunder had, and the others had . . . *deposited* . . . upon her. In more places than she cared to recall.

In the dark, the only warning she now had that it would happen yet again, was the sound of the key turning in the lock on the door.

It turned now.

It seemed just one too many times for it to turn, and Charmane begin screaming. Like she'd never screamed before.

* * * *

They just came out of nowhere, and they came so damned quickly. Scully felt like an idiot for falling into the trap, and hated to die feeling such emotions. Four of them. All carrying automatic rifles, and Scully suddenly hurt for Mark Penn, and his wife, Martha. He'd let them both down. Like Penn, he struggled to release the seat belt in order to get to his weapon on his belt, hidden and obstructed by a suit coat. It simply took too damned long.

One of the four let loose with heavy rounds from a powerful assault weapon, but they did not tear into the sedan's passenger compartment. The man aimed instead at what lie beneath the hood. What Scully guessed was a thirty round magazine tore and ripped into the radiator and engine, surely disabling the sedan. Instinctively, both detectives sought cover behind the dash as lead pounded the front of their car. Neither had yet managed to free their inferior service automatics.

"Are you hit?" Penn screamed.

"No! You?"

"Not fucking yet!"

The firing stopped. Scully raised his head with Penn, and no doubt viewed the same thing. One man on each side of their car with rifles pointed just feet away from their heads.

"Get you're fucking hands up," the one on Penn's side shouted.

"Die now or die later?" Scully bellowed to Penn.

Penn raised his arms. "I want to take my chances, Sean."

If Scully tried to retrieve his Glock again, both would die. He could not do that to Mark Penn. He put his arms up as well.

"Skinheads," Penn said without moving his lips.

A third one stood in front of the car with his rifle at the ready, while the initial shooter reloaded his rifle.

"I do believe so," Scully whispered just before their doors were jerked open.

The one on Scully's side pulled him out of the car and pushed him around to Penn's side of the car with the barrel of his rifle. The one in front of the car moved around with the others, and became the spokesman.

"We want your guns and badges. Hand them over."

Scully beat Penn to the punch. "If I pull my gun, I'll be using it. The only way you get my badge, is off my dead body."

"Can't work that way. You have to surrender them."

Funny what can make a man chuckle when about to die.

"Says who?" Scully asked around the chuckle.

"Says Sampson."

"You boys are too young for this shit," Penn spoke up. "Too young to spend the rest of your lives in prison."

"Fuck you," the spokesman, or spokesboy, spat at Penn before turning back to Scully. "I want your guns and badges."

"Then try taking them, asshole," Scully replied, sounding much calmer than he felt.

"Sampson said it might come to this, and told us to tell you, that it can end here, or it can end at 3238 Pulaski."

"That's my address!" Penn nearly choked.

"Okay," Scully immediately decided, "You can have my gun and badge." He started reaching for them as Penn's eyes fell to the ground.

"I've always promised myself that I'd never surrender my gun," he mumbled solemnly.

Scully turned his head to look him face on. "Hell, old friend, didn't you see the movie? Never say never. Let's do it for Martha."

Penn turned tortured eyes on Scully. "You shouldn't have to remind me of my wife."

"What are friends for?" Scully found the courage to grin.

Both detectives handed over badges and guns, and Scully asked, "Why would Sampson want this done?"

"Damn he's one smart dude," the spokesboy laughed. "He said you would probably ask that, and told us what to say. See, he wants to get the Outlaws before you do. And, he wants your dying to be a message to the Outlaws. Shows his power."

"You're not thinking straight, son," Scully said. "Don't you get it? This is the very type of thing that brought the Outlaws to Chicago in the first place. It won't happen here and now to do us any good, but you can bet they'll come after you. We've seen the people they go after. You don't want to be one of them."

"I'm not your son, motherfucker," the boy grinned. "And I'm tired of hearing you talk. You get it first."

The kid, so intent on being a man, stepped up to Scully and put the barrel of the rifle to his head. Scully looked closely at him. Studied his face, just before it simply disappeared. What had been eyes, nose, and lips, evaporated into a mist of red and gray.

A single shot sounded.

And three more followed in quick procession. The other three youths writhed on the ground with less than life-threatening wounds. Scully and Penn, out of instinct and training, moved quickly to kick their firearms aside.

Mark Penn just happened to be the first to look up, point, and cry out, "The Outlaws!"

Scully jerked his head in the direction of the pointed finger. Two men, on horseback, slowly approached with Remington rifles pointed to the heavens. Scully dove for the nearest weapon.

* * * *

Remington called out, "Don't disturb the crime scene, detective!"

He'd seen enough photos of the two to know it was Sean Scully going for a gun. Thankfully, Scully obeyed the command. He spurred his horse into a trot, and Ledford stayed right with him. They didn't stop until practically on top of the two cops.

"Did you set this up?" Scully shouted angrily.

"We don't put cops in danger, Detective Scully," Remington said from behind his bandana.

Scully spun in place to view the carnage. "Well, you damn sure didn't show up a second too soon! You fucking killed a kid!"

"That's regrettable," Remington replied, and meant it, "but we miscalculated the escalation. He was supposed to rough you up before killing you. He didn't follow the plan, and we couldn't afford anything other than a head shot." Remington drew in a deep breath. "Better him than you."

Remington observed that Detective Mark Penn looked still in shock, and remained silent, and it took a few seconds for even Scully to respond.

"The plan? Whose plan?"

"Just like you were told. Sampson's plan. We liked the part where they disabled your vehicle first. Helps us in making a safer exit."

"How did you know about the plan?" Scully asked.

Of course, Remington couldn't tell him about Dan Hick's specially equipped communications van. "Let's just say a geek birdie told me about it."

Scully seemed to struggle for the right questions to ask, but made a statement instead.

"You two are under arrest."

Ledford reined his horse up closer to Scully. "Did you see the movie Tombstone, Detective Scully?" He said in his taunting way of speaking. "At one point, right after the shootout behind the O.K. Corral, Wyatt Earp tells Sheriff Behan, something along the lines of, 'I don't think I'll let you arrest us today.' That's kind of the way I'm feeling right now."

Scully did not press the point. "So, what do we do now?" Scully asked, as if actually perplexed.

Remington replied, "You are going to do whatever cops do with a crime scene, and we are going to . . . ride into the sunset."

"I take it that means you are going to leave Chicago?" Scully asked.

"Not quite yet, Detective," Remington smiled behind his bandana. "We got just one more rodeo to ride."

Remington and Ledford started backing their horses, and were about to rein them about and spur them into a gallop when Mark Penn evidently found his voice.

"Hey, uh . . . Outlaws . . . Thanks for saving our lives."

Both Remington and Ledford tipped their hats before spinning about to ride "hell bent for leather."

* * * *

Sampson sat in the back seat of a plain four-door Chevy behind darkened windows. Slick Ray occupied the driver's seat, and had the car parked in a secluded place a mile away from the ambush site.

"Thunder should be calling any minute now," Sampson said.

"Wish the fuck he would. This waiting is hard on my nerves, man. Don't know how you can remain so calm."

Sampson liked that Slick Ray thought him calm, and appreciated the fact he couldn't see beneath his skin. On the inside, he squirmed. No move could be bolder than the one he'd selected. If all went well, the next step would be a piece of cake. If his men didn't pull this off, Sampson would lose face.

He'd stationed Thumper in one of the abandoned buildings at the selected killing site, giving him a bird's eye view of the action. Sampson instructed him to call the very minute the last cop died.

"Hey, uh, Sampson," Slick Ray said as he sat up straight in the driver's seat.

"What is it?"

"Thumper's car. Headed this way in a hurry."

Something went very wrong, or overwhelmingly good. Thumper tended to forget specific instructions when excited.

Seconds later, Thumper jumped into the backseat beside Sampson.

"Tell me it's good news," Sampson ordered. But, he could tell by the look on Thumper's face that it wasn't.

"The Outlaws showed up. On fucking horses. They blew Jack Boy's head off, and wounded the other three."

"After they killed the cops, right?" Sampson bellowed.

"No," Thumper winced.

Sampson threw a fist into seatback in front of him with enough force to make Slick Ray groan.

Then he grabbed Thumper by the throat. "You're telling me, that the Outlaws saved the detectives?"

Sampson evidently cut off his air, because Thumper only seemed able to nod. Thumper dropped his hand before dropping a dozen or so fucks in various formats. Not feeling satisfied with ranting, he grabbed the pistol in the seat beside him and thrust it to Thumper's forehead.

"We have a fucking snitch, Thumper. A fucking snitch that knows every move I make. You're the only one who knows every move I make."

Thumper's eyes grew wide with fear. "Are you shitting me, Sampson?"

Sampson lowered the gun. "No, Thumper. . . I'm killing you."

Sampson jammed the gun into Thumper's ribs and pulled the trigger until all rounds were spent.

Slick Ray had fallen over in the front the seat and now shouted, "Motherfucker, Sampson!"

"You want to be next, asshole?" Sampson shouted back.

"No! No please! You know I don't, Sampson! I'm loyal to the core!"

Sampson tossed the gun to the floorboard.

"You're my new Thumper, Slick Ray. Congratulations. Get someone to get his car out of here, and get me the fuck back to the farmhouse. Oh, and you'll be in the house with me the night the Outlaws come to die."

Slick Ray started working his cell while turning a key, shifting gears, and pushing the accelerator to the floor.

* * * *

Lieutenant Ely Elmore leaned across his desk to bury his head in his large hands. "I fear I am living some horrible nightmare. I'd ask you to pinch me, Scully, but figure you too homo-phobic to lay hands on me."

Scully didn't feel in the best of moods. "I almost died today, Lieutenant, and so did my partner here. You don't want me to start laying my hands on you."

Elmore raised his head, and nodded it solemnly. "Yeah. Sorry Scully. This is not a time for lame gay jokes."

His sentiment almost made Scully sorry for making the remark.

"So, you two met the Outlaws," Elmore sighed. "Anything all that spectacular about them?"

Scully shrugged his shoulders. "Oh, only just everything, boss."

"I don't even know where to go from this fucking point," Elmore grumbled.

Penn raised his head and opened his mouth for the first time during the briefing. "I do, Lieutenant Elmore."

Scully and Elmore responded by simply turning heads to study Mark Penn. As they did, he pushed to his feet, and reached into both lapels of his suit coat. Scully all but gasped when he pulled his gun and badge to place them on Elmore's desk.

"I'm putting in for retirement, Ely. Starting right now."

Scully didn't have words, but Elmore did.

"You sure about this, Mark?"

"I am. Been shot once. Stabbed once, but my wife was never in danger. She was in danger today. I intend to keep her close."

Scully could only emit a loud and mournful sigh. Penn turned to look down at him, before extending his right hand.

"You've been a good partner. Best I ever had," Penn smiled.

Scully stood to grip his hand. "You too. Like to say more, but don't care to give the boss the wrong impression by crying."

"Fuck you," Elmore grumbled.

Penn dropped his hand and cocked his head to look hard at Scully. "Don't know how you can stay on the case. How do you pursue men that saved your life?"

Scully could only shrug his shoulders and shake his head. "Don't really know, Mark."

Penn gave him a warm smile, turned to shake Elmore's hand, and then just walked out of Scully's life. For long seconds, Scully and Elmore remained silent.

Elmore broke the silence, "Can you stay on the case, Sean?"

Scully considered the question long and hard before responding. "You know, LT, if we had a chance in hell in apprehending them, I'd tell you no."

Surprisingly, Elmore seemed to understand, but still had one more question. "How did they know Sampson planned this hit?"

Scully plopped back down in the chair. "Only one good answer, sir. They are keeping tabs on Sampson. They know where he is.

Maybe they have a snitch, but I'm willing to bet they have the ability to intercept communications."

"So, it's now just a matter of time before Chicago is rid of one more piece of shit?" Elmore asked.

Scully liked the way he put it. "Yes, sir. Won't be long now."

Elmore seemed to dwell on the response. "Do you know what I think would be the best outcome to all the murders committed by the Outlaws?"

Scully couldn't help but chuckle, "Sure. You'd like to see them behind bars."

Elmore chuckled back at him. "Not even. I'd like to be give authorization as soon as possible to send this case to the cold files."

Scully smiled and nodded his appreciation for the statement.

Elmore stood and extended his hand toward Scully. "Detective Scully, please don't make a joke out of this, but I must say, you are one fine man, and a hell of a cop."

The sincere words humbled Scully as he stood and accepted the hand, and found it firm almost to the point of painful. "I, uh, appreciate that, sir, but I do intend to, uh, not understand those different from myself."

Elmore chuckled again. "Hell, son, we are all that way. But, living in a so-called civil society, we are required to act as if we do."

Sean Scully had long been jaded by his choice of careers, but left Elmore's office feeling something he had not in years.

Enlightened.

* * * *

Sampson grabbed up the phone on the first ring. "I can't wait to kill you motherfucker," he thundered.

"Hello to you, too, Sampson," the voice on the other end responded calmly.

"You won today, but you will not win again, 'Wyatt,' or whatever you real name is. Probably something more like Mikey or Benny."

"Jeez, Sampson, you seem awfully bitter this evening."

Sampson so wished for the magic powers to reach through the phone and pull out the tongue talking on the other end. This he could not do, but he could drop the phone and crush it beneath his feet. But how stupid would that be? He tried to calm himself.

"I eliminated your source of information today, Wyatt. Now you will only stumble in darkness until I invite you to the party."

"Hmmm. What source would that be, Sampson?"

Sampson pulled in deep breaths. "The only source you fucking had. I killed Thumper."

"Thumper was not our source," the voice on the other end laughed. "Seriously? You killed your closest associate, Sampson? Sounds like you are coming unraveled, Sampson."

"You fucking liar!" Sampson stormed, feeling as if he might foam at the mouth.

"Think about it. My response came too quickly. I'm good, but had I lost my link to you, I'd paused or stammered, or acted like you're acting now. No, I'm glad Thumper is gone. He seemed too willing to give his life in order to protect you."

Sampson grabbed his face with a hand and squeezed it until hit hurt.

NO. NO. NO. Do not let the bastard fuck with your mind.

"Well, Wyatt," Sampson said with forced calm, "Fuck that shit. Let's go to the next rung on the ladder. Earlier today, I made special plans and arrangements for our sweet little Charmane. Do you care to stay on the line while I bring them to fruition?"

"I think we've had this discussion, Sampson."

"So, you going to hang up, pussy?"

"Make your move, Sampson. You've had fair warning."

Sampson held the phone away from his face, but intentionally did not cover the receiver. "Go get the little bitch, boys."

He brought the phone back to his lips and chuckled. "Wish I could let you watch this, but this special phone restricts my ability. Guess you will have to just imagine from her screams what it is we do to her."

Wyatt did not offer a response.

"You still there, asshole?" Now, the tables turned, allowing Sampson to emit the laughter.

"I'm still here," a very serious voice responded.

Then, Slick Ray returned, and spoke too loudly of his efforts.

Wyatt spoke up again. "Did I hear that right, Sampson? The girl's not there?"

Sampson struggled to sound confident. "Oh, we'll find her motherfucker. She's here someplace."

The phone connection went dead. Sampson threw the device across the room before turning to glare at Slick Ray.

"That fucking Thumper!"

Slick Ray did little but stand and stutter his incomprehension.

"Yeah, he's dead, but still could be fucking me. He was the last one out of here today. Did you by any chance check the trunk of his car?"

"Uh, no, Sampson, didn't think to."

"Where's the car now?

"In a garage, going to be taken apart to piece out."

"Get someone to check that trunk, and start searching around this place. If she's in the trunk, she's already dead. If you find her around here . . . then she soon will be."

* * * *

P-Wac paced within his spacious and expensively furnished new pad. Well, not exactly his, but it served as home sweet home for now. The man he knew only as J.D., brought him here earlier today.

"We need to keep you safe," J.D. had said, "You're not safe in your own house. Sampson now has even greater reasons for wanting you dead."

"Why's that? What happened?" P-Wac recalled asking.

"Just watch tonight's news," had been J.D.'s only response.

P-Wac did watch it. Someone tried to make a hit on the two detectives assigned to the Outlaw's case, and the Outlaws ended up saving them. It amazed P-Wac as much as he knew it amazed other viewers. Probably even more, because P-Wac felt certain about who set up the blotched ambush.

Sampson.

P-Wac had almost felt like laughing at Sampson' blotched plans, but knew Sampson might have the last laugh.

The motherfucker still had Charmane.

So once again, P-Wac found himself in a situation where he could only worry and pace. He did just that until the doorbell rang. He ran to the door to look through the peephole.

Two visits in one day?

P-Wac jerked the door open to see in person the solemn look on J.D.'s face.

"Charmane?" P-Wac gasped.

"Yeah," J.D. nodded.

P-Wac fought to keep his knees from buckling.

Then, J.D. stepped aside and Charmane shot through the door and straight into P-Wac's arms. They hugged, and they cried, and P-Wac could not let her go. J.D. gently moved both further inside the safe house so he could shut the door.

"You're alive! You're here!" P-Wac cried out loud.

"And she will remain safe, P-Wac, and so will you," J.D. smiled. "When your mother is released from the hospital, we'll bring her here as well."

P-Wac hung on to his sobbing niece as he asked, "How you get her out?"

J.D. pulled in a deep breath and let it out slowly as he seemed to study P-Wac. "P-Wac, I don't imagine at this point that we have to worry about you having loose lips, do we?"

"Hell no, J.D., you saved my life, and more importantly, you saved her life. I'm now as loyal a friend as you'll ever have."

J.D. nodded his belief. "Did you watch the news tonight?"

"Yeah, I know what happened."

"Okay. Well, we knew Sampson intended to be near the ambush site when the hit was made. We knew his hideout would be empty. That's when we went in to get Charmane."

"You know where Sampson's hidin'?" P-Wac gasped.

"We do."

"Then it's almost over?"

"Almost."

P-Wac babbled a string of thank-yous at J.D., and just before he walked out the door, P-Wac called his name.

"Yes, P-Wac?"

"Thank 'em for me. Thank Wyatt and Doc. Thank the Outlaws."

J.D. grinned at P-Wac. "Don't know a Wyatt or a Doc, but I'll thank John and Trey. And, uh . . . they're anything but outlaws."

SIXTEEN

"I don't want to buy into this," Ledford stormed. "I want to do it *right* now."

Remington forced himself to remain calm. "John, you're not hearing what it is that J.D. wants us to hear."

Ledford turned to the Chief of Operations. "No, offense, J.D., I hear what you're saying, but the girl is safe, and I want to move in."

"And I damn sure don't want to offend you, John," J.D. grinned. "but I don't think you'd do too much damage to an old war buddy with two artificial legs. So, I'll be bold. Donning has already approved the plan. And I'm not changing it."

Remington watched as John drew in a deep breath. "Run it by me one more time, J.D. Make it good, because if I don't like it, you will change the plan."

J.D. turned to look defiantly at Remington.

"Hey, J.D., you know how he is. I can't whip him for you, and I can't out shoot him. Guess you will just have to woo him." Remington really didn't care either way it went, but he did see the virtue in J.D.'s plan. Still, he didn't care enough to aggravate either of his comrades. He decided to simply let the best man win this pissing contest.

J.D. pulled up a folding chair and took a seat in front of Ledford. "Surely you won't hit a crippled man sitting down." Then he reached into his pocket, retrieved his reading glasses and stuck them on his head, "Surely not a crippled man sitting down and wearing glasses."

It surprised Remington when Ledford laughed. "J.D., run it past me again, please? I do want to work with you here."

"John, Sampson is spreading the news of the magnificent way he is going to take down the Outlaws. It's spreading amongst the street gangs. All of them. He intends to be some kind of living legend, and even those who don't ally with him, hope he can pull this off, because you two have destroyed their worlds."

Remington nodded and grinned at J.D.'s new approach on making his point.

"Right now, John, he's still putting his pieces in place. If we hit him before he *thinks* he's totally prepared, before he can initiate his grand plan, then all the others will always be able to say, 'Yeah, but what if?' What I want to do, is take away the *what if.* I want those left standing to believe he had every opportunity to carry out his grand design, and that you two still squished him like the slimy cockroach he is. You two, amongst this city's underbelly, will then always be the two legendary bad-assed duo that no force could stand against. So, he can die today as somewhat of an unsung hero to the street thugs. Or, he can die tomorrow or the next day as a pathetic moron who couldn't win in the best of situations. And, that will eventually get out to the good citizens as well, strengthening their resolve to keep this movement on the move."

Ledford grinned at J.D. "Why didn't you say that in the first place?"

J.D. pushed to his feet and removed his glasses. "At this very moment, John, if you were sitting down with two artificial limbs and wearing glasses, I'd still slap the shit out of you."

* * * *

"I haven't heard from you in nearly a week."

"What a coincidence. Haven't heard from you in the same length of time."

The word *touché* popped into Marge Myers' mind. The last thing she wanted was for this call to go south.

"Well, so I'm calling you. You didn't call me, Marcus."

A long silence followed from the other end. "Didn't see no sense in calling, Marge," Marcus finally responded.

"I feel totally out of touch. Did you know anything about the Outlaws saving those two detectives before it happened?"

"Are you grilling me, Marge?"

"Just asking."

Another period of silence. "No. Didn't know a damned thing about it. Believe it or not."

Marge felt undecided, but went for the safe response. "I believe you."

"Good. I don't know anything at this point, Marge, but I believe this thing is almost done. Soon, we'll have no excuse for calling each other."

Marge had no idea if that might be the case, and needed to hang on to her source at all costs. Still, she carefully chose her words. "That's rather final, Marcus. I don't want to see it that way."

"Okay, then let's go out together. Let's have a real date. Show me I'm more to you than a confidential informant."

At this point, to be a responsible professional, Marge could only lean on the truth. "I do consider you a true friend. Someone I care about."

"And we'll never be more than friends?"

Marge took moments to consult with her heart and conscious. "I don't think so, Marcus."

A soft humorless chuckle sounded from the other end. "I appreciate your honesty. I really do, but truth is, I'm past the part of needing only friendship."

The line went dead, and Marge sincerely regretted the feeling that she'd never speak to Marcus Jones again.

* * * *

"She wasn't in the trunk, Sampson, and we've searched every inch of this property. She's gone," Slick Ray said while keeping a safe distance from Sampson.

Sampson didn't blame Slick Ray for the girl's absence. He still blamed Thumper. His dead friend evidently saw the writing on the wall even before Sampson started to scribble it. He'd known Sampson would find out about his treachery, and used the girl as his last chance to get back at him. Whatever he'd done with her, didn't truly make a shit now. He'd had enough discussions with the so-called Wyatt to know that the man and his partner would come after him whether he had the girl or not.

"Thanks for all your efforts, Slick Ray. I consider you a true friend. You did all you could." Sampson observed Slick Ray exhale a sigh of relief.

"You fear me, Slick Ray. I can tell. You shouldn't. I'm depending heavily on you to help me to win this war with the Outlaws."

"I want to help you get it done, Sampson."

"I know you do, and . . . it's time to get it done. Do you fully understand what I have planned? At this point, we can't afford another fuck up."

"I do, Sampson. I have no questions. If I did, I'd ask them."

Slick Ray did not have Thumper's ego, and Sampson believed him. "Okay. Get all the players in place. That 'Wyatt' fucker is calling every morning now. When he calls in the morning, I'll invite him out tomorrow evening. They won't even know what hit them."

Slick Ray turned and started toward the door.

"Hey, Slick Ray, do you know where Thumper stashed the lever-action rifles?"

His new lieutenant turned and smiled triumphantly. "I know where they are. They're ready to go, and we have plenty of ammo."

For the first time in many hours, Sampson threw back his head and let go the mighty Sampson laugh.

* * * *

Melinda Lollar drew tired of chasing sleep, and pushed from her bed to go out on the porch for a cigarette. The clock had not yet struck midnight, but it seemed much later to Melinda. All through the day, even more than most days, she'd missed her Trey.

She stepped out on the porch and looked up at a nearly full moon as she thumbed a Bic to light her Marlboro. She found some comfort in knowing the same moon hung over her man's head. It served to connect them.

Not until she lowered her head to exhale her first deep drag did she notice the lone figure way out in the drive, facing the north. She immediately recognized the slouched form of Bingo, doing some kind of strange dance. He looked to be stomping things on the ground while waving his hands over a head that bobbed and swayed.

"Bingo?" she called, "What in God's name are you doing out there?"

He turned and started to jog her way. Melinda could not help but laugh. He seldom took a walking step.

"You're up awfully late, Mrs. Remington," Bingo said as he stopped at the foot of the steps.

"You are, too, Bingo. What were you doing out there?"

Bingo smiled in a shy manner. "Did I ever tell you that I have pernitions?"

"Pernitions?" Melinda repeated.

"Yeah, sometimes I can see into the future."

Melinda had to think about it a moment. "Do you mean, premonitions, Bingo?"

"Uh-huh, that's it. Have problems remembering how to say it."

Melinda took one long final drag off the cigarette and flipped it away. "Okay, what kind of premonition did you have, Bingo?"

"I saw in my mind that things are coming to a head up there in Chicago. So, I was making a good-luck offering to the boys. When you hollered at me, I was doing a Comanche war dance for John.

Melinda swallowed back an urge to giggle. "How did you know how to do a Comanche war dance?"

"Don't really. Just let the spirits move me."

Melinda did allow a fond smile. "Well, Bingo, looked like you were doing a fine job at it. What, uh, good-luck offering did you have in mind for Trey?"

Bingo displayed an index finger in the air before turning to jog back to where he'd stomped and jiggled. He bent to retrieve something from the ground and jogged back. He held the bottle of whiskey up for Melinda to observe.

"You know how Trey likes his whiskey. Was going to take some mighty swigs for him."

As she'd found herself tempted to do over the past weeks, she just wanted to hug and squeeze Bingo. She would of too, if he only bathed more often. Or ever.

"Bingo, if I go in and get a glass, could I swig some with you?"

"Why you damn sure can," Bingo grinned.

"Would you like a glass to drink from, too?"

"No, ma'am, think it might lose some of its power if I didn't swig it from the bottle like I've seen Trey do."

Melinda nodded her head a couple of times before moving down the steps. She sat down on the bottom one, and patted the vacant spot beside her. "Have a sit, Bingo, and we'll just pass the bottle."

They both took several swigs apiece before she asked a question that burned in her heart even more than the whiskey burned in her throat. "Bingo, do you have a feeling they'll need a lot of good luck?"

"Aw, heck, Mrs. Remington, everybody needs some good luck, but those two, they don't need all that much. They'll be back. I seen that in my pre . . . uh . . . that word."

He handed the bottle back to Melinda, and she took another hit.

"I'm ready for them to be back, Bingo."

Bingo nodded his head with enthusiasm. "Me too . . . except . . . "

Melinda waited for him to continue, but he didn't. "Except what, Bingo?" she asked.

"Except, I sure am going to miss this place. Never had such a nice house to live in. And . . . I'm going to miss you, too. Never had a little sister, but if I did, I'd want her to be just like you."

She'd drank from the same bottle, so what the hell? She swiveled so she could wrap both arms around Bingo to give him a most hearty hug. He sure needed a bath, but at the moment, it didn't make any difference to Melinda. Bingo nearly dropped the bottle.

"Bingo, you aren't going any place. This is your home as long you want it to be."

Bingo bent to place the bottle in the ground, and then wiped at his eyes with both hands. "Darn it, Mrs. Remington, think I got something in my eyes. I ain't crying or nothing."

Melinda let go with the giggle, "Think I got something in mine as well, Bingo."

* * * *

Marcus Jones moved silently through his dark apartment with a tall glass of whiskey in one hand and his departmental issued Glock in the other. He walked back into Trisha's room and sat down on the chair he'd moved to the side of her bed a few minutes earlier. He placed the glass of whiskey on the floor at his feet and laid the pistol in his lap in order to remove a pack of cigarettes from a shirt pocket. Jones tapped one out of the pack, put it between his lips, and lit it with a Zippo. He drew smoke deep into his lungs, held it there until it stung, and then exhaled toward the ceiling.

He brought the cigarette up to his face to stare at it, then he looked toward the still form sleeping in the bed. Trisha struggled to breath. She always did. Jones turned his eyes back to the burning cigarette.

"Guess the last think you have to worry about, baby, is second-hand smoke," Jones whispered. He picked the glass up from the floor and took a long swallow.

"Haven't told you, dear Trisha, but we're rich now. We have all the money we could ever want," Jones paused to chuckle bitterly before continuing. "But, sadly, there's not enough money in this whole world to fix you. To make you whole. To make you where you don't hurt all the time. And, there's not enough money anywhere to change what Daddy has done . . . or what Daddy's thinking about doing right now."

Jones stared down at the gun resting on his lap. "Sweet baby, Daddy has done just a horrible thing, and if the right people find out about it, Daddy will be going away. Probably forever. And you? Poor little innocent you? Well, they'll put you away, too."

Tears started to stream down Jones' face. "I've always feared that you are like you are, because I'm like I am. That's the reason I've always done my best to take care of you."

He began to sob. "I just can't imagine you being in a *home.* Because where they'd put you is not really a *home.*"

Jones swiped at his nose and eyes before snuffing out the cigarette in a tray on Trisha's nightstand. He took another gulp from the glass. Then he picked the gun up off his lap and studied it closely before closing his eyes. He started to quake.

"Oh, Dear God, I know what I should do, but I never have done what I should do, or *should not do.*"

Jones slowly pushed to his feet, leaned over the bed, and placed the barrel of the Glock to his daughter's head.

"And now, once again, I'm just too much of a coward to do what should be done."

Detective Sergeant Marcus Jones, raised the gun, and stumbled from his beloved Trisha's room. Because of his inadequacy, they would *both* live to struggle through yet another day.

* * * *

"So sorry. Did I wake you up?"

Sampson rolled over to look at the clock beside his bed. "It's five a.m., asshole, what do you think?"

"Think I'm ready to dance this dance, Sampson."

Sampson sat up in the bed. "You mean, Wyatt, you're ready to die?"

"Did you ever see the movie, Tombstone, Sampson?"

"As a matter of fact, I watched it in prison."

"Good. Then you'll understand when I say . . . *I'm your huckleberry.*"

Sampson forced laughter. "I never knew what that meant, Wyatt. Explain it to me."

"In this case it means this, Sampson. Unless you're just a punk-ass coward, a sniveling bitch, a frightened little . . . "

Sampson shot out of the bed and bellowed into the phone. "Tonight, motherfucker! You be here at eleven. I want you two dead by midnight. Are you ready to copy down where to find me?"

"Got a pen in hand," Wyatt chuckled.

Sampson gave explicit directions, and then said, "Tonight, you meet your match."

Then he cringed at the sound of Wyatt laughing heartily.

"Tonight, Sampson . . . you meet *The Outlaws.*"

* * * *

"You don't have no pen in your hand," Ledford grinned.

Remington laughed at the comment. "Well, guess I lied. Had to. Couldn't tell the silly son of a bitch that we know where he's at, and we're only minutes away."

"Liked the huckleberry part," Ledford smiled.

Remington liked the fact John proved to be in such high spirits. "Well, I enjoyed it when you quoted a line from the movie to Detective Scully. Thought I'd try my hand at it as well."

J.D. Roach jumped in to ruin the fun. "Well, if it's okay with you two to drop the O.K. Corral horseshit, I'll let you know that all is a go. Every team member and all equipment are here on the ground. The Hummer's special provisions have been inspected and tested, and we've vacated and closed out all locations within Chicago proper. Final recon of the kill site will be conducted at 2130 hours. We'll do a complete comms check at that time. Air transportation is scheduled for 0600 in the morning to carry your happy asses back to the Brazos. Any questions?"

"Will you be flying back with us, J.D.?" Ledford asked.

"Do you want me to?"

"Not really," Ledford grinned. "I intend to be in one hell of a fine mood and don't want you pissing on my parade."

SEVENTEEN

"One hour to go, Sampson," Slick Ray said as walked in the front door with his lever-action rifle in hand.

Sampson didn't need the reminder. This day seemed to have the life span of three. "Everyone and everything is in place?" he asked.

"Sure is. The drive is blocked. They'll have to park that magic Hummer way up front, and walk in. Unless it can fly."

Sampson chuckled, and it worked to release a little tension. "You blocked it with the two big fallen trees and the log chain?"

"Just like you said to do, but also parked that giant old tractor behind all that, and removed the battery."

Sampson nodded his approval for good thinking. "And the men?"

"Lined up on both sides of the drive. Five on one side, five on the other. Lying flat on their bellies outside the reach of that old light on the tall pole. I stood beneath the light, and could not see any of them. When the Outlaws walk beneath that light, they'll open fire. Once they hit the ground, they'll stop firing. With any luck at all, both will still be alive for you to finish off."

Sampson liked the sound of that. It would be his pleasure, and he would do it in a grand way. And the word would spread. Sampson would be the newly crowned king who reestablished street gang control of Chicago.

"Could you see me at the window earlier?" Sampson asked.

"Nope. The lights in this part of the house leaves that far room dark as hell. You'll have a great view from there, Sampson."

"We, Slick Ray," Sampson grinned. "We will have a great view. You'll be right at my side."

"That makes me proud," Slick Ray grinned back.

Soon enough, in less than an hour, Slick Ray wouldn't be the only one trying to stroke Sampson's ego. Everyone loves a king.

* * * *

Remington opened the rear door of the Hummer and used the small flashlight to illuminate the interior. Any small army in the world would envy the arsenal arranged on secure racks. So far, they'd used very little of the "provisions" they'd asked for to stock the moving gun safe. Still, it'd been there all along just in case it was needed. Tonight, some of what had not been used would be. Not necessarily because it was needed, but just to make a statement.

Remington took out the two small wonders of technology first, then reached back in and removed the first impressive weapon, and handed it back to Ledford. He heard his partner whistle approval. Remington removed another for himself and handed it back to Ledford to hold. He then removed the final selection for the first stage of the assault, and used the sling to attach it across the back of his shoulders. He closed the door and turned to take his weapon back from Ledford.

"Are you ready?" Remington asked.

"Couldn't be more ready."

Remington moved his head in close to Ledford's face to once again gaze at the alteration of his appearance.

"Damn, must say again, partner, that is some wicked camouflage."

"No," Ledford grinned. "Powerful medicine."

Remington grinned back at him before taking a few steps away. He pushed the button on the device attached to the lapel of his duster. "Alpha One to Control One, radio check."

"Loud and clear, Alpha One," Remington clearly heard J.D. Roach respond through his earpiece. Then he heard Ledford.

"Alpha Two to Control One, radio check."

"Loud and clear, Alpha Two."

Remington walked back over to Ledford. "Care to join me in a little shock and awe?"

"My loins tingle to do so," Ledford deadpanned.

* * * *

"One minute to go," Sampson exhaled heavily as he squatted at the right side of the window.

"Should see their headlights anytime now," Slick Ray replied.

Sampson picked up on the slight quiver in his voice, and damn sure understood.

"I'd expect them two to be right on time," Sampson said, fighting to keep his own quivering at bay.

Sampson had his attention focused on the small piece of drive lit by the light on the pole. He knew Slick Ray did the same. At that spot, they'd get their first glimpse of the Outlaws just before all hell broke loose.

Then the light just went out.

"What the hell happened to the light?" Sampson bellowed.

"Don't know," Slick Ray truly quivered.

Longs seconds ticked by without anything happening. Just enough time to allow Sampson to almost believe the light simply burned out.

"What do we do now, Sampson?"

What they'd done so far seemed to be the only alternative. "We continue to wait," he grumbled.

"Oh shit," Slick Ray moaned.

"What is it? You see something?" Sampson rattled off loudly.

"A couple of our guys . . . They're moving around."

"Fucking idiots!" Sampson bellowed.

"Sampson, I told them over and over just like you said. I told them not to move for a damned thing. I told them . . . "

And *there was light.* But not from on top the pole. This light flashed and spewed in quick bursts from both sides of the drive, and it had a sound.

TRRRUPPP . . . TRRRUPPP . . . TRRRUPPP . . . TRRRUPPP . . .

"Fucking machine guns!" Sampson screamed as he dove for the floor.

Slick Ray pressed facedown beside him. "The Outlaws using machine guns?" He screamed. "But that's the reason you wanted . . . "

"SHUT THE FUCK UP, SLICK RAY!"

The automatic weapons fire continued only for a few more seconds, but Sampson knew it went on long enough to leave ten dead. When the noise stopped, silence reigned for or so long, that Sampson wished for more noise, but not from Slick Ray.

"What do you think they're doing out there, Sampson?"

Sampson had a good idea, and maybe sharing it would shut Slick Ray up so Sampson could think. "They are cutting off balls, Slick Ray."

He felt his lieutenant start to shiver next to him.

More silence and more waiting, and nothing came to mind for Sampson to do about it. He considered slowly rising up to peek over the window ledge, but didn't care to take a bullet to the forehead. Suddenly, his true leadership philosophy kicked into gear.

"Slick Ray!"

"Yeah?"

"Peek out the window. See if you can see them."

Slick Ray didn't offer a response and didn't move a muscle. Sampson pulled the big revolver out of his waist band and jabbed it into Slick Ray's ribs. "Get up and peek out the window."

"Hell, they might shoot me!"

"And you don't think I will?" Sampson hissed.

Slick Ray didn't get a chance to respond before a phone started ringing in the living room.

The Wyatt phone.

"Forget the window, Slick Ray. Go get that phone," Sampson ordered.

"I'm going to crawl on my belly!"

"I don't give a damn if you do somersaults, just get the fucking phone!"

Sampson seethed during the time it took for Slick Ray to retrieve the phone. His guts boiled with hatred. He would not let this be the end. Slick Ray thrust the phone in his hand, and Sampson stuck it to the side of his head.

"You just won the first battle, Wyatt," he stormed. "But this war is far from over!"

A long silence, and then light laughter. "Lever-action rifles, Sampson? What the hell were you thinking?"

Sampson clamped down on the grips of the revolver in his hand.

A fucking revolver?

He'd chosen it for the same reason he'd chosen the rifles. Now he so wished for an automatic with a fifteen-round magazine.

"Fuck you, Wyatt!" he spat.

"Oh, there is so much you need to know, dear Sampson. First of all, my name's not really Wyatt. The second thing, we intercepted all your calls, and bugged that house. We knew everything you planned. I know that until the bullets started flying, you were watching from a window in the far east room. Oh, and Charmane, she's safely back with P-Wac. Now, go ahead and rant and rave like the lunatic you are, Sampson."

Sampson could feel his mouth hanging open. All those facts just numbed his mind. At the moment, he couldn't work up a rant or a rave. "So what happens now?" he asked.

"One of two things. You can come out, and we'll go ahead and kill you. Kind of in a nice way. Or, we'll give you a fighting chance."

"Why would you do that?"

"Which one, Sampson? Kill you or give you a fighting chance?"

"Both. Why don't you just turn me over to the cops?" Sampson expected laughter in return, but the other man's voice sounded solemn.

"You've been to prison before, Sampson. Didn't help you none. You're an evil man that deserves to die. Best I can do for you, is let you choose how it happens."

"Well, I'm damn sure not going to let you just kill me. I'll take that fighting chance, and I intend to send you to hell. You made me kill Thumper, MOTHERFUCKER!"

"Okay, Sampson. You'll get your chance. The dude in there with you, Slick Ray, if you want him to come out the front door, we'll let him live. Just to tell the tale."

"He stays with me," Sampson hissed between gritted teeth.

"Have it your way, Sampson. By the way, are you familiar with a M23A1 MSGL?"

"What the hell are you talking about?"

"I'll take that as a no. So, first you might hear a pop, and then . . . hang on to your ass. Oh, and the next time we talk, it'll be face to face."

Sampson slung the phone across the room.

"What did he say, Sampson?" Slick Ray nearly panted.

Sampson thought a few seconds before responding. "He said if we come out the front door, they won't kill us."

* * * *

"Sounded like you tried to talk him into the easy way of going, Trey" Ledford objected.

The two stood side by side behind a huge tree standing about forty yards from the front of the farmhouse. Remington had felt John tensing up as he talked to Sampson on the phone. "Yeah, kind of varied from the script, but there for a moment, he sounded so pathetic, but then he went back to being an asshole. He's willing to let the other man in there die for him."

"Well, I'm glad he didn't choose option one," Ledford grumbled. "We could have killed him the easy way days ago. We waited to make an example that other scum would not forget. I'm determined to make that example."

Remington handed John his M4A1, just like the ones they'd used in Afghanistan, and removed the M32A1 Multi-Shot Grenade Launcher, or MSGL, from his shoulder.

"Okay, you'll sure get to make that example, Trey."

Although the grenade launcher could hold six rounds, this one only contained one 40-millimeter low velocity grenade.

"Are you ready to take off for the horses?" Remington asked.

"Yup, but want to see the fireworks first."

"Then get ready to giggle," Remington said, as he raised the launcher to his shoulder and stepped from behind the tree.

* * * *

Sampson did indeed here a "POP."

A moment later the living room seemed to erupt like a volcano.

The sound deafened Sampson to a point where he could barely hear Slick Ray, lying next to him, start screaming. The lights in the living room went out, but were replaced by the bright glow of blazing furniture.

Sampson jumped to his feet, and pulled Slick Ray up with him. He shoved him out in front of him toward the enflamed living room.

"Run to the front door, Slick Ray!" Sampson bellowed. "It's over! Let's get out of here!"

They dodged the things that burned. The smoke seemed to singe Sampson's lungs, but he made the effort to step around Slick Ray just before they reached the front door.

"I have to save you, Slick Ray. They won't shoot. Get the fuck out!" Sampson screamed as he jerked the front door open, gave Slick Ray a mighty shove . . . and slammed the door shut behind him.

TRRRUPPP . . . TRRRUPPP . . .

Sampson both heard and felt Slick Ray's body being slammed back against the shut door.

Fuck him. A casualty of war.

Once again dodging the flames, Sampson sprinted toward the back of the house, and didn't slow down when he reached the back door. He practically ripped it off its hinges, and sprinted into the darkness toward the woods at the back of the old house.

* * * *

"Control Two to Alpha Team, Dead Man took primary escape route."

Remington pushed his button, "Alpha One to Control Two, roger that."

Remington and Ledford quickly passed off the M4A1s to J.D. in exchange for their Winchester rifles. They both leapt onto their horses, and engaged the small devices Remington first retrieved from the back of the Hummer. The night vision goggles suddenly turned the dark into a glow of green.

"Control Three to Alpha Team, have Dead Man in sight . . . "

Remington and Ledford noted the direction of travel as both spurred their horses to take different routes at a slow trot.

Remington pushed his button again. "Let the games begin!"

"Alpha One this is Control Four. Already began. First obstacles now in place."

* * * *

Dumb asses concentrated all their efforts on the front of the house.

But Sampson knew they'd eventually look for him in the woods. For now, he continued to jog down a dark and narrow trail once travelled by cattle. Deep undergrowth had spread beneath the trees over the years since the livestock were removed, making it difficult for a man on foot to do anything but stay on the trail.

Sampson could not run forever. He had nowhere to run. But he did have the pistol, and he did have six bullets in the .357 magnum. His only chance of survival dictated that he set his own ambush. He only needed the right spot to wait in hiding. He planned to keep jogging until stumbling into the right spot.

Then he did stumble. Too dark to see the form on the ground that tripped him, and sent him tumbling until he landed face down on another form.

A dead body.

No. Ten dead bodies, stacked in a line.

Sampson's men. He suddenly felt if the fall paralyzed his ability to reason. How in the hell did they get the bodies back here so quickly? A fact quickly trumped the question.

They expected me to run down this path.

Sampson spun in circles while struggling against near panic. It made no sense. How the hell did two men always know his next move? Now that all but Sampson was dead, how did they know he'd run out the back and into the woods? How did just two men get ten bodies deep into the woods so damned quickly?

His mind settled on answering the only question it could. They knew he'd run out the back door for the simple reason that he had nowhere else to run. On the other questions, his mind sent him to the recent past words of a dear friend.

". . . I mean, there are all kinds of people everywhere now that believe they have like super powers. Or super natural powers . . . "

For the first time, Sampson believed such as well. It had been these powers that tricked him into killing dear Thumper, and that forced him to sacrifice Slick Ray's life. Sampson shared no responsibility for any of the deaths of his men. The two super beings were totally to blame.

Sampson might have stood idly in tortured contemplation longer had he not recognized a sound he'd only heard on television and movies.

The clomping of horses' hooves pounding the ground.

His peripheral vision provided movement to his right. Sampson spun to catch a fleeting glimpse of a shadowy rider on horseback. Far too late, Sampson brought up the pistol and fired his first round. The explosion of the heavy round still reverberated in his ears when motion on his left caught his attention. He swirled in place and shot another round at a quickly disappearing silhouette of horse and rider.

"Fuck! Come out and fight, you bastards!" Sampson screamed.

Behind him, and no doubt on the trail, he again heard the pounding of fast moving hooves. Sampson tore off in a dead run straight ahead. The sound grew in intensity behind him, and he didn't make it far before he made out the terrifying site of a mounted man coming straight at him on a stampeding horse. Sampson stopped, raised the pistol and jerked off another round, but not before the horse and rider to the front shot off to his left into the heavy underbrush. Sampson spun in place and fired again toward the one he'd heard behind him, just as that one leaped into the brush on the opposite side of the road.

Now his mind and heart raced as fast as the two men on horses. He gave no thought about taking off in a run in the same direction he'd moved since vacating the burning house. He ran until his legs simply gave out, and he crumbled to his knees. Sampson dropped his head and fought to pull air into his lungs. Just as he started to realize some relief, a voice called from the darkness on his left.

"Over here, Sampson!"

Sampson shot at the spot from which he thought the voice called. The echoing of taunting laughter proved he'd not struck his target. He pushed to his feet, and just started again, when a voice rang out from his right side.

"You missed him, Sampson."

"FUCK YOU!" Sampson bellowed as he fired to his right.

No one laughed this time, and Sampson took that as a hopeful signaling of a shot well placed. He started off in a run again, but every bone in his body ached, slowing him considerably. He ran until . . .

. . . nearly running smack dab into a horse's ass. He could not help but laughing out loud as he raised the revolver and aimed at the back of the very close rider.

Click. Click. Click.

He'd not counted his rounds. Sampson slung the revolver into the woods and turned to run in the opposite direction. He took only steps before spotting the mounted man that blocked the path.

"Turn around and follow the horse in front of you, Sampson," a voice he'd never heard ordered. "Try to run off this trail, and I'll have my horse stomp you to death. It's a brutal way to go."

It wasn't "Wyatt," that spoke, but Sampson did not doubt his warning. Wearily, he turned, and followed the horse and rider to his front.

"Wyatt! Is that you in front of me, Wyatt?" Sampson exhaled heavily.

It took long seconds, but a response finally came.

"I told you, I'm not Wyatt. My name is Trey Remington. The man behind you is John Ledford."

"What are you going to do with me?" Sampson shouted.

"We are going to give you that fighting chance," Remington chuckled.

"What if I don't fight?" Sampson responded.

The horse to his front stopped, and the rider turned the horse slowly in place in a tight circle. For the first time, Sampson looked into the face of his opponent.

"I thought you dudes wore bandana's," Sampson sneered. "Not night vision goggles. Doesn't do much to cover your face"

"No sense in doing so now, Sampson. Dead men don't give descriptions."

"So, what are you going to do if I don't fight?" Sampson snarled again.

The man leaned forward in his saddle to rest in a relaxed manner on the knob like thing that jutted up from the front of the saddle. "You're a rapist, Sampson, and a murderer. How many women have you murdered?"

"Ain't none of your business, asshole," Sampson thundered.

"Oh, yes it is. Consider this your last chance to stand before judge and jury. What's the worst way you ever killed a woman, Sampson?"

Sampson forced loud laughter. "I'll play your game you, motherfucker. You name it, I've done it. One time made one drink battery acid. Stomped another to death. So the fuck what?"

"What was the youngest age of girl or boy you ever raped?"

Sampson threw back his head and laughed. If they wanted the truth, they'd get it. "As best I remember, she was seven."

"As the jury, Sampson, I find you worthy of death," the man on the lead horse said before sitting up straight in the saddle and raising his head up high. "John," he called to the man behind Sampson, "being the judge, if Sampson here decides not to fight, what do you declare his punishment?"

A stern voice responded at Sampson's back, "If he will not die like a man, I declare a rope be tied to each leg, and he painfully be ripped in two by slow moving horses."

Before Sampson could reel about and curse his "judge," the lead man laughed heartily. "So, Sampson, do you wish to die like a man, or be torn apart by horses?"

Sampson pulled bitter breath into his lungs. "I'll fight you two bitches!" he bellowed.

"No," the lead man chuckled, "You'll only fight one of us. And may God have mercy on your pitiful soul."

"I only have to fight one of you?" Sampson questioned.

"You will fight only John, the man behind you, Sampson."

"And if I win, I'm set free?" Sampson again questioned.

"That's a tremendous 'if,' but we will grant that."

Sampson threw back his head and bellowed out laughter. He'd never met a single man he could not best in one-on-one combat.

"Let's do it right here and right now," he thundered.

"No. Not in the plan, Sampson," the lead man said. "We are going to fade into the darkness, but you will continue down this path. You will know where to stop. If you turn and run in the other direction, we will let the horses do the privilege of ripping you into two gory pieces."

The man at his back, John, spoke again. "Consider this lone walk you will take as your path to the hereafter. Use it to contemplate the horrors you've committed . . . and the fires of hell that wait to consume you for eternity."

Sampson spun around to tell the asshole to go fuck himself, but he viewed nothing but darkness. He wheeled back around to spew profanities at the lead man, but he'd disappeared into the black of night as well.

EIGHTEEN

Sampson didn't contemplate a damned thing about his past as he stomped down the dark trail. He concentrated instead on the very near future. He didn't fear dying, but only because he didn't think he would. If those assholes were the crusaders for the good and upright that everyone thought, Sampson depended on them to keep their word. All he had to do was win some kind of fight, and he'd be set free. Sampson had not lost any kind of fight since the age of fourteen. He fantasized about this one being a fight to the death. Sampson found he currently held a lot of pent up anger. He longed for a release. He'd discovered by the life he led that nothing released anger like beating a man to death. Or, a woman, as far as that went.

Sampson stomped and fumed and flexed until the moment the trail spit him out into a large clearing. From where he stood and what he could see, it seemed like some sort of arena. A killing field. Just yards in front of him, Sampson could make out a tremendous brush pile, as if someone expected a bonfire. The thought barely came to mind, when Sampson heard something like an electrical popping. Right in front of his eyes, the mountainous pile of branches and logs ignited, blazing as if doused with gasoline. The flames lit up the night.

Startled, Sampson jumped, but landed in a crouch. He surveyed the area lit by the inferno. Seconds later, a lone figure stepped from the outer shadows and into the light. Sampson could make out the western style hat, and the long coat that nearly touched the ground. The figure started his way, taking long and confident strides. The man did not stop until Sampson could clearly see his face, but did stop short of Sampson's reach.

"I'm Trey Remington. The man you knew as Wyatt," the man said in an eerily calm voice.

"So, you're the one I get to fight?" Sampson said, adding a chuckle.

"No. I already told you that you will fight John. I'm here now only to prepare you for what lies ahead."

"Well, then, get to preparing me, bitch," Sampson snickered, but then could not help but ask, "But first . . . how did that fire start on its own? How the *fuck* do you two do the things you do?"

"You will soon know all, Sampson."

* * * *

Remington so wanted to be the one who ended the scum's life, but knew John wanted it even more.

No. John needed it more.

Remington pulled back his duster to expose the two pistols carried in cross-drawl fashion, butts forward in Slim Jim holsters. He reached with his right hand to remove the one on his left hip.

"Fuck this shit, man," Sampson bellowed, "I don't have a fucking gun!"

Remington slowly removed the Colt .45 and extended it butt first toward Sampson.

"Take it, and you will have a gun," Remington said, and could not help but grinning. "This one that I offer, has killed many of your kind."

Sampson proved damn weary of taking the Colt.

"Don't worry. I won't kill you with the other, unless you force me to."

Please force me to.

Sampson slowly reached to take the old revolver.

"Now, here's what we are going to do," Remington grinned again. "What you hold is a single-action army Colt. That means you have to cock the hammer before the trigger can be pulled."

Remington watched with amusement as Sampson studied the gun in his hand.

"I am going to allow you, Sampson, when you are ready, to raise the gun, point it at me, cock the hammer, and try to pull the trigger."

"What the fuck?" Sampson exclaimed. "Why the fuck are we doing this?"

"Just to prove a point," Remington chuckled, before starting to slowly raise his right hand until it hovered parallel with the ground. "See, here's the deal, you have the gun in your hand. All you have to do is raise it, point it, cock it, and pull the trigger. I am at a disadvantage, because I have to lower my hand, pull my gun, cock it, and pull the trigger. I'm ready when you are, Sampson."

Sampson started with, "Fuck, man, I don't know the first thing about . . . "

. . . Before he abruptly turned his effort toward using the old Colt.

His tactic did not deceive Remington. Before Sampson could as much as raise the Colt, Remington dropped his arm to reach across his body, pulled, cocked, and leveled his revolver mere inches from Sampson's forehead.

"If this had not been a test, Sampson, what few brains you have would be scattered to the winds."

"And what exactly are you testing, motherfucker?" Sampson spat.

The flames of the fire illuminated the concern in the giant of a man's eyes.

"A test of your dexterity and quickness, Sampson. When compared to my partner, I'm damn slow. Way I see it, big man, you're in a hell of a fix."

"So, I go through this same bullshit with him?" Sampson stormed.

"No," Remington laughed. "John Ledford won't use a gun. He's very proud of his Comanche heritage. He's chosen a more traditional way to kill you."

Remington watched Sampson draw in several deep breaths before asking, "Well, where the hell is the bastard?"

Remington extended his hand. "Give me my gun."

Sampson seemed all too ready to give it up. Remington thrust both Colt's back into their holsters before slowly raising a hand to point at the blazing brush.

"He's right there."

* * * *

Sampson cut his eyes toward the bonfire, and did not at first see anything but roaring flames. Then a form moved from behind the inferno to make its presence known.

The intense glow of burning brush illuminated a man nearly Sampson's size, with shoulder length hair, and bare from the waist up. Sampson's eyes were initially drawn to the deep cuts of muscularity that defined the man's upper torso. Only when the man stepped closer did Sampson notice the bright colors that decorated his face.

War paint.

Sampson had seen it in movies, and recognized it now, but forced himself to deny the psychological impact.

"Didn't now I'd be attending a masquerade party," he huffed, forcing his voice to remain calm.

"You jest about the customs of my people?" the man all but whispered.

"It doesn't mean shit to me," Sampson lied.

"My white man's name is John Ledford. Easier for you to remember than my Indian name. When you enter hell, you can tell them John sent you."

"You have a lot to do that hasn't been done to send me to hell, Indian," Sampson found the gumption to say.

"You have a knife on you that you always carry. Feel free to pull it now," Ledford announced serenely.

Sampson had not failed to see the large knife sheathed on Ledford's waist. "Don't need no knife, unless you pull yours," he announced.

"The knife I wear took the life of someone dear to me, and then it ended the life of one of your kind. I will not pull it until you are finished."

"Fuck this bullshit!" Sampson bellowed before rushing the long-hair wearing silly make-up, and talking like some asshole from the past.

* * * *

At the last second, Ledford simply sidestepped the charging man, and turned in preparation for Sampson's next move.

Sampson spun as well, but did not charge again. Instead, he stood in place snorting like a bull before bringing up powerful hands to literally rip his shirt right off his back.

"When I get my hands on you, I won't need horses to rip you into two pieces," Sampson shouted.

Ledford observed the man's heavily muscled torso, and didn't doubt his ability to cause great damage. However, he also knew Sampson could not rip what he could not hold onto. Ledford moved in close.

Sampson lunged with his arms posed to grab. Ledford ducked beneath the reaching arms and landed a stout jab to Sampson's left kidney. The huge man arched his back and bellowed in pain. Ledford circled to use only an index finger to compound his agony.

Sampson screamed in pain and pressed a hand to his left eye that Ledford gouged. Ledford took steps backwards and simply waited for Sampson to recuperate. He did not move an inch when Sampson lunged again. This time the raging hulk used his fists. He threw a hook with the left. Ledford block it with a forearm. He threw a hook with his right that Ledford blocked with his other forearm. Sampson jabbed with first his left fist and then his right. Ledford just bobbed his head to escape both attempts. Then Sampson tried to land an undercut with his left, and Ledford did not choose evasive action.

He caught Sampson's left wrist, brought up a knee, and used it to snap Sampson's arm like a twig. Ledford spun to the side as Sampson bent to cradle the broken arm while screaming in pain. Now behind the bent and wailing man, Ledford delivered a crushing hatchet kick to Sampson's coccyx, and Sampson crumbled to his knees.

Ledford circled to Sampson's front. "I hoped you'd be more of a challenge."

"Fuck you," Sampson gasped.

"Are you so soon ready to die? You're not even bleeding yet."

Sampson slowly raised his head to glare into Ledford's face.

"No. But you soon will be."

* * * *

Sampson could barely see out his left eye, and his kidney still ached like living hell. Severe pain radiated through the entire length of his left arm, but he let go of it with his right, allowing it to drop to his side. He could not help but scream once again at the pain this caused. He used his one good arm to push to his feet, and cried out yet again because of the intense torture of a crushed coccyx bone. He managed to stand, but swayed on his feet.

"Are the voices of those you've destroyed calling your name yet, Sampson?" the painted man asked.

Sampson saved his strength in order to remove the knife from his belt.

"I was hoping it would come to this," the white Indian said, but he did not pull his knife.

Sampson lunged.

He jabbed.

He slashed.

And his blade never touched skin.

In a final act of desperation, he brought the knife over his head, and slung it with all the strength he had left.

And it stuck.

* * * *

Ledford stumbled backwards. Momentarily, his mind could not grasp the turn of events, but pain served to bring him to his senses. He craned his neck to look down at his right shoulder. The knife protruded from the space between his shoulder and chest, buried to the hilt. He looked up just in time to see Sampson stumbling toward him. Ledford moved in to make contact.

His right arm now did him no good, so he could no longer continue this game of cat and mouse.

"Now you are mine, motherfucker!" Sampson declared.

Ledford's neck fell prey to a very large hand that grasped and squeezed like a vice.

Still, Ledford managed to laugh.

Then he effectively went to work with his left forearm and elbow along with legs and knees. The forearm dislodged the hand that grasped his throat. As a continuation of that maneuver, he crushed his elbow into Sampson's left temple while simultaneously sending his right knee into Sampson's crotch. Ledford spun in place to practically drive his left foot clear through Sampson's right knee. The giant toppled and fell face forward to the ground.

* * * *

Sampson now only knew his face rested against the ground. He did not know how he'd ended up here. Moments before, he moved in to finish off the man with a knife sticking out of his body. What followed was just a blur, but Sampson did know that his body might as well be dead. Nothing on it seemed to work. All it could do was provide terrible, awful pain. Pain that he could only relate to . . .

Inez Kelly

He could not prove it at the time, but the sixteen-year-old bitch snitched him off to the cops. Even after he'd taken her in and taught her the fine arts of pleasing a man. Oh, did he give her a beating that day. Once she lay on the floor unable to move, he slowly twisted and snapped each and every finger of both hands. Then he poured a pitcher of ice water on her face to rouse her. He needed her to be awake for the "love making." After he finished, she hurt so bad, that she begged him to kill her. Instead, he used a butter knife to slowly and deeply carve a swastika into her forehead. Later, the weak bitch ended up killing herself.

At the moment, Sampson still felt no remorse, but he did now understand how much she must have hurt. He now realized how one could welcome death in order to be free of a deep and ugly hurt. Yet . . .

I don't want to die.

Because maybe . . . death is not the true ending.

Suddenly a dreaded realization tortured Sampson more than his left eye, and kidney, and broken arm, and crushed coccyx, and smashed balls, and destroyed knee.

"I don't want to face God," he heard himself mumble.

"I don't want to see *Inez Kelly,*" he babbled.

Then Sampson felt his head being turned and felt hands grasp his ears. He wailed in torment as the grip on his ears was used to pull him up and onto his knees. He felt himself teeter, but the hands on his ears held him upright. The different kind of torment of being lifted by his ears, helped to clear his mind and eyesight.

"John" kneeled in front of him, both on their knees, face to face. Sampson momentarily averted his eyes. Yes, the knife still protruded from John's upper chest. Sampson again looked him in the eyes, but did not note a trace of pain.

"Look over my shoulder," John ordered.

Sampson did not immediately understand. John briskly slapped his face.

"Look over my shoulder," he repeated.

Sampson understood this time, and did as told. He counted. Several yards behind John, nine men stood shoulder to shoulder. Sampson only recognized the other outlaw, Trey something. Realization slowly penetrated his groggy mind.

"Ten of you . . . hell, you're not . . . super human. It never was twelve of us against two of you. It was ten of you against twelve of us. That's, uh . . . fucking unfair."

"Look at me," John hissed.

Sampson looked from the line of men and back into the serious eyes surrounded by war paint. He watched as John raised a wicked looking hunting knife, and waved it beneath Sampson's nose.

"A woman, who would of one day been my wife, took her life with this knife because of a wicked man like you."

Sampson looked from the knife and once again concentrated on the eyes of the warrior. He forced a smile.

"Fuck you, John, and . . . fuck her as well."

The words did not change the expression on the face in front of him.

"Kind of expected that from you," John said before offering his own smile. He then raised his empty hand, and placed it around the handle of Sampson's knife stuck deep in his flesh. Without as much as a whimper or grimace, he slowly pulled the knife out of his body.

Sampson stiffened and inhaled a jagged breath as John brought up a knife in each hand, one dripping with his own blood, and inserted just the sharp tips into the opening of Sampson's ears.

"Sampson . . . go to hell."

Sampson felt the slow and initial pressure of the knives penetrating flesh. He brought up his one good hand and placed it for a second time around John's throat. Before he could apply pressure . .

.

The flames from the bonfire somehow penetrated deep within his head.

Like sharp metal, they ripped, and gorged and somewhere far off . . .

Sampson heard screaming.

And laughter.

As a thick liquid poured down the back of his throat, in his final excruciating seconds, he knew the screams came from his own mouth, and it had been a long while, and even then he'd heard it so infrequently, but he still recognized . . .

Inez Kelly's laughter.

NINETEEN

S ean Scully stood over the slumped forward body of Clint Demont. He crouched on his knees and used a gloved hand to tilt the head forward. After studying it for a minute or so, he dropped the head, and stoop upright. Sean summed his findings by looking skyward and laughing heartily.

"You find this funny?" Detective Tim Onan scowled.

Scully turned to face the newly assigned rookie investigator of violent crimes. "Damn, boy, that is some fine deductive skills. Was it my laughter that gave it away?"

Onan shrugged his shoulders sheepishly.

"No, Onan, I don't really find it funny. I find it hilarious. This dead bastard once known as Sampson, was a sadistic and murdering piece of shit. Looks like he died by having his brains skewered on a knife inserted into each ear. It would have been a most slow and terrible way to die. And, too, he looks as if he'd been run over by a truck beforehand. Now, tell me, what's not hilarious about that?"

Onan dodged the question by pointing at the knife lying on the ground beside the dead man. "You don't think they used just that knife in both ears?"

"I know they didn't. The insertion point on the right ear is larger than the one on the left. Additionally, it's just so much cooler to use two knives. Remember, Onan, I met them? No two cooler humans ever walked this earth."

"They're cold blooded murderers," Onan objected.

"Sure, if you want to nit-pick."

"You seem to be a fan, Detective Scully," Onan sneered.

"You better bet your ass I am. Chicago is now a much better place because of them," Scully paused to point at the body, "a hell of a lot fewer of this type to spread their disease. Yeah, I'm damn sure a fan. They shoved aside political correctness, and did the things our society doesn't have the balls to do."

Onan clearly looked appalled, and changed the topic. "Maybe we can lift prints off the knife."

"Did you read all the reports like I told you to?"

"I read them twice."

"Then you didn't pay attention. You won't get a damned thing off that knife or anything else on this property."

Onan sucked in oxygen. "We don't even know that it was the Outlaws. All the rest of the bodies are riddled with bullets. That didn't come from single action revolvers or even Winchester rifles."

"Don't fool yourself. It was the Outlaws. Do you have any idea why they'd use assault rifles on this final hit?"

"No. I mean, I haven't given it . . ."

"Let me tell you then," Scully butted in. "It's called 'finesse.' You can look the word up later, but for now just know it's a prime quality of cool."

Onan remained silent for seconds before repeating, "This final hit? You think they're finished?"

"Guess you missed that part in Penn's going away report. Does 'one more rodeo to ride,' ring any bells?"

"I didn't know that meant . . . "

"Yeah, Onan, it meant this was it. They're done now. You can bet your pension on the fact they are as far away from here as they can get. We might as well forget working this scene. Won't turn up shit, and we'll definately never find those two."

Onan started shaking his head, "I'm sorry, Detective Scully, I don't think I can work with you. Your attitude, well, it sucks."

Scully busted out in laughter again. "You know you're right. My attitude does suck. And, no, you can't work with me. See, I've worked with the best, and you couldn't even wipe Mark Penn's ass. Get the fuck off my crime scene."

Onan bowed up, sneered angrily, and started to open his mouth.

"Onan, don't make me go Outlaw on your ass."

* * * *

Remington stepped out of the van and into the open arms of Melinda Lollar. They kissed and hugged and exchanged loving words in whispers. There would be much more of the same to follow, but now Remington pulled out of her embrace to help Ledford down from the van.

"Oh, my God! What happened?" Melinda shrieked.

"Oh, not much," Remington chuckled. "Ninja boy, here, just needs to practice getting out of the way of flying knives."

Melinda stepped up to assist Remington in helping Ledford. "Are you okay, John?" she gasped.

Ledford looked down at his arm in the sling. "My ego hurts more than the wound, and of course your loving man here can't help but rubbing salt in it."

Remington laughed about it – now that it was over. "That which does not kill you, just makes you hurt like hell."

Ledford cut his eyes at Remington. "Once we are not in the presence of a lovely lady, remind me to tell you to go have sex with a goat."

Buzz and Bingo stood off to the side grinning. Remington nodded and smiled at both. "Thanks for filling in, boys."

"We took damn good care of Mrs. Remington, Trey," Buzz advised.

"Mrs. Remington?" Remington questioned.

"Don't waste your breath, Trey," Melinda giggled.

Remington looked from Buzz to his woman. "Well, I like the sound of it."

Melinda didn't get a chance to respond before Bingo stepped up to Ledford.

"Wanted to wear my wig to welcome you home, John, but it caught on fire yesterday."

"In other words, boys," Melinda grinned, "I burned the filthy son of a bitch."

Remington stood idly, and simply watched and listened as home welcomed them back. From this perspective, it would fall on John to convince him to take a new offer just recently placed on the table.

* * * *

Kenneth Donning sat alone in the dark remembering the much earlier conversation with Charles Atkinson.

"So, the boys are back on their way to Texas! That calls for a celebratory drink, Ken," Atkinson beamed.

"It's seven a.m., sir, don't think my stomach can handle liquor at this hour of the day."

"I hope you will not object to me having one?" Atkinson said as he moved toward the bar. "I've saved a special bottle of Scotch for this moment."

"I certainly don't object, but, your doctor, sir . . . "

"Oh, nonsense, what do doctors know?" Atkinson said in a joking manner.

They know you have three to five years to live . . . If you watch your drinking.

Donning pushed the thought aside. How could he put a damper on his dear friend's desire to celebrate a truly phenomenal accomplishment?

Atkinson returned with a double in hand. "Can you believe it, Ken? It worked. Just like we planned. Mission accomplished!" Atkinson beamed, raising his glass to toast Donning.

"It certainly did, sir. All across this nation, people are taking back their neighborhoods from street gangs. Mission accomplished, indeed."

Donning spoke the words, and faked a smile, but for him, one task remained, and it proved a grim one. "I will be flying out this morning in the other jet to tie up the loose ends in Chicago. I'll be back late, but not too late to then celebrate with you, Sir Atkinson."

Atkinson raised his glass again, "I could not have done it without you. You are a fine and honorable man, Colonel Donning."

At that time, Donning felt anything but honorable.

He felt even worse now, sitting in the darkness, hundreds of miles from the mansion, in a place starkly opposite of a mansion. He now so wished for some of that fine Scotch that Atkinson offered, but knew he needed sharp wits to conduct the final act of the mission that brought him here.

Moments later, he heard a key being inserted into the lock on the front door. Donning braced himself as the door swung open. He tensed when the switch flipped to illuminate the room.

"Smith? What the fuck . . . Where is the nurse? Where is Trisha?"

Donning remained seated as Sergeant Marcus Jones sprinted across the living room toward the girl's room. He drew in a deep and calming breath when Jones reappeared with his service weapon in hand.

"Where is Trisha? What the fuck have you done with her?"

Donning stared into the barrel of the pointed automatic. "Your daughter is safer than ever before. Please, Sergeant Jones, look at the material on your dining table."

Clearly dazed and terribly confused, not to mention frightened out of his mind, Jones did not bother keeping Donning in his sites as he scurried to the table. Donning gazed at Jones' back as he sorted through the literature stacked on the table.

"I'm familiar with this place. Hell, I can't afford this. Not even with the money you paid me."

"May I approach you?" Donning asked.

Jones plopped into a chair at the table. "I don't give a damn . . . I just don't understand," he mumbled while sorting through the brochures.

Donning stood and walked over to stand at Jones' back. He placed his left hand gently on the father's right shoulder. "I knew you would want the best for her. Consider it a gift. Trisha will be treated like a princess for the rest of her life."

"But why would you do this?" Jones' voice warbled.

Donning reached with his right hand to remove the .22 caliber automatic with a silencer from inside his suit coat. "I owe you at least that much."

Donning did not wait for a response before firing a single bullet into the back of Marcus Jones' brain. The police sergeant's head came to rest on the table, and Donning fired a second time to insure there would be no suffering.

Donning stuck the gun back in his coat, and took a step back. "Please forgive me, Sergeant Jones, I'm simply protecting the well-being of someone very dear to me."

* * * *

Three wonderful days passed on the Brazos, and Remington knew the conversation could not be held at bay forever. He sat in a lawn chair in front of a blazing fire, and Ledford sat next to him.

"So, you are ready to talk about it now?" Ledford asked a second time.

Remington took a hearty swig from a bottle of whiskey before turning to grin at him. "Can you believe Buzz and Bingo are here to stay?"

"Not hard for me to believe, Trey, since I'm sharing my trailer with them," Ledford scowled.

"Well, we'll soon start building the underground complex. We'll have all the space we could ever want," Remington chuckled.

"All the others are in bed, are we going to discuss the proposal or not?" Ledford pressed.

"Jeez, John, you're as demanding as a dog wanting a belly rub."

"A dog that bites when ignored," Ledford reminded him.

Remington pulled in a deep breath and let it out slowly. "You know, John, we're not filthy rich, but we are very wealthy men. We can live a very comfortable life from here on out, and never have to put our ass on the line again."

"Yes, you're right, Trey. We can sit back and live the easy life while watching the world around us just go to hell."

John always knew the exact buttons to jab. He knew Remington too well to think he might enjoy a good life in a bad world. "Are you saying we're too young to retire?"

"Nope," Ledford grinned, "I'm saying were not the retiring types."

Remington could not argue that fact, so he turned to another. "I'm going to ask Melinda to marry me."

Ledford displayed a big smile. "Glad to hear that. I'm sure she'll accept." Then he grew solemn, "So, does that mean you're hanging up your guns?"

Remington brought the bottle to his lips and took a mighty swig. "No. But I do sometimes wish I could. But it does mean I'd like the time for a very long honeymoon."

"Wouldn't deny you and your bride that much, but then what, John?"

"Well, old buddy, after that," Remington paused to hit the bottle again, "I'll fight the next fight with you. We'll accept the mission."

Remington looked up to gaze at the stars overhead, thought about all the foul things they shined down upon, and found confirmation on the decision he'd just made.

The Outlaws will ride again.

ACKNOWLEDGMENTS

To Henry P. (Pat) Scully of Scully and Associates for the cover design. Pat, thanks yet again for the work of art that draws the eye to my novels.

To David Shupe for line and story editing. David, thanks for finding all my mistakes and making the suggestions that improved this story.

To Sohail Liaqat for formatting and technical support. Sohail, thanks for taking my manuscript and doing all that technical "stuff" to turn into a real book.

ABOUT THE AUTHOR

Keith Remer is a retired Army colonel. After thirty-two years of service in the Army, he taught various courses as an adjunct professor before buying a horse ranch. He has to date written twelve novels and is the recipient of the *International Indy Book Award for Best in Fiction* for his thriller, *The Hiding Place of Thunder*. Keith lives on his horse ranch in rural Oklahoma City where he writes his novels and tends his horses.

To connect with Keith, visit his Facebook page @KeithRemerAuthor, or his webpage: keithremer.com